Published by wrotelio™.

Image Courtesy: light source

Tess Tobias – Anna: A Story About A Crime

ISBN-Print: 978-1-77181-045-6

ISBN-E-Book: 978-1-77181-046-3

May the missing receive justice.
May the innocent receive freedom.

- PROLOGUE -

A chill runs down his spine. He knows what he has done. His fingers are tingling and his breathing is heavy. The sound of air escaping his lungs is loud and he instinctively tries to calm himself down. A huge breath of ice-cold air fills his lungs and he slowly lets the air escape through his nostrils. As he inhales again, he closes his eyes. The adrenaline rushes through every vein. She's right there.

The keys are still hanging in the ignition switch and the sound of them jangling brings him back to reality. He opens his eyes and he can faintly hear her cries. Without looking at the car door, he grabs the door handle and slowly opens it. One leg swings out of the car. The foot hits the ground and out of habit, he swings out the other leg. In a swift motion, he stands up and turns his head towards the front of the car. He can see her, lying on the ground in front of him. There's that tingle again.

"Help," she cries. It almost sounds like a whisper. She's not moving but tears are coming from her eyes. She seems scared. It's frightening and exhilarating at the same time.

"Help," she cries again. "Hurts."

She's scared. He can sense it. Her facial expression is fearful and her skin shines from her tears, as the headlights of the car face her. He takes a deep breath and then takes one step towards her. He doesn't say anything as her eyes widen. She doesn't know what's about to happen.

"Help," she cries out.

She's paralyzed from the neck down. He can see it without even trying to lift her limbs. She's going into shock. He knows she can't attack him. She's helpless. He lowers himself down next to her. Without saying a word, he scoops her into his arms. She's light as a feather, much lighter than the other children he has held. He looks up to the sky as he gives her a hug and for a minute, he convinces himself that she feels a moment of peace. In a swift move, he snaps her neck.

He lets her lifeless body fall to the ground. There's nothing but silence. She's dead. She won't be able to identify him. Problem solved. Now it's time to dump the body before anyone notices she's gone.

- CHAPTER 1 -

It was cold in the trailer as the sun rose and shone a light on the glistening straws of grass that surrounded the home. It was a quiet morning. The birds had left town for the season and the tree branches hitting one another was the only sound breaking the silence of the white landscape. The gravel road leading up to the property had patches of frost and small water puddles that had turned to ice. A colder season had arrived and it seemed like everyone was prepared for it, except Maple. Her neighbors had thought about salt for the road, removed the patio furniture from their yards, and had insulated their homes. She never thought about these cold mornings when she rented the trailer. That wasn't on her list of priorities at the time. Things moved fast and the property had provided a sanctuary for her. Plus, this was only supposed to be a temporary home for her and her daughter, and she didn't think that she would be spending a cold winter in a poorly constructed bungalow with no heat.

The morning sun made the trees look black on the horizon as Maple looked out the window. The window was small and it didn't keep the cold out. There were still traces of brown streaks where someone had attempted to clean up the mold from the window - or perhaps hide it from a tenant. Maple knew it was there, but chose to ignore it for now. She had no choice. There was no money to get a new window frame and she had already postponed rent twice with her landlord, so asking him to fix this could result in consequences she didn't need. She had finally found a home, and she didn't want to lose it over some minor mold issues she could easily turn a blind eye to.

Maple scouted the grass, the trees and the forest in the distance. Glancing left, then right, she realized she was alone. It was quiet, and even from inside the home she could hear the trees in the distance, dancing in the wind. She spotted the newspaper on the ground. For a moment, she contemplated whether she should venture outside to get the morning paper. On one hand, it would be nice to read the daily news. On the other hand, she would have to go outside, exposing herself to the cold temperatures with the frost underneath the soles of her shoes. The little heater in the trailer didn't work well. Sometimes it wouldn't even turn on. Plus, if the newspaper was completely soaked from the frosty weather, it would be ruined. The pages would stick together and the ink would run.

The rolled-up newspaper paper was further away from the trailer this morning than it had been every other day this week. It was close to the road, making her journey longer than usual. It would take Maple a few extra steps in both directions to get the paper. Suddenly, Maple felt uneasy about the situation. Why was it closer to the road? Was it the mailman's fault? Or did someone move it? Now, her fear wasn't the cold. It wasn't about the weather, winter's unforgiving winds, or the little space heater that may not provide her with heat when she returned. Her fear was him.

He was the biggest problem in her life and whatever she did she couldn't make it work. It had been a two-year long relationship, but it hadn't been good after a few months. Maple had tried to talk to him, work things out. She wanted them to stay together for her daughter, even though he was not the biological father. Maple wanted to give her daughter the family unit she didn't have growing up, and she was willing to do anything for it - even accept domestic abuse. But when he had almost killed her, she ran away in the middle of the night with her daughter on her arm. She had packed nothing, taken nothing from the shared home, and she only had the clothes they were wearing. When Maple had found the trailer, she was going into hiding.

Maple wasn't exactly proud of her past. While the latest boyfriend had been the worst of them all, she didn't have the best record. They had all been abusive in some capacity, and the majority had mug shots for various offenses, including break-and-enter, assaults, and even robberies. She would fall for their sweet words, their soft touches, and their kind gestures. But once she was committed, they would turn on her.

She had been left in a ditch, beaten black and blue, and after her latest ex-boyfriend had threatened to kill her and put a noose around her neck, she escaped. He truly wanted her dead but she couldn't understand why. She had asked him but he could never justify his desire to kill her. Maple had wondered what his reaction was when he learned she was gone. It scared her at times and had given her nightmares, but her nights were improving. With every passing day, her sleep got better and her thoughts more positive.

It's not like she tried to go for the bad guys. She genuinely wanted a sweet man who could be her companion in life. A part of her felt that it could happen and that this man would accept her daughter as his own. Another part of her felt that she was doomed to be with these abusive men as a punishment for her own choices earlier in life. Over the course of a few years, she had gone from being a straight-A student to a dropout with a drug problem. The wrong people took her in and she had regrets from when she turned her back on her family for a life of drugs. But things changed when she got pregnant. She got sober and after four years, she chose to leave her abusive boyfriend. She had her daughter to think about. She was all that mattered.

Picking the trailer hadn't been hard. It was buried in a trailer park far away from what many would consider civilization. There was a small town nearby called Beaverville, but the nearest city with any form of entertainment, including a cinema, was over an hour away. And her home was just one of several trailers. No one wanted to live here – willingly. It seemed like all of her neighbors wanted to escape and hide for their own reasons. Some were criminals and others just didn't like being social. Even the landlord had questioned why such beautiful girls would want to live here. Maple hadn't answered his question, but she could sense that he knew it was serious. Since moving in, no one had bothered them. Everything had been good. It had been quiet. Her bruises had healed. Her daughter had hugged her every day, never mentioning her ex-boyfriend or the violence she had witnessed. Maple didn't have much to offer her daughter, but everything had been perfect – until now. Now the newspaper was far away. It was too far. It all seemed staged.

Maple took a step back from the window. For a moment, she feared she had been spotted. Maybe he had found her. Maybe he had a gun pointed right at her. She stood completely still by the window, paralyzed by fear. A minute passed. Another minute went by. It was silent. Maybe he hadn't found her after all. With every passing minute, Maple felt a sense of calm. The trailer started to feel safe again. She snapped out of it when she saw her own breath. The temperature inside had dropped overnight as well and she had been so worried about getting the paper that she hadn't realized how cold it truly was. She spotted the space heater on the floor. The frost was creeping inside, but Maple had been too occupied to notice.

"Shit," she mumbled as she grabbed the cord to the space heater.

It wasn't plugged in. It made an odd sound when she turned it on, but she eventually started to feel the heat, hugging her toes. The heat felt nice and she wanted more. Her body needed to warm up. Maple turned to her cupboard and grabbed her mug. They only had a few cups and she used the same one for her coffee every morning. Her daughter had her favorite cup too. It had a big white bunny on it.

Two scoops of the cheapest grounds that Beaverville had to offer and four cups of water would make the worst cup of Joe Maple had ever tried. But it didn't matter. It was her coffee that she had brewed for herself in her own home. It was the beginning of something new and when the funds would present themselves, she would buy the better beans. As the coffee dripped through the machine and the heater warmed the kitchen, Maple went back to the window to see if the paper was still in the same spot. It was. She peeked left and then right but saw no one. She told herself she was overreacting. He hadn't found her. How could he? She had left with nothing and she had no plans in mind when she closed the door to their shared home. If she didn't know she would end up here, how could he have found her?

Maybe it was the smell of the fresh dark roast or perhaps the calming effect of the heater that gave Maple a boost of confidence. Over the course of a few minutes, she had gone from being scared of the past to being ready for whatever the day may bring. In a single swoop, she threw on her pink-faded housecoat and jumped into her worn-down sneakers. She was getting that paper, no matter what.

She unlocked each of the three locks on her door. In a single movement, she grabbed the door handle and swung open the door. The cold air hit her instantly and in shock, she inhaled the freezing air, letting out a gasp. Her lungs hurt as she was overcome by the crisp and sharp feeling in her chest. But Maple was on a mission. She was getting the paper. She was out and exposed, and she wasn't willing to turn around and hide inside. New beginnings required courage and this was her first step.

Maple walked fast, the housecoat swinging in the wind and with determination on her face. For every step she took, she looked around to see if anyone was there. She was looking for a man, a rifle, a car – anything that could potentially come at her at any second. Once she reached the paper, she swooped it up and ran back to the trailer. She got inside, slammed the door, and locked all three locks. The window was completely covered in fog, as the door had been open during her short trip outside. She couldn't see if someone was chasing her. She sat down at the table and just listened.

Silence.

No one was chasing her. There was no car screeching away or the sounds of gunshots flying around her trailer.

All quiet.

The coffee machine broke the silence with three beeps. The brew was ready. It was black and steam rose from the mug as soon as it was poured. While the beverage was bad, Maple was thankful that it was hot. During these cold months, her crappy drink would at least keep her warm. She spotted some grounds dancing in the mug, but rather than pick them out, Maple just flashed a smirk. It was still her brew in her kitchen – being enjoyed on her own time. Independence at its finest.

She quietly rolled out the newspaper, trying to avoid the wet areas. Some of the ink had started to run in certain spots, as the newspaper had been out in the freezing cold for at least a few hours. Luckily, her daughter hadn't heard her rushing out to get the paper and accidentally slamming the door behind her. The last thing she wanted to do was wake her daughter. She had been through enough the last few months, seeing her mother beaten up, with bruises, and even with a noose around her neck. She was only four years old but she had seen more than an average adult. There was nothing healthy about those situations. If she wanted to sleep in, she could. A new life also meant new rules – and Maple was ready to let her daughter call the shots for a while.

The stress of getting the newspaper was slowly easing. Maple was proud of being protective, but a part of her felt silly for overreacting and letting the fear slip in. The newspaper wasn't in the same spot and she immediately thought the worst. Surely that wasn't healthy. As the coffee cooled, and she flipped through the pages of the paper, she noticed that her shoulders were down and her body was less tense. It was so relaxing to just sit and do whatever she wanted. She never had that luxury before. Maple grabbed a cigarette and lit it using the space heater. What a great way to start the day. Maple glanced at her daughter's bedroom door and smiled. Maybe this day would be the best one yet in their little home.

- CHAPTER 2 -

The pain was coming from right behind the eyes. It was a pulsating pain. With every heartbeat, the pain seemed to circulate in his head - again and again. It wasn't the first time he had felt this way. In fact, he knew exactly how to deal with this kind of a headache. Detective Richard Morgan had often had these headaches after nights of drinking. Every time he woke up, there were instant regrets. He never intended on consuming so much alcohol in one sitting that he would be battling a hangover. After years of drinking, Morgan was convinced that his body could handle it and he could feel just fine the next day. But it seemed to get worse. He knew he couldn't do it much more, but sometimes he lost control.

Morgan couldn't open his eyes. The sunlight was too bright as it bounced off the fresh frost covering the leafy landscape that lay beyond his large bedroom window. His wife had already opened up the curtains to let the light in. That was usually a signal for him to get up, as she hated seeing him in bed. He didn't have to open his eyes to know that she wasn't in bed next to him. They used to get up at the same time, enjoy breakfast together, and joke around in the morning. His drinking changed that, as he was now sleeping in during the week, skipping breakfast with his wife, and the jokes had turned to awkward conversations – if the two even crossed paths.

Without opening his eyes, Morgan started moving his tongue around. It tasted horrible. He tried to remember what he had consumed the night before. When nothing came to mind, he tried to guess based on the tastes in his mouth. He always started his list of alcohol in alphabetical order, possibly to extend the time he could stay in bed. This was a game he used to play after a night of binge drinking as a way to feel better about the situation. He may have been drinking but it wasn't so bad that he couldn't have a little fun. That – to him – made him a person enjoying an occasional drink. His wife would disagree. She would call him a functioning alcoholic.

Morgan slowly opened his eyes and tried to adjust to the bright room. He felt no motivation to get out of bed. He glanced over at the bedside table in hopes that he had several hours of sleep to go. The alarm clock told him he had exactly 43 minutes until he had to be at the station. He extended his arm to his wife's side of the bed, knowing she wasn't there. Her side of the bed was cold. She had been up for hours. Morgan hadn't even felt her move or heard her shower. He used to feel her slightest movement and he used to wake up when she got into the shower in the morning. But since he started drinking, he fell into a deep sleep. He believed he slept better and could, therefore, focus better at work. The drinking wasn't ideal. He knew that. But it helped him cope. Plus, it would be over soon.

Detective Richard Morgan was planning his retirement. In actuality, he already knew when his last day would be. And when that day came, he would proudly walk out of the station and into retirement - unless a case came up that took longer. Since he was the only detective in town, he had to stay on a case until it was solved or officially became a cold case. But Morgan wasn't too worried. The cases in Beaverville were few and far between and they were usually the same: a runaway teenager, a drug-fuelled burglary, and the occasional bar fight. It wasn't something he couldn't handle before his last day.

Morgan stretched out his body while still in bed and glanced at the clock again. He now had 35 minutes to get to work. He rolled out of bed and had a quick shower. The goal wasn't to get clean – the goal was to remove the smell of alcohol.

His brown uniform hung on a chair in the bedroom. It was the same uniform that he had worn the day before. He didn't have many shirts to wear and he had no interest in looking for a clean one. Without granting it a single thought, he pulled up the pants, stuffed the button-down shirt into the trousers, and closed the belt. There was nothing spectacular about his appearance. It was completely brown and not very flattering. But he liked it. It was neutral, professional and it reminded him of better times. He fixed the collar and used his hands to straighten out his hair. He was going for presentable, not perfection.

As he walked down the stairs to the kitchen, he could hear her. His wife. She hadn't left for work yet. She was usually gone by now and he was a bit confused as to why she was home. Morgan felt a slight bit of excitement, as he hadn't seen her the night before. As he stepped into the kitchen, he hoped to see a smiling wife, ready to embrace him with a hug.

But she stood over the kitchen sink, looking out the window at the glistening landscape.

"Morning," Morgan said, feeling the raspiness of his voice.

He hadn't said a word since he got up and the simple vocal acknowledgment of his wife was enough to cause a cough. Morgan now felt the effects of the alcohol he had consumed the night before. It was rough. His wife said nothing as she continued to stare at the white landscape that dominated their backyard. Realizing that she may be angry with him, Morgan decided to ease into the conversation.

"Did you sleep well?" he asked her, scared to look up at her.

She sighed and he could hear it. He knew that she wanted him to hear it. Morgan also knew what it meant. She was tired. His beloved Jules was tired – of him. She wanted so much more than a drunken husband, passed out in bed. She wanted her husband back, the one who enjoyed getting up early, flirting in the kitchen before work, enjoying romantic dinners at night, and hiking with her on the weekends. He was none of those things anymore. He knew he was a disappointment, but he felt betrayed. She should be there for him, no matter what.

"Jules…" he started before being interrupted by her.

"Don't," she said firmly, clearly not interested in hearing his excuses.

Morgan knew that he had broken a promise. Last time he had come home drunk and passed out, he had promised her the following morning that it wouldn't happen again. Jules had threatened to leave him, but her threats of divorce hadn't stopped him. Those threats hadn't been on his mind the night before. With every drink he had ordered at the bar, he only thought about the good times. Morgan thought about their early years together and how beautiful they had all been. He chose to never think about one thing – that one event that changed it all.

"It will change," he promised. "You know, once I'm done work, it will all be over. I'm just trying to cope here."

She turned around to face him. She looked straight at him in disbelief.

"Cope? Cope with what?" she questioned with frustration on her face. "I've never heard of a detective, who drinks to deal with runaway teenagers or drug busts."

She had a point and he knew it. He knew that he couldn't use work as an excuse and he never meant to. She knew deep down inside what was bothering him, but they never talked about it. It was too painful. Morgan felt like a coward because he couldn't deal with the pain as well as Jules could. But that didn't change his frustration at that moment. Why couldn't she just understand?

They stood silently in the kitchen, the frustration building within him. His face got tense.

"You don't know what you are talking about," he blurted out, but immediately wanted to take it back.

"I know it all," she said. "I was there."

"It will change, I promise. I just have a little while longer and then I'll retire. We will go on walks, I'll get up early, we'll have breakfast together – it will go back to the way it was," he said, trying to sound apologetic.

Morgan had never really apologized for his drinking. He knew it was a big problem in their marriage, but whenever he felt an ounce of guilt, he would go to the liquor store and buy a bottle. When he got home, he would start drinking and he wouldn't even notice when Jules would go to bed. It had become a sad life for him, and his work was the only thing that kept him going. While he was determined to change once he retired, he knew she was worried that he would spiral out of control. Without work, he had nothing to get sober for. There was no one holding him accountable.

"You've promised that before. You just don't care," she said, looking down at the sink.

A single tear slowly rolled down her cheek. Morgan knew that she wasn't being dramatic. She wasn't the kind of woman who would say such things to get a reaction. She was serious. She truly felt that she wasn't important anymore and that she wasn't a priority in his life. Nothing could be further from the truth. There were days where he felt that the threats of divorce were justified. On mornings like these, he was thankful she was still there. She had given him too many chances and he knew he was lucky.

"Just..." he started. "Please just be here when I get home."

She didn't look up when he talked and he realized she wouldn't. Without touching her, he stepped out of the kitchen, grabbing his badge and keys on the way out. It was a cold way to say goodbye, but these goodbyes were common now. He hadn't been the same for a while and Jules didn't know how to deal with it. It was clear to see and while he wished he could fix it, he felt he couldn't.

Morgan rushed into the car and immediately turned it on. He sat for a minute, waiting for the heat to come on. He knew he had to stop drinking. It was time. He needed Jules. Even though these awkward morning conversations had become a common occurrence, he didn't like them. He had never felt more distant from his wife. When they met one another many years ago, things were so much easier. Now, things were complicated. There were unwanted feelings. Morgan never expected to be in a situation where he couldn't work through his feelings. In fact, he never expected to have these damaging thoughts.

He had 11 minutes to get to the station and the icy roads didn't make it easy. Being at the station gave him something to do. His work kept him busy. Morgan could focus on people who needed his help and not on his marital problems. In fact, Jules was often out-of-sight out-of-mind when he was at work. It had always been like this. Being a detective was part of Morgan's identity and he never wanted anything or anyone to get in the way of his career goals. His career was something he was proud of, even though Jules had played a supportive role throughout the years.

He pulled up to the dark building, the Beaverville police station. It was a brown structure. It was outdated and bland, but the style suited Morgan just fine. He was an old-school detective so the look went well with his brown uniform. As he sat in his car outside, he looked at himself in the rear-view mirror. He looked tired with the skin sagging underneath his eyes and his grey hair.

"Just a little while longer," he mumbled to himself before getting out of his car.

- CHAPTER 3 -

The trailer was warming up and Maple felt the warmth all around her. She couldn't drink all of the coffee. Even though she had been optimistic at first, it was simply too gross to finish. It was giving her a horrible taste in her mouth and she knew that the aftertaste would linger for hours. This could be her next goal – get some better coffee beans from the town next time she went in for groceries. This was the way she lived her life now. Baby steps. Step one – get a home. Step two – get a better coffee. Step three – independence and no fear.

Sometimes, a life without fear seemed unattainable. For years, Maple had lived in fear with her abusive boyfriends. She would go from one boyfriend to another and they never got any better. But now, she was done with men and done with relationships. Her blissful time was now.

After getting the paper, Maple would occasionally look up at the window to see if she could spot someone outside. She had only gotten up once to look out the window since returning inside. Her front yard was empty and there was no one in sight. She chuckled a bit at herself, realizing that she may have overreacted. He hadn't found her and her daughter. Hopefully, he would never find them.

The paper wasn't too thrilling. There were articles about the weather and a two-page feature on how to prepare your car and home for winter. The paper also had articles about local politics and business, but it was all about the bigger city an hour away. Nothing happened in her little town worth writing about. There was a gas station, a diner, a liquor store and a grocery store nearby and nothing else. A paper couldn't function here and be profitable. No one cared whether Bob bought a coffee or a tea at the diner, or that the grocery store now carried buttermilk. But the paper did keep her entertained while she enjoyed a quiet morning. This was a new beginning for her, and she loved that she could read the paper first if she wanted to. She didn't have to cater to anyone and she didn't wake up to a fist in her face or being grabbed by the arm.

Maple looked at her daughter's door once again and smiled. She imagined her daughter sleeping in her bed, hugging the stuffed bunny that she had kept with her as they ran away. She hadn't told her little girl that they would be leaving that night. When he had passed out from alcohol, Maple snuck into her daughter's room with their coats in hand, wrapped her up in her blanket, and had walked out the back door. Her daughter had been sleeping with her stuffed bunny, not waking up as Maple carried her away from the house. She was hugging it in comfort as Maple placed her in the car's backseat. To avoid being detected, Maple had shut off the car lights as soon as she had turned the key in the ignition switch. She had watched the backdoor as she switched it into reverse. If he woke up from the sound of a running car, it would only take him seconds to run through the living room, the kitchen and open the back door. But the door remained closed. Maple backed out of the driveway and slowly drove down the alleyway to the main road. Without stopping to check for other cars, she made a right-hand turn and drove away.

She had planned this escape for about a week. They needed to get out of the house while he was passed out from drinking. He would usually get abusive the following day because he wasn't feeling well. He would be irritated from headaches, bad breath and having spent money on alcohol the night before. Maple knew his pattern all too well and he had been curing his hangover with a fresh bottle of whiskey when he put the noose around her neck that final night. Her daughter had been right there. The noose had been the result of his frustration with a sandwich she had made for him. He didn't want butter on the bread. For a moment, Maple wasn't sure if she would make it out alive. All of the planning could have been for nothing, but luckily he passed out before making good on his promise to kill her.

The plan had been simple. Get her daughter out of the house, get in the car and drive it to the bar where he would go to drink with his friends. Here, she would leave the car, making it seem like he was the one who had driven it there. Sometimes, he would take a cab home and other times, he would drive himself. He never remembered how he got home, so he would probably believe that he had driven himself there. The hope was that he wouldn't put two-and-two together and realize she had set him up.

The good thing about this plan was that she would have a head start. Should he wake up while she was driving, it would take him some time to get a cab and come after her. The other good thing was that he would check the bus terminal and the train station first, as these two options would be her only ways out of the city. But Maple had another plan. During her visits to the library with her daughter, she had been emailing a close friend of hers. She wasn't allowed to have friends and she couldn't access her email from the home, but when she was at the library, she could send a quick message or two. Her friend would meet her at the bar and drive her to another city. From here, she would get on the Amtrak just minutes after arriving at the station and be about 300 miles away from her boyfriend before the sunrise.

It was a bit of a gamble. If her friend was not waiting at the bar, blending in with the other bar visitors, it would be for nothing. She would be forced to take the train or bus near their home, and the public transportation didn't start running until the morning. That would give him about six hours to realize that they were gone and come looking for them. But luckily, she was there. She had been waiting for half an hour, just to make sure that she could remove Maple from the situation. She didn't even know about the noose or that Maple's little girl had witnessed it all.

Maple had quickly placed her daughter in the backseat, letting her sleep wrapped up in the blanket. She was holding on to the stuffed bunny, as they tried to hide in the dark. But she managed to sleep through most of the escape. While driving through the dark landscape, Maple hadn't said much to her friend. She had constantly looked in the side mirror, checking to see if he had figured out her plan. Despite the planning, she felt it was too easy to figure out. Maybe someone had spotted her at the bar. Perhaps someone had recognized her friend, though it was unlikely. Maybe he had hacked her email account. Maple was convinced he would find her and kill her.

Even though her friend kept telling her not to worry, this move would be fatal if he found her.

After being dropped off at the Amtrak station at 3:42 am, Maple wrapped her daughter in the blanket once more and held her close to her chest. She wanted to feel her breathing. She needed to feel some comfort, even if it was a four-year-old girl. When she had given birth to her daughter, she had been shaking all over. She couldn't speak and she could barely hold a conversation with the doctor. But when her baby was placed on her chest, she calmed down. Her daughter had always been able to calm her down. It was a special bond they had. She thought about her daughter's future that night when she boarded the train at 4:00 am, leaving for a stop over 300 miles away. They would arrive in a few hours and then she had no further plans.

The only time Maple could sleep was on the train. She held her daughter close to her and rested her head on the window. She could sense the light every time the train came to a stop in a new city or town. Maple would open her eyes and look at the platform to see if he would be standing there. He was never there, but every time the train stopped, her eyes opened wide, scouting the oncoming passengers.

During the morning commute, Maple and her daughter arrived at a busy train station. It felt overwhelming due to her fear and concerns that he would find them, but she had planned it all out. It was better to be in a big public space and big city, so she could get lost in the masses. She had found a small diner near the station, where they could get some breakfast. Her friend had given her $100 to get some food, so she splurged on pancakes. Her daughter had loved those chocolate chip pancakes with syrup. Maple had eaten some scrambled eggs with bacon and some toast. People had glanced at them, perhaps judging her as a mother, as her daughter was eating breakfast at a diner in her dirty pajamas. But she didn't care. She wanted to remember this moment: two girls enjoying their first few hours of freedom.

On the way out of the diner, Maple grabbed every newspaper she could find. The plan was to find a playground where her daughter could be entertained, while she looked for work, a place to live – anything to start over fast. It was here she found an ad for the trailer and had borrowed a phone from a library to call the landlord. It had taken her a few hours to find a bus that would take her to the trailer park so she could look at the place. It would also cost her the rest of the money she had.

When she finally found the place, the landlord seemed upset. He had waited for them for over an hour, but Maple apologized fiercely. Perhaps it was her sweet little girl napping in her arms in the same pajamas from the night before or Maple's exhaustive appearance, but he quickly changed his attitude when she asked if they could start renting the trailer right this minute. At the time, Maple didn't know how she was going to pay for it, but she was hopeful that he would understand.

"There won't be any trouble now," the landlord had said, both as a request and as a question.

"No," Maple had replied. "We're alone."

He put his hand on her shoulder, sending a sideways smirk her way. She knew immediately that he understood that she was running from someone. He must have known that she was scared and that her daughter was her priority. For a minute, Maple felt she could count on him. He was on her side. That was the first time in a long time that a man had given her any kind of support. It felt nice.

The landlord had been nothing but supportive. He had accepted it when she couldn't pay her rent and he had brought them the space heater when the temperatures started dropping. He knew they had nothing and that Maple was doing everything possible to pay rent. She had gone into Beaverville to use the library services to file for financial support from the government. She was learning how to live her life and it felt good.

Maybe Maple was reading the paper simply to avoid any sort of routine that reminded her of the past. Or maybe she was reading it to see if her past was out looking for her. She wouldn't put it past him to put an ad in the paper, asking people if they had seen her and her little girl. If he couldn't have her, she couldn't stay alive. For him, it was simple. For her, it was scary.

She turned over the last page and read the cartoons and horoscopes. She never believed anything her horoscope said, as it had predicted money, fame, and good family relationships while she had been abandoned in a ditch, beaten and bruised. But the cartoons always gave her a good chuckle.

Maple turned over the last page of the paper and realized that she had read the whole thing from beginning to end. What was even more surprising was the fact that she had read the paper without her daughter waking up. She would usually make some sounds around the mid-way point but today she hadn't said a word. It had been quiet. As she stared at her daughter's door, wondering why she had slept so much this morning, a branch hit a window facing the backyard. Maple jumped out of her chair. A strong gust of wind had slammed the branch into the plastic window and several gusts kept the branch banging into the trailer. The home was no longer quiet.

But these new sounds were not enough to wake her daughter. If the branch had scared her, it must have scared her little girl. Without taking her eyes off the door, Maple got up and walked over to her daughter's bedroom. She grabbed the handle and opened the door. She just wanted to make sure her daughter was safe and sound.

The bed was empty. The sheets were wrinkled and pushed aside. Maple knew she had been there, as she had tucked her into bed the night before. Her favorite stuffed bunny was abandoned near her pillow.

"No, no, no, no!" Maple whispered quietly, as she rushed over to the side of the bed. She hoped her little girl was just playing peek-a-boo or hiding under the bed. She called out her name repeatedly with an increasing sense of panic. Her whispers were turning to screams. Maple ran through the trailer, checking every room and opening closets, screaming her daughter's name.

"Can you please come out to mommy? Game over, okay?" Maple pleaded as the tears streamed down her face.

Nothing. Her daughter was nowhere. She wasn't in the trailer at all.

It was him. He took her.

Her chest began to tighten and her throat became dry. Maple struggled to catch her breath, and she found herself shaking. She screamed out her daughter's name, hoping she would surface from her hiding spot.

He came for revenge and he knew Maple's daughter was her weakness. He knew that she would be devastated. Her little girl was her motivation to run and her reason for living.

Without her, she would be nothing. She knew it. He knew it. He took her.

In the middle of her screams, Maple remembered the newspaper from this morning and suddenly went quiet She ran back to the window and looked out. Maybe he was messing with her, moving the newspaper to distract her from her daughter. He must have taken her, but how? The only way into the trailer was through the front door and then the creepy sliding door located in her bedroom. Could he have gotten through there? Maple ran back to her bedroom, shaking from the thought that he could be here. She placed her hand on the doorframe of the sliding door and immediately felt the cold air escaping through. The door was open just enough for air to get through. It had been locked when she went to bed. Nothing made sense. Could he be coming back for her?

Maple ran out to the kitchen and grabbed the phone. Her hand was shaking as she struggled to dial 911.

"Operator here, what is your emergency?" the voice on the other end asked.

"She's gone, my daughter is gone!" Maple screamed into the phone. "Please, send an officer. He's dangerous!"

"What's her name?" the operator asked, trying to calm Maple down.

"Anna!" Maple cried, wiping away the tears from her face. "Her name is Anna."

- CHAPTER 4 -

Detective Morgan opened the door to the station and was greeted by silence. The dark walls and the dimmed lights didn't exactly provide a welcoming feeling, but he always felt at home here. Morgan was only one of nine people working at the station, and one of them was a receptionist. She would take calls from 911 and assign the cases to one of the few police officers there or Morgan, depending on the kind of case it was. There were also a few administrative workers, but he never saw them.

The station's interior was nothing to brag about compared to the police station in the city. The building contained wooden paneling on the walls and tiring fluorescent lights. It hadn't been updated since the station was built back in the 1970s. The reception area had a poster of Beaverville and the surrounding areas, and there were some articles hanging near the door about staying safe in the countryside. There was also a water cooler and a table with a coffee thermos with a stack of foam cups. Morgan personally liked the darkness of the station. He had often thought about it as a dungeon, a place where he could shut out the real world. It helped that he didn't have a window in his office.

There was a sense of slowness in the atmosphere. The receptionist wasn't in her chair to greet him as he walked into the station. She was probably talking to the administrative workers about something that had happened with her boyfriend. She did that often. The coffee in the thermos was hours old. He could almost smell the bitterness coming from it. Plus, the donuts were almost gone. Maybe he had missed an entertaining morning meeting. While Morgan had always thought eating donuts at the office made him a stereotype, he couldn't refuse a vanilla crème donut with a hint of raspberry jam on top. Luckily for him, there was one left in the box. Maybe the receptionist had saved it for him, as she knew it was his favorite. Morgan looked around and since no one was in sight, he grabbed a chocolate donut as well.

His office was located closest to the main lobby out of all the offices, so he could often hear people coming and going. That was both a blessing and a curse. The windowless office was a personal space for him, which he enjoyed. He could hide when he needed to. He could shut the door and when people knocked, he could ignore them. Plus, it was a bonus for him that he was right next to the interrogation room. It was rarely used but it was entertaining for him when it was.

The walls were covered with old pictures, case file documents, and random pins. The pins were connected with red string as if he was trying to make connections between cases. There was no connection. Even though he was a small-town detective solving minor thefts and making small-time drug busts, he still wanted to feel like a big shot detective. He always dreamed of standing in a conference room, briefing his team about all of the wonderful discoveries he had made in a case. However, Morgan had always been a small-town detective and this was all he would ever be. Even though the cases he had worked on were not complex, the red string on the wall, connecting seemingly random people and places, made him feel legit.

Morgan looked at his desk and saw a folder. It had a yellow post-it note on it with the word, "Urgent!"

This is how he learned about a new case. Since he often missed the morning briefings, he would learn about the day's events on a post-it note. It hadn't always been like this. He used to spearhead the morning briefings and he was proud of the single murder they had solved. He still remembers how he announced the suspect during one of these morning briefings. He had never felt more proud. Plus, he had a handful of missing person cases that he had solved as well. He was just tired and he couldn't get up for the briefings anymore. He told his co-workers that he was letting them take the reigns, but in reality, his drinking was the reason why he didn't get there on time. Morgan knew it too. He was just too ashamed to admit it.

He flipped open the file folder.

"Girl named Anna has gone missing. Mother is Maple. She's frantic. Talked about a man on the 911 call. Call made at 8:42 am to the central switchboard."

He had expected to receive a case before his retirement, but not a missing person's case. He had suspected to be placed on a traffic violation or maybe assist in planning a drug raid at a local hangout, but a missing person's case? These cases could drag out and he wasn't eager to go search for people who willingly ran away, which was so often the case.

"Girl named Anna," he quietly read out loud while taking a bite of one of the donuts.

Morgan had received these cases before. The girls were usually runaways. He had often tried to justify why someone would run away and it was easy to come up with an answer. This town was a dump and it didn't offer much to its residents. There was nothing pleasing about living here as a teenager, as there was a high level of drug use and drinking. There had been a few missing person cases where the victims were children, but in two cases the mother had been responsible and in one case, the child had been shipped off to a trafficking ring. It amazed him what people were willing to do for a drug habit.

"Slam dunk," he mumbled to himself.

He noted the address on the file and he knew that the trailer park was filled with drug users and sex offenders. The answer had to be straightforward. It would be one of several outcomes. Maybe this was karma giving him a freebie before retirement. He would be going out with a bang. The last case he worked on ending up being a robbery, where the store owner was guilty of insurance fraud. The owner wanted him to file the necessary documents, so he could claim insurance. Morgan had felt odd about being a pawn in a larger scheme, a scheme he wasn't able to figure out before it was too late. He didn't want to end his career on this low note. He wanted something much grander. This could be it.

Morgan grabbed the case file and walked into the lobby of the station again. There was no one there. On the way to his car, he grabbed another donut. He needed the treat, as he had no desire to go out to the trailer park to interview Maple. It was cold and he had hoped for a silent day in his office.

Given his past experience with these kinds of cases, he had a feeling he could solve it from behind his desk. It was like a multiple-choice test. Anna was either killed or hurt by her mother – on purpose or accident. Anna was kidnapped and killed by a sexual offender in the area. Anna was kidnapped or taken as a pawn in a drug-related scenario. Anna ran away from home, or Anna was alive and well. It was hard to say upfront, as he didn't know a lot about Anna. But after he had talked to Maple, he felt he could confidently give his theory.

Morgan got in the car and looked in the rear-view mirror again. He still looked exhausted. The donuts hadn't cheered him up. The smell of bitter coffee from the lobby hadn't influenced him in the least. The drinking had taken a toll on him. It was as if he was just realizing this today. It's not like he had looked younger or healthier the day before. But today, it seemed like the past mistakes were catching up with him. There was a sense of relief that no one had spotted him in the office, as he didn't want to explain himself and his choices. Like he had told Jules on the way out the door, he just had to deal with the situation a little while longer.

He didn't need to look up the address. He knew where the trailer park was, as he had been there several times. No one wanted to live in the trailer park, surrounded by people who only had their own interests to think about. Morgan had always thought that the trailer park was a dangerous place to live and the file folder on the passenger's seat in his car proved him right.

The trailer park was in the middle of nowhere and he had to drive a good 20 minutes before he spotted the first trailer in the distance. Those 20 minutes had been nothing but cornfields. He had often thought about how many bodies were buried in these cornfields. While he never had to deal with these cases himself, he knew that it would be a good hiding place for those who were looking to hide a body. If he had killed someone, he would bury the body here. The fields expanded so far that it would be nearly impossible to find bones after several years. It wasn't looking for a needle in a haystack. It was looking for the haystack. Hopefully, this wouldn't be the case with Anna. He just wanted a motive. With a motive, he could solve the case. Maybe Maple could provide him with one.

He pointlessly turned on his signal to turn into the trailer park. There were no oncoming cars. There were no signs of people either. The trailer park looked abandoned. Only criminals wanting to go underground would come out here, or people who wanted to die alone. Perhaps that's why he had been out here a few times. Maybe someone had died and a mother was trying to cover it up. He scouted the trailers to see if he could find the one that housed Maple and her daughter.

- CHAPTER 5 -

Maple ran the scenarios through her head one more time. She had gotten up, made coffee, gotten the paper, enjoyed a quiet morning and then the branches had gotten her nervous. She had checked on her daughter to see if she was awake. She knew she had to explain her nervousness, but maybe she didn't have to go into too many details. It was hard to think when all that was on her mind was Anna.

She ran through the morning's events in her head one more time, trying to put time stamps on every action. Maple wanted to have all of the answers ready for the police officer that would be showing up to take her statement. She didn't want to forget something that could prevent her from getting her daughter back. She didn't know what her answer would be if he asked her why she hadn't checked on Anna when she got up. Part of her just wanted her daughter to sleep and relax. Maple had only checked on her daughter when they had moved in. It had been a few weeks before she trusted Anna to sleep in her own room.

Pacing back and forth inside the trailer, she felt scared, angry, and sad. Emotions ran high, as she tried to remember the details from that morning. Had she seen or heard anything unusual? He couldn't have come in through the sliding back door while she was reading the paper in the kitchen, as she could see Anna's door from her chair. She would have seen him. That scenario was impossible. There wouldn't have been time for him to come inside when she bolted out to get the paper either. And he couldn't have come inside in the middle of the night, as she had locked both doors before going to bed. She was certain of this. Nothing made sense. She closed her eyes for a second and tried to breathe. She was shaking, her thoughts were unclear and she was jumping to conclusions. Frustration was building within her and she wanted to scream. But screaming solved nothing.

Keeping her anger inside wasn't good. She felt her heart beating fast, her chest tightening. For the first time in a while, she felt like she was losing control. She tried to slow her breathing. She needed to be strong for her daughter. It had already been a long morning even though noon was hours away.

As she waited inside the warm trailer, she looked at her daughter's drawings. Anna had created many drawings of the landscape surrounding the trailer and Maple had hung them up in every room. She would have loved the frosty landscape from this morning and would have asked to draw it. Maple would have grabbed the blue, black, purple and yellow crayons and Anna would have started with their new home. She always drew the trailer first. When Maple asked about it, she would say that it was her home – her happy place. That was joyful news to Maple, who felt that her running away made it all worth it. The drawings brought life to the home. They provided a sense of innocence in what had otherwise been a scary and dark life for Anna.

Anna was still here. Maple felt it. Her drawings gave the property life. But she couldn't stop thinking about her ex. Maple was convinced he had found them. Her thoughts were running wild with questions. How could he have found her? What had he done with Anna? He wouldn't hurt her – would he? Where could he have taken her?

She looked out at the cornfields. Anna could be anywhere. She seemed so close and yet so far. The emotional stress started spreading through her body, her muscles tightening up, and the adrenaline running through every vein. Her skin was hot to the touch. She didn't know whether to run out to the fields or stay home until the detective arrived. She looked at the clock. It had already been over an hour since she called 911. Why was it taking so long? Why was so much precious time being wasted?

Maple grabbed another cigarette from her stash and lit it using the space heater. It had become a bad habit. She needed to calm down. She needed to tell the detective everything she could remember, so she could get Anna back. She couldn't forget any important details. She looked out the window. It was quiet.

She suddenly felt a jolt of energy go through her body. If he had been there, there would there be footprints outside of the home. Would she be able to see his footprints in the morning frost? The sun had come up and the frost was turning into water drops, but maybe there were still some footprints left. That would help her prove her theory that he had come to find her and had taken Anna in an effort to hurt her. She grabbed her coat and rushed outside. Her heart started to beat fast again at the thought that she may get a clue.

The temperature was gradually increasing and Maple wasn't as startled by the cold air this time. She ran around the entire trailer, stopping at the sliding door that she had found to be slightly open. Nothing. There was nothing. The grass was wet, but there were no footprints there. The grass wasn't flat. It hadn't been stepped on. The green stands of grass stood proudly in the sun, looking nearly perfect. Maple closed her eyes and started to cry. For a brief moment, she thought there was a chance that she could find her daughter. Anna had felt close. Now, there was a different feeling inside. It was the feeling of Anna being ripped away from her.

Back inside, Maple went to Anna's room and lay down in her bed. She cried inconsolably and hugged Anna's clothing from the day before. Maple held the clothes right up to her face, smelling her daughter's scent for every breath she took. The scent of Anna made the pain more real. Maybe it was the cold weather or maybe it was her emotional mindset, but she was exhausted. Crying was exhausting. She closed her eyes and slowly started drifting off. She never wanted to leave. She never wanted to get up. This was the closest she could get to Anna. No one was going to take this away from her.

A car pulled up outside and the engine could be heard from inside the trailer. She opened her eyes wide, thinking that Anna had returned. Maybe someone found her wandering around. Maybe her neighbors had spotted her. Maple jumped out of the bed, rushed out to the kitchen, and flung open the front door to the trailer. She spotted a man in a car, wearing a brown uniform. She immediately looked inside the car, but there was no girl. The backseat was empty too.

An older man got out of the car. He had grey hair and he looked tired. He moved slowly. If it wasn't for his brown uniform and badge on his belt, Maple wouldn't have thought he worked with law enforcement. He didn't exactly seem upbeat and ready to work on a missing person case. She was ready to give him everything she knew, but she was also ready to snap at him if he wasn't doing what she wanted. He wasn't going to be the reason why Anna didn't make it home.

"Mrs. Maple?" he questioned as he walked up to her front door.

"Just Maple, Maple is fine," she replied as she extended her hand to him. His handshake was weak. A weak handshake meant a weak spine. Internally, she sighed. Couldn't they have sent someone else? She was already ready to yell at him, even though he was there to help.

"Please, come inside," she said, using her hand to show him the way. Without saying a word, he walked into the kitchen.

Maple noticed how he looked around the trailer once he was inside. He methodically glanced at the ceiling, at the walls and even at the floor as if he was looking for something. He walked over to the window that faced the front yard and dragged his finger along the brown streaks that resembled old mold stains. With his back turned to Maple, he started speaking.

"Where is she?" he asked Maple.

"I don't know. That's why I called you," Maple replied confusingly.

"Anna you say," he started, turning around mid-sentence. "How old is she? Is she into the whole prostitution thing?"

Maple looked shocked, her mouth opening slightly in disbelief.

"She's four," she replied, feeling no need to reply to his second question.

"Four," he said slowly. "Four, four, four," he added, stretching each word out as if to add suspense to the conversation. Her age didn't seem to change his approach to finding her.

"Is this her?" he asked while looking at a small photo of her, hanging on the fridge door.

It was the only photo she had of Anna. It had been in her wallet the night they ran away. It was now the only way she could see her daughter's beautiful face. If the detective asked her if he could have the picture, she would refuse. The way he was acting, Maple felt she had a better chance at finding her daughter.

"Yes, that's her," Maple said, but was quick to follow up her answer with questions. "Where is she? Where do we start looking for her?"

Maple looked directly at him, thinking that it may be a good idea to offer up her ex-boyfriend as a suspect. He didn't inquire about Maple's question as to Anna's whereabouts. It's not like he was asking her questions about what had happened. Asking if a four-year-old girl worked in prostitution didn't exactly help the case.

"I think I know who may have something to do with her disappearance," Maple added.

He turned around to look at her.

"I had an abusive boyfriend and we ran away. We are here in hiding. Maybe he found us. Maybe he took her to get even," she explained, but then she ran out of thought. "Maybe he…"

The detective looked at her, waiting for her to say more about her missing girl. He didn't exactly seem excited about this suspect that had just surfaced. She was feeding him clues and he didn't seem to care. Anna could have been thirty years old instead of four and it wouldn't matter. Maple encouraged him to sit down at the kitchen table and she told him everything that had happened. She explained how they had a shared home, how he got drunk, how he had put the noose around her neck, and how they had escaped using the Amtrak in the middle of the night.

She pointed to her landlord's phone number and address, which was displayed on the fridge. He could corroborate her story about showing up alone with Anna, looking scared, and being on the run. Maple even made a point to mention the newspaper this morning and how it had been in a different location. She had gone through the story a million times in her head and she didn't leave a single detail out.

He sat down at the kitchen table, right across from her as he listened to the story. As she was telling it, he would look around as if he wasn't listening. He even picked his teeth at one point. But he was her only connection to law enforcement and she owed Anna to do everything possible to get her back.

"Are you going to write any of this down?" Maple asked him, providing him with a pen.

"No, I got it," he said, adding in the same swift breath, "Were you guys having a fight?"

"No," she replied. "Not at all. What would we fight about? She's a child."

He ignored her question.

"You know, sometimes people do stupid things," he began his sentence, but was interrupted by Maple.

"Yes, my ex-boyfriend did some stupid things. And if he took her, it would be the stupidest thing he has ever done! But you not taking notes about anything I'm saying is pretty stupid too," she said with aggression in her voice, her teeth almost grinding together.

Why wasn't he prioritizing Anna? What could possibly be more important? Wasn't he a detective? Wasn't his job to solve these kinds of situations and bring peace to the community around him?

"You know," he said slowly, "I've worked a lot of these cases, even in this trailer park. And you know what? They often end up the same. Someone is missing. Someone is responsible. And it's always close to home."

Maple had a feeling he was trying to put the blame on her.

"What are you getting at?" she asked him, challenging him to be straightforward with her.

"Do you have a reason to not want a daughter?"

Maple's tone went from helpful to defensive.

"That girl is the reason I'm alive today," she said angrily. "I'm not going to fall for your games, Detective. I didn't hurt my daughter. I didn't cause her to go missing. I'm not that kind of mother!"

Maple slammed her hand down on the table, frustrated with him for not listening to her. She was trying to help and he was using his investigative tactics, pushing every single button he could find.

"You have a temper," he pointed out, taunting her a bit with his comment.

Maple sat quietly, the anger fueling within her. Her breathing was loud and her chest kept rising with every breath. She knew what he was doing. She had lived with a domestic abuser, someone who fueled his own anger and behavior based on her reactions. She knew what he was looking for and he wasn't getting it from her.

She took a few breaths, trying to calm herself. She thought about Anna and what she would want from her mother. Getting angry with the man who was supposed to help her wasn't the way forward. She thought for a moment before putting forth her request.

"Just find my daughter," she told him, realizing she would have to go elsewhere for help.

"I don't think I introduced myself when I came in," he said. "I'm Detective Morgan. If you need anything else, let me know. I'll see what I can do with the people I have available at the station. I'll be in touch."

He got up from the chair and walked over to the front door. Before walking out of the trailer, he stopped and looked back at Maple.

"Take it easy. We don't need more people getting hurt."

The detective glanced at the picture of Anna once more before he decided it was time to leave. He closed the door behind him and Maple immediately reached for the phone. After three rings, someone answered.

"I'm Maple, Anna's mother. I need someone other than Detective Morgan to take my case."

- CHAPTER 6 -

He closed the front door behind him, noticing the three locks on the inside of the trailer door on his way out. Morgan had only spent about an hour with Maple, but he already knew that she was emotionally charged and she would do anything to get her daughter back. But Morgan also had a theory. Maple had done something to her daughter and she was emotional because she was now starting to realize what had happened. She lashed out in anger at him, because she couldn't forgive herself for what she had done to her daughter. It was a classic example of someone snapping and then realizing the consequences of her actions later.

He was slowly getting used to the cold air as he started to walk away from the front door. The sun started to come through the clouds, as it had been overcast while he had been inside with Maple. Over the past couple of days, he has seen nothing but a continuous overcast. He opened his jacket slightly, exposing his neck and throat. He immediately felt the warm sun on his skin. Maybe this was a sign that everything was going to work out in his favor.

Morgan walked around the trailer but he spotted nothing out of place. There were no signs of an intruder as she had suggested. If someone really wanted to get inside and take a child, wouldn't there be some kind of damage? Wouldn't there be a broken window or door? Even the flowerpots from the summer stood upright. Nothing had been tipped, cracked or flipped over. Maple hadn't even tried to stage anything. She was clearly not a professional criminal.

He took out his notepad and skimmed through the notes he had taken inside. There wasn't anything of importance. He crossed out every line and wrote in capital letters, "LIAR!" on the notepad.

Morgan got back into the car, which had cooled down thanks to the chilly weather. He had only been gone an hour, but the car was freezing cold and it felt like the leather seat was completely stiff. He turned on the car and sat there for a minute. As the car heated up, he thought about Maple and the case. He just needed one piece of evidence to prove that she had done something. As for motive, it could be anything, but out here, a financial motive was often a compelling reason. People were so poor that they couldn't afford to feed people, so it was often a solution to limit the number of mouths that had to be fed. Maybe that's what had happened. Morgan's plan was to drive back into the station and see if he could come up with some new theories.

He could still taste the chocolate from the donut he ate earlier that morning. It had given him a joyful reaction, something he had often desired over the past couple of weeks.

He checked his cell phone to see if Jules had called him. There were no messages or missed calls. Morgan had secretly hoped she would reach out to him, telling him that she missed him and looked forward to seeing him that night. He missed those sweet gestures. Now, those sweet gestures were replaced with an emptiness that was often filled with alcohol. Being in this dirty trailer park didn't help either. He put the car in reverse and drove back out to the main road.

Morgan knew that his marriage needed to be a priority. Deep down, he wanted to put Jules first but the drinking just seemed to take over once he got home from work. Some days were just fine. They would both be at home and they would spend time together in the same room. But there was no conversation and they rarely looked at one another. It was awkward.

Over the past couple of years, Jules had prepared herself for retirement. She had gone out with new friends, had taken up new hobbies, and she was slowly gearing down at work. She looked forward to retirement. Morgan also wanted to look forward to retirement, but a small part of him was worried about kicking his habit to the curb. What if retirement only resulted in more drinking? He kept telling Jules he would quit, but he truly didn't know if he could. He was lying to her to keep her close. It wasn't fair. Morgan was being selfish and he kept telling himself it was the right thing to do.

He drove along the cornfields, watching every row go by. He wanted to think about anything but his marriage. Morgan was reminded of their troubles every morning when he woke up, and whenever the day was over and he headed home. Perhaps that's why he ended up at the bar more often than at home. He closed his eyes in frustration, giving his head a little shake. Think about something else. Anything else.

Maple did it. Anna is gone. What could be a good motive? What would be worth exploring?

His cell phone started ringing and he struggled to get it out of his pocket. He hoped it was Jules calling him, but he knew that it wasn't. She wouldn't call after the confrontation in the kitchen this morning. As much as she wanted to work things out, she wanted him to make the next move. He knew this. He knew he needed to drop the drinking, get up early in the morning, and show Jules that he was committed to her.

He recognized the number on the phone immediately. It was the station calling him.

"Morgan here," he said when he answered, not really sure who from the station was calling him.

"Yes, Detective Morgan. Christina calling," the voice on the other end said. She was the receptionist at the station.

"A body has been discovered by a jogger. Are you free to go out there and take a look?"

It was rare that he received calls like this. There had only been a handful of bodies discovered in his entire career within his county but the crime scenes were in neighboring counties. That meant he didn't have jurisdiction, so he never got to work those cases.

"Yeah, where is the body?" he asked.

"Out by Lander's Lake. The man who called it in said he would meet you at the entrance, right by the sign."

He knew exactly where the jogger had found the body. It was a remote area that was rarely visited by the locals. He thought that it could be Anna. If it turned out to be an adult or any other person, he would have his hands full before retirement. A missing person's case and a dead body could keep him at work for another six months. At least if it was Anna, he may be able to find some evidence to prove that Maple had committed the crime. The idea of a slam-dunk case made him step on the gas a bit more as he sped through the remaining cornfields before entering Beaverville again.

Lander's Lake was on the other side of town, so he had to go through town to get out to where the body had been found. It didn't take him long, as he sped through town. The police station wasn't located on the main road, so he wasn't too concerned about running into any of his co-workers.

For years, he had hoped he would get to solve another murder. He had been so proud that very first time that he had hoped people would commit murder more often. Now he finally had his dead body, but the timing was off.

Morgan knew there was a possibility that this wasn't Anna. It could be someone who had died from an overdose and had been dumped there. Morgan had seen these kinds of cases before and they rarely worked out in his favor. He was never seen as a great detective, solving cases - another failure in his books. At times, he would get phone calls from other counties to see if bodies had been found because family members were persistent. Maybe this was one of those cases.

As he left town once again, the landscape started to change. The trees started to tower over the road and before him lay thousands of acres of forest. His car seemed so small in comparison to the two-lane road, swirling through the tall pine trees. He also felt his ears clicking, as he was entering a higher altitude. Jules always admired this landscape, but he had never taken the time to really enjoy it. Now, as he was driving to one of his last crime scenes, he stopped the car at the side of the road. He shut off the engine and rolled down the window.

In the distance, he could hear a few birds chirping. Despite the cold weather moving in, some of the birds were sticking around. He glanced at the trees, trying to take in the silence of nature. Some of the pine needles were shinning, as the frost hadn't disappeared due to indirect sunlight. It was only a mild start to winter and he knew that it would only be a matter of weeks before this landscape would be covered in snow.

He closed the window again, as he noticed he could see his own breath. As the sound of the window closing snapped him out of his daze, he thought about the woods as a possible hiding place. This would be the place to hide a body, as no one really came out here. He was surprised to hear that a jogger had found a body. Why would a jogger be out here now?

Maple didn't have a car. Maybe the jogger had the car. Maybe the jogger was her accomplice. He put his foot down on the gas and sped out to Lander's Lake. Morgan turned off the main road as he approached the area where he was told to meet the jogger. The further away he got from the main road, the taller the trees appeared. It was an area that wasn't visited by residents of Beaverville, and no one maintained the area. Trees had fallen down during storms and they had rotted in the same spot for years. Most of the area looked brown and muddy. This wasn't a place where you would put a loved one to rest.

He had to drive a few minutes inland from the main road before seeing a car. There was a person sitting inside, waiting for someone to come along. It was parked right by a small wooden sign that read "Lander's Lake" in faded yellow paint. Morgan pulled up right behind the car and shut off his vehicle. The person got out of his car and Morgan rolled down his window.

"Did you call in a body?"

"Yes, I'll show you where," the man said with a sense of shock in his voice.

The two men started walking away from their vehicles and into the forest. The trees were still bright green underneath the frosty exterior. While Beaverville was covered in brown mud thanks to the vehicles, the forest looked unprepared for winter. The ice hugged the pine needles, devouring them so the needles had no chance to breathe. There was something beautiful about it all. Ice killing nature.

"It's down there," the jogger said, pointing down a steep hill.

Morgan looked at the jogger, irritated. At the bottom of the hill was a small pond. Some would call it a lake. It wasn't Lander's Lake, but a smaller pond just nearby. It wasn't a place where hikers would come often, as there were no identifiable trails nearby. There were large patches of leaves from the autumn season, blanketing the ground they walked on.

Rocks, fallen leaves, and branches surrounded the pond. But there was one area near the pond's perimeter, where some bushes had grown out of control. These bushes appeared larger than they were, as they reflected in the water. Underneath one of the bushes, a little foot stuck out. A wave of relief washed over Morgan. He knew this was Anna without ever seeing her face. It had been a few years since a girl had gone missing. It must be her.

Morgan thought about the photo of Anna that had been on Maple's fridge. He had a vague idea of what she looked like. He was confident he could identify her. His pride was quickly overpowered with grief. His confident smirk turned into a sad frown. The past came washing over him. And he felt his anxiety kick in as the dead body slowly came into view with every step he took.

The little girl was near the edge of the water. With mild wind gust, the water would be pushed just enough to touch her foot. Her body looked mangled. She had bruises on her body and her head was forcefully turned to the right. Simply by the way she was placed, Morgan knew her neck had been snapped. Her hair was knotted, as if she hadn't brushed it in weeks. He could tell her hair was long. She was wearing yellow pajamas with unicorns on it. She literally looked like she has been taken straight out of bed and placed here.

The bruises looked violently blue and black, but she looked oddly at peace. Her body was pale, but showed no signs of decomposition. It must have been dropped there recently.

"This is a good place to hide a body, don't you think?" Morgan asked the jogger, looking directly at the terrified man.

"Uh, yeah I guess. I mean I've never had to hide a body before. It was a miracle that I spotted her," he stuttered.

"Are you nervous?" Morgan inquired.

"Well, I don't know about you, but seeing a dead girl freaks me out."

Morgan could tell that he was shocked. He had never seen a dead body before and it didn't help that it was a young child. His skin was pale and he looked like he could throw up any minute. Taking a few steps back, the jogger was doing everything to avoid looking directly at the body.

What a wuss, Morgan thought. There was no way he could have carried the body out here to dump it without feeling queasy.

"What were you doing out here?"

"I...I, I was just running," he said, stuttering. "I've been training for a marathon and these hills are great for training. I just happen to look down at the pond when I spotted her. It was a coincidence."

"Hmm," Morgan said loudly.

"Can I get out of here? I can't really stomach this. I wasn't made for this."

Morgan nodded, signaling for him to head back up to the cars. As he walked behind the jogger, he knew that this small-framed man couldn't have done it. He wasn't a cold-blooded killer or an accomplice. He could barely look at her pale feet. How was he supposed to have carried the body down here for Maple? It takes a certain kind of person to do that, and he didn't fit the profile.

In disappointment, Morgan asked him to leave his name and number with him, and then head straight to the police station for further questioning. There was really no point in him going to the station, but it was protocol. They needed an official interview on file for the person who had found the body. It was a possible crime scene so the jogger couldn't just disappear.

Grabbing his phone from his pocket, Morgan called the station to get a crime scene unit from the city, and he told his fellow officers about the jogger coming in. He instructed them in what he wanted them to do. As soon as he hung up the phone, he could hear just how quiet it was out here between the pine trees.

All he could hear were the trees swaying in the wind. When the light wind gusts stopped, it was silent. The dark green pines danced slowly, as they settled down after each blow of wind that would circulate around them. At times, he could hear his own breathing, his lungs struggling to get fresh air in and expel it again. He could feel the cold air pinching his lungs.

Suddenly, a pack of birds took off from a wooded area right next to the car and Morgan jumped. It was loud. The birds lifting off could have deafened the sound of a child screaming out here. His heart started to beat fast. Suddenly, the beauty of the woods turned eerie. A child killer had been out here.

Morgan opened the trunk of his car and took out his crime scene tape. He needed to secure the scene before crime scene investigators came in from the city. It would be a while before they arrived because of the remote location, but he could help out by putting up the tape. The last thing he needed was another jogger coming through the scene and vomiting thanks to a dead body.

There were plenty of trees to choose from as he started his walk. He tied the crime scene tape to the tree and walked in a wide circle around the lake, so he could secure a large area, including the hill. Since the killer had dumped her near the water, there was a chance something had been left behind.

As he was walking, he kept an eye out for anything that could be considered evidence. Morgan kept thinking about Maple and the trailer. Maybe Maple had been here.

If she had been out here early this morning to dump the body, maybe there would be some clothing or a toy. Perhaps even a hair clip. Or a cigarette butt. Maybe Anna was alive when she was taken out here. The body hadn't been here long. It looked fresh. But the cooler air kept it that way too. There were many scenarios. While he was convinced that Maple had something to do with the crime, he struggled to find the evidence to fit his theory.

When Morgan had been in the trailer, he hadn't spotted any drug paraphernalia. But that didn't mean anything. All it took was Maple putting it in a drawer. It didn't take much to hide a bong, a syringe or white powder. Maybe Maple had been high on drugs, killed her daughter and now she was crying because she remembered what she had done. A psychotic rage. She snapped. It wasn't a far-fetched theory. It had happened before. Maple was just another mother, who had fallen victim to drugs.

It took Morgan almost an hour to secure the perimeter. It wasn't a big crime scene, but the landscape made it difficult to get around. It was beautiful in some places, but near the lake, many of the trees were rotting. Some trees were completely dead. There were bones of animals, including skeletal remains of birds and mice. It was a lake of death.

It would take all day to comb it for any additional evidence. Plus, he needed a medical examiner to look at the body. Getting a cause of death would help a great deal. He knew he would have to wait a long time before getting any useful information from crime scene investigators, so he decided to take a few photos of the body using his phone for his own investigative purposes.

He went back into his car to warm up. He checked his cell phone for missed calls, emails and text messages. Nothing from Jules. She wasn't going to make the first move. Maybe he had to step it up. Maybe he should go home after work and not to the bar. And maybe he could skip his trip to the liquor store. Just straight home. Morgan opened up his text message app and sent a text to his wife.

"Let's talk tonight over dinner," read the text. Within a few seconds, she replied, "Ok."

No liquid courage tonight. Jules needed him and he would make the effort. Morgan settled into his seat. It would be another hour before the crime scene investigators would pull up to examine the body and the scene.

- CHAPTER 7 -

Magnolia Watson felt the sun on her face as she lay in the bed next to her husband. The sun warmed her face and she enjoyed the brief moment of silence before the day's beginning. It was a new type of day for her and she knew these relaxing mornings would soon come to an end. She struggled to open her eyes, as the sun beamed. The cars on the streets below honked and the sound of the streetcars meant that the world had come alive. People were commuting to work. They were active, busy and ready to provide for their families. And here she was – in bed.

As she lay in bed, she looked over at the clothes she had put out the night before. Her police uniform had been traded in for a boring brown uniform. Sure, it didn't match her personality, but it meant she was moving up the ranks. No more traffic violations. No more undercover to bust teenagers doing graffiti. It was time to live out the dream of being a detective. She was leaving the police headquarters in the city and she was starting her new career as the main detective in a nearby town of Beaverville. The town was over an hour away, but it would give her more time with her husband.

Watson turned her head and saw her husband sleeping peacefully next to her. Doctor Sam Watson. It was still early and he didn't have to be at the hospital until tomorrow. His crazy work schedule had often conflicted with hers, so they rarely saw one another. But these days, he was working somewhat regular hours and with her new promotion, there was a chance that they could see each other more. He had high hopes that she could provide him with that family he had always wanted. He had come home early this morning and she knew that he would tell her that he had been called to the emergency room for surgeries. This happened frequently during the winter months, as there were more car accidents on the roads. Despite working for 10 hours or more, he would always jump in and help. He was a giver and a helper. She smiled at her husband, who appeared to be in a deep sleep. No need to wake him up.

The cold tiles in the bathroom surprised her as she stepped out of her pajamas and turned on the water in the shower. She let the warm water run and she looked herself in the mirror. Detective Watson. What a name. She smiled at herself, straightened her back and pulled her hair back in various styles to see what would work. Hair up it was. Better to look professional than young for this job.

She let go of her hair, letting it fall down. It rested on her shoulders, as the steam from the shower started to spread. Soon, the mirror was completely fogged up. She stepped into the shower, letting the warm water run down her body. She usually took her time in the shower, perhaps because she dreaded going to work in the city. Here, she was just one of many officers. She hadn't solved any cases or she didn't have the chance to prove herself to anyone. But today, a new chapter would start. Today, her shower would be short.

She shut off the water, and quickly dried herself with a nearby towel. Her hair hung wet on her shoulders, so she gave it a good rub before brushing it through. No need to glam it up. She was a detective now. It wasn't about appearances, but more about her skills. The brown uniform hung on a chair in the bedroom. Her husband hadn't moved. She quietly got dressed and pulled her wet hair back in a ponytail.

The apartment was modern and sleek. It was exactly what people expected to see when she told them that her husband was an ER trauma surgeon. Big responsibility, but an even bigger paycheck. The apartment was an open concept in the living area. The large kitchen had an island and from the kitchen, she could see both the dining room and the living room. It had been perfect for their dates at home, where he would cook dinners for them and she would catch up on the latest crime documentaries. And it would be perfect for the day when kids would start to fill their lives.

The kitchen lit up as she flicked the light switch. Over the island hung three large lamps that provided ample light for her. She grabbed the coffee beans, some water and had quickly made a fresh pot of coffee. With two pieces of toast in the toaster, she would soon have a complete breakfast that would keep her full for a while.

"Good morning Detective," her husband said, hugging her from behind.

She hadn't heard him get out of bed. He hugged her tight, as if he hadn't seen her in days.

"Good morning," she said with a smile, turning around to face him.

They embraced and kissed each other good morning. She knew he was proud of her and she was happy that he had remembered her special day.

"What are you doing up? You can go back to bed if you want," Magnolia told her husband, who looked extremely tired.

"It's just until you leave. I can sleep all day if I want to," he smirked.

"Busy night at the hospital? What time did you even get back?"

He looked at the clock on the stove. It read 10:14 a.m.

"About two hours ago," he said, smiling through his exhaustion.

"Wow, that crazy!"

"Guess you didn't see the news this morning," he said, pushing their iPad towards her.

As she put butter on her toast, she read an article about a massive car accident, involving at least six cars.

"More than 20 people severely injured, 3 people dead," she read out loud. "Doctors saving lives right on the pavement."

She looked up at him.

"You were there?"

He nodded, stretching his arms above his head.

"I've never done CPR on someone who was laying on concrete," he said with a low voice. "It was crazy. We had to drive there and we had doctors coming in from three hours away to make sure we didn't lose anyone."

"Where was this?" she asked. "In the city?"

He shook his head.

"No, no, some small stretch of road east from here. In the middle of nowhere. They suspect a deer started it all and with the icy conditions and all..."

Magnolia nodded.

"But enough about dead people," he said. "Are you ready for your big day my love?"

"Oh yes, I was born ready for this," she joked, flashing him a smile.

She poured the coffee and added some milk with her back to him to avoid answering any of his questions about her ability to be a detective. Secretly, she was a bit nervous about the day, but the last thing she wanted was to make him nervous too – especially after his long night.

She sat down at their kitchen island and Sam joined her, sitting in front of her. As she took a bite, he snatched a piece of her toast.

"Did you see those?" he said, pointing to the flowers that had been there for two days.

"Yes, thank you."

"Big day, big flowers," Sam beamed.

Even with his busy schedule, he still managed to get her flowers to celebrate her promotion. Sure, they surfaced two days before she was to start, but it was the thought that counted.

"So, you are alright to do this," he asked in a way that sounded like a statement rather than a question.

"Yes of course. I've been ready for this for a while."

"I know, but Noles – if something happens to you…" he began but took a break. "Look, I just know that town well. We get gunshot victims from there all the time."

Magnolia loved that he called her Noles. It took away the feminine aspect of her name, and Noles seemed like an officer name. A detective name. Detective Noles Watson.

"You don't need to worry," she said, reaching her hand out to hold his. "Chances are I'll be doing paperwork for a long time before I get to hit the field. Starting from the bottom, remember?"

Sam smiled at her. She knew that's what he wanted to hear.

"Good, I love paperwork," he smiled. "I don't need you laying on the pavement like those people last night."

But paperwork was far from her job description. Noles knew that she would be training under the current detective to take over and detective work rarely meant paperwork. She hoped she would have admins to do that for her. This was the only thing she had lied to Sam about since they started dating years ago. She had told him that she had gotten this job because no one wanted to take a position so far away from the city.

This was, in part, true. They did have a hard time recruiting police officers out there as there was no real chance of promotions, career growth and experience. Out there, there were only limited types of cases. But for Noles, this would be a career start for her. She was tired of being overlooked in the city and she looked forward to this opportunity. But Sam thought she was working for the detective, not training to be the main detective of the town.

She chowed down on breakfast while looking at him. He didn't know she was looking at him, thinking about how she was lying to him. There was a sense of guilt within her, as she knew he was concerned about her. Sam worked in a similar field. He saw death everyday. But as he had previously pointed out, there was a big difference in seeing a dead body in real life versus in a textbook.

But this was her passion. This is what she had prepared for. When she was doing traffic violations, she would study at home at night. She would try to solve cold cases by going over evidence, seeing pictures of dead bodies, studying bloody crime scenes, and even going to jails to talk to accused killers. She wanted to explain to him that her work was different, but she had never bothered to have the talk. It was best just to shoot him a little white lie and hope he would adjust over time.

"When are you leaving?" Sam asked as he looked up at her again.

"Oh, I'll be out the door in a few minutes. Can't be late for my first day."

She had been asked to be at the station at noon, so she could meet as many people as possible. She didn't really know where it was, but she knew it was a long drive through hundreds of cornfields. She hoped it was beautiful, as she needed to drive this route daily.

Pushing out the chair behind her, she grabbed another sip of coffee from her mug. Noles kept chewing the toast, as she reached out for her bag that she had packed the night before. As she got ready to head out the door, Sam surprised her with a thermal mug.

"For the road," he said with a smile. "Drive carefully out there. The roads could be slippery."

"Two milks?"

"Always."

She smiled as he handed her the mug. Noles was thankful for Sam. He took such good care of her. In fact, at times, she felt spoiled by him. But it was time to leave Sam at home so she could get on the road. She kissed him goodbye and closed the door behind her, knowing he would go straight to bed again.

The frost was visible on her car. The parking garage was underneath the building, but was leveled with the street. It was partially opened, so people walking by could see the parked cars. The interior of her vehicle matched the outside. The temperature had dropped from the day before. It had been moderate and had reflected what she loved about autumn. But this frosty morning was a sign of things to come. Noles turned on the car seat heater and took a sip of the warm coffee.

As she waited for the car to heat up, she looked at the mug and smiled. How lucky was she to have Sam? He could have easily stayed in bed and slept this morning, as his shift at the hospital had run into the morning hours. She thought to herself that she should try to repay him. Maybe she could rush home tonight and make him dinner. He would be home tonight as he wasn't due back at the hospital until the next morning.

The cornfields appeared in the distance as Magnolia raced out the two-lane road. It was therapeutic to be away from the big city. No traffic, no undercover, and no boss telling her what to do, especially when she didn't want to do it. There was something calming about the chilly landscape. Perhaps this was the pace out here. Slower. Relaxing. Old school.

It took about an hour before she saw the small town in the horizon. She hadn't gone out to Beaverville before she accepted the job. Noles had picked the job over the location because of the experience it would bring. As soon as she got into town, she pulled over to the side of the road and got out her phone. While she could guess her way to the town, she hadn't located the police station. A quick search for the station on the Internet and she had the address on hand. She opened up her email and found the email with instructions.

"Detective Morgan," she mumbled out loud.

He was her point of reference. He was the one she had to see. She put the car in drive and slowly rolled back out on the road, the ice from the ground breaking underneath her tires.

The dark police station didn't look nearly as modern as she had imagined. The brown building looked like a blast from the past in the frosty landscape that surrounded the town. As Noles pulled up, she frowned a bit. Maybe she was used to the glamorous architecture of the big city. She tried to remember where she had seen a similar building. It looked like a run-down version of the police station from the television show, *Twin Peaks*. She shrugged. At least it was a good show. She parked the car, grabbed her bag and walked up to the front door.

The interior of the police station didn't impress either. The dark wood paneling on the inside needed to be replaced. The lighting would surely give someone a headache at the end of a long day, and there was no sound other than someone coughing in the distance. Noles took note of the coffee thermos and the foam cups. She also noticed that the receptionist was missing. She looked around for a bit, browsing the map of the town that hung on the wall, and reading through some articles about safety – just in case she ran into a bear.

"Oh hi," a voice said from behind her. It made her jump. "Can I help you with anything?"

The receptionist had popped out from a room in complete silence. Noles had been so surprised that she couldn't find the words.

"I…hi," she started. "I take it that you aren't Detective Morgan."

"Oh no, that's not me," the receptionist said. "I'm Christina, the receptionist. He's out right now. It could be a while before he's back. Can I get you someone else?"

"Oh, he knew I would be coming," Watson explained. "I'm Magnolia Watson. I'll be working with him."

The receptionist lit up. She brightened up the dull police station in an instant with her smile.

"Oh, you are the new detective," she said, quickly adding, "…in training."

She smirked at Noles as if she had made a mistake in titles. But Magnolia didn't want to make a big deal of it, smiling at her as a way of accepting her apology.

"Well, I'm not sure if I'm supposed to tell you, but he was called out to a crime scene. Apparently, someone found a body. Oh, and there was a missing person this morning. It's a bit busy around here."

Noles nodded. She had prepared herself for a slow week. From what she had been told, she shouldn't get her hopes up about this job. She didn't think that there would be missing persons, killings, and these extreme crimes out here. They happened daily in the big city, but out here, she had expected to work on a murder once every few years. Not on her first day.

"Do you mind if I sit and wait?" Magnolia asked, while pointing to the chairs next to the table with the coffee.

"Not at all dear. Knock yourself out."

Noles spotted herself in the mirror in the lobby. She adjusted her brown hair, so she had a straight ponytail resting on her back. Her bangs looked even and they rested just above her eyebrows, allowing her blue eyes to stand out. She wanted to look clean and organized when she met Detective Morgan.

It would be another two hours before a tired-looking man walked into the station. He didn't look up at Noles, but she knew exactly whom he was. It had to be Morgan. He was wearing the same brown uniform as her and he looked old enough to be close to retirement. Maybe Noles blended into the brown wooden walls because he didn't acknowledge her at all until she stood up. With a straight back and her hand out, she asked him if he was Detective Morgan. He looked surprised. He looked at Noles, then back at the receptionist. She nodded at him and he turned to face Noles.

"And you are?" he asked, waiting for her to finish the sentence.

"Magnolia Watson - or Noles for short. People call me Noles. It's easier."

He didn't answer her and didn't shake her hand. He simply started walking towards his office, gesturing for her to come along. Maybe she didn't need to explain that she would be taking over for him. He seemed like he already knew why she was there. Morgan invited her into his office and pointed to the chair in front of his desk.

Noles took in the atmosphere of his office. She was overwhelmed. There were documents, papers, pictures and red string all over the walls. The documents overlapped one another. She couldn't tell whether they represented one case or several cases. One newspaper clipping stood out. It was about a case that happened in the city years ago. It wasn't even in his jurisdiction. Why would he have this hanging in his office? Did he have a personal connection to the case?

She remembered the case. It had been a double homicide. The husband had killed the wife and her lover. The story had garnered headlines for weeks, but she didn't recall him being on the case. Noles browsed the wall to see if there was anything else she could spot that didn't fit. He interrupted her.

"So, you are my replacement," he said, leaning back in his chair.

"Yes, I'm excited to be here. I can sense you have a lot of experience."

She pointed around the room at the articles. He looked up at his walls and smiled. Noles could sense he was proud of everything he had done throughout his career, but she wondered why he was taking credit for cases he didn't work on. She tried to think of him as someone who may just have done research. She was guilty of having old cases hanging around her living room for months while studying to be a detective. It was a personal choice to live such a lifestyle. Maybe his wife wasn't as supportive as Sam had been in having autopsy photos hanging in the dining room.

"Please sit, we have a lot of work to do today," he said, pointing at the chair again. "A little girl has just been found dead."

The chair in front of Morgan's desk was old. It was clear that it hadn't really been used. It was hard and the leather was stiff. Morgan tossed her the file folder with the label "Anna" on it. He started to tell her about his day. Within minutes, Noles had a breakdown of the case, including a briefing on Morgan's meeting with Maple and his theory about her dumping the body at Lander's Lake.

"This is my first case. I may need you to tell me what you expect from me."

Morgan looked up at her. He looked surprised and almost disappointed that she didn't address his theory.

"Well, I'm fairly certain the mother did it," he explained without addressing her need for help. "I don't know how she got the body into the woods without a car, but I'm pretty sure she's guilty. The circumstances fit. She's poor. The motive could be plenty of things. I've seen it all."

Noles looked up from a notepad, as she had been ready to write down some instructions. Morgan was sitting with his hands over his stomach, leaning back confidently in his chair. He was convinced the mother had done it, even though he had no evidence and no admission. Surely, he wouldn't be able to get a conviction on just a theory.

"What about the body? Where is it now?" Noles asked him, looking back down at her notepad, ready to write down whatever he said.

Morgan took out his phone and located the photos he had taken of Anna. He pushed his phone across his desk to Noles, asking her to swipe to see all of the photos he had taken of the body. He could tell she was examining the photos, looking at the natural landscape and the yellow unicorn pajamas.

"Crime scene technicians are transporting it to the city. A medical examiner will have a look this afternoon. Hopefully, we will have some answers before the day is over," he told her without taking his eyes off her.

"But look, this is your first day. I'll give you some free reigns. You can do some investigating, find some motives. But mark my words - she did it," he pointed out. "She's guilty. We just have to figure out how she did it."

Magnolia sat in silence, not sure how to react. It was one thing to be certain with evidence, such as DNA, but certain because of a gut feeling? He had worked many more cases than she had, but she believed in fair justice. The mother may be guilty, but Noles wasn't ready to arrest her without the proper evidence in place. Instead of addressing his theory, she wanted to keep the conversation going. She looked at her wrist to get the time.

"So maybe this afternoon...the medical examiner will have something for us," she asked quietly, pretending to take his theory to heart.

He nodded and sat silently looking at her. Noles felt odd about the whole situation.

- CHAPTER 8 -

Morgan sat in his office looking at this young woman in front of him. He had completely forgotten that she would be showing up. He leaned back in his chair, examining her. She looked like a young girl, straight out of the academy. Could she really handle his job? It was almost an insult that they would send her out here, a young woman with no experience to take over for him – someone with almost forty years of experience.

There was something really irritating about her, but he couldn't quite put his finger on it. She questioned him. How could she learn from him if she kept questioning his authority? Did she not know that he had been a successful detective? The frustration started building within. He found himself not listening to her asking questions about the case. Why couldn't she just take some direction from him and just do as she was told? Find evidence or a motive to nail Maple.

Morgan rubbed his eyes, irritated that she was sitting in his office, avoiding eye contact. He wanted her out of his personal space.

"When you are not working on the case, or if you come in early in the morning, you can work with Christina and the admins to learn everything you need to know," Morgan explained, already knowing that she would show up before him in the morning. "Do you have any questions?"

The more he could place on other people, the better. He only had a short time left before retirement and he was determined to solve this case. Anna deserved it. He deserved it. This new detective wasn't going to ruin it for him.

"These photos on your phone…" she began. "How do you know it is Anna?"

"I saw a photo of Anna in her mother's trailer this morning, just hours before seeing this little girl. Trust me, it's her."

He noticed Noles nodding, not quite as convinced as he had hoped she would be. Part of him thought she would be more of a pushover, more eager to learn from him.

"Since you think she's guilty, what do you think happened? I mean...I feel like I need your theory so I know where to go from here," Noles asked him, looking up from the notepad.

He looked at her in silence, examining her question. Maybe she was starting to realize that he was right. Perhaps she was willing to learn from him. Her question made him smile after an awkward period of silence. Before answering, he glanced at his walls. He wasn't sure if he wanted to send her a signal, but she looked in the same direction as him.

"She did it. The motive could be anything and that's what we have to find out. But she's poor. Finances could definitely be it. Maybe there was a debt to a drug dealer. Maybe she couldn't afford to get her daughter food. This is where you come in. You need to work on the motive."

Magnolia Watson nodded slightly, pretending to write everything down. The two sat in silence, waiting to see where the conversation would go.

"Don't you want to explore other suspects? I mean, I respect your theory and I think it's worth looking at, but I feel the scope is too narrow at this point."

"Don't bother," he said in a relaxed tone of voice, looking once again at his walls.

He wanted the walls, the cases, the photographs and the red string to send the message that he was a damn good detective and his gut feeling was always right. He could tell that she had hoped for a more direct response.

"But I don't feel we are…" Noles began before he interrupted her.

"Look," he said in a firm tone, leaning towards her as if to intimate her. "I've been doing this a lot longer than you. I'm telling you that she's the one. We need to find a motive. You can help me find the motive so we can charge her with first-degree murder, or you can go file something in the file room with the admins. If you want to be a detective, you need to listen, young lady!"

She sat back in her chair in shock, nodding before grabbing her bag and leaving his office. He could hear her asking Christina about a workspace and listened as the receptionist showed Noles her own office. Eventually, she would take over as the lead detective for the town, but for now, she was under his command.

His office went silent again as he sat there by himself. They had talked for just a few minutes and Noles was already annoying him. In many ways, Magnolia reminded him of his wife. Both Noles and Jules were nice and kind, but then they started to have opinions about things. And those opinions never really worked in his favor. He felt that they were both working against him. Why couldn't they just listen?

The sound of the fluorescent lights rattled above him as he sat alone in his office. The frustration grew within him, and his teeth started to grind a bit. He caught himself with a tight jaw and tried to relax his entire body in his old chair. The thought of leaving work now and going to the bar was enticing.

These angry emotions were familiar. He felt them every once in a while and they often ended up in the bottom of a bottle. He licked his lips and shook his head. She was not going to get the best of him. Noles would not be the reason why he ended up at the bar today. No. Today was for Jules. She deserved more than to be railroaded by a young wannabe detective.

Jules deserved more. Morgan knew she deserved so much more than he could give her, but he wanted her all to himself. He would never willingly let her go. She deserved a husband who was mentally and emotionally there, someone who cared about her feelings. She deserved someone who put her first. Morgan closed his eyes and leaned back in his chair. Why this case? Why this detective? Why now?

It would be the anniversary of the crash next month. 20 years. He took a deep breath and rubbed his eyes as if to avoid getting emotional. It had been 20 long years of pain and suffering with a few smiles creeping through the cracks. Just 22 years ago, it had been bliss. He was working as a detective, solving random crimes around town and he enjoyed diving deep into these cases. He would have pictures of criminals on his walls at home. Morgan often stood in front of them, pretending he was a big shot detective from the big city.

Jules supported him, smiling whenever he thought he had found a connection. She would sit on the couch beside him, flipping through magazines, pretending she knew what was going on. Sure, perhaps she knew he was making a big deal of nothing but it gave him confidence. It gave him an egotistical personality. She didn't care and it was who he wanted to be.

Jules was pregnant at the time. Morgan remembers how she would interrupt his thinking whenever the baby would kick.

"Oh," she would suddenly say, putting her hand softly on her belly.

"Helping his dad solve the case," Morgan smiled, putting his hand on her belly.

"What did you say? He knows the suspect? Thanks, buddy," Morgan joked.

He had been thrilled about becoming a father. It was never something he had dreamed about until he learned about the pregnancy. It had been an accident. Jules had been told that she wasn't able to carry a child, so they hadn't used protection. Then one day, Jules threw up. She went to the doctor as she had no other symptoms and a pregnancy test came back positive.

It was a boy. Morgan had been in the delivery room when his son was born. It was cliché, but he couldn't stop saying to everyone he knew that it had truly been the best day of his life. His entire career was about a tough image. He was a detective. Morgan didn't let anyone in. But this little baby had him wrapped around his little finger in seconds. Everything faded away. It was just Jules and this baby. These two were his world now.

People had come by to visit, so he could proudly show off his son. For months, Jules had been hesitant about bringing the baby outside of the house. She would take him out for a stroller walk, but would quickly come back home. She was very protective of this baby. He had always suspected it was because of her infertility diagnosis and this baby was possibly her one and only child. He was truly her miracle baby.

But life for Morgan went on. Months would pass at the station and he was eager to bring his son out for everyone to see. Then, an invitation came through the door. It was an invitation to celebrate the retirement of one of his co-workers and Morgan really wanted to go with both Jules and the baby. He knew how soft, gentle and caring Jules was with him, so he had no doubts that she would be able to rock him to sleep when he was tired. Jules felt more comfortable having the 8-month old baby with her than with a babysitter. She wanted to protect him.

And oh, did she ever. Morgan found himself smiling in his dark office just at the thought. Jules left the party to walk around with the baby, quietly singing lullabies to him until he fell asleep in her arms. The party would continue without her, but she always stayed within reach so Morgan could see her. He remembers standing with his friends, drinking a beer and being joyful about his life. He had never been happier than at this very moment. He had everything. His career was on the fast track to success, he had a loving wife, and he had the most adorable son who would grow up adoring his father and his work as a detective. He couldn't wait to hear his son say that his father was catching all of the bad guys. He remembered thinking that he was the perfect role model.

It was that same night that things went wrong. One minute he had thought of himself as the perfect role model and the next minute, he was the worst kind of role model. Morgan had strapped his son into his car seat and the baby had slowly fallen asleep. Morgan was proud of being a good father and his son could now rest as they drove home. It had been a cool summer night and he had been watching the fields as they drove home with the window open. Jules had been sleeping in the seat next to him. She was constantly up with the baby at night, so she was resting up, preparing for another sleepless night ahead. Morgan had thought about his life once again, smiling as he sped down the highway.

But something had gone wrong. Within seconds, the car had flipped and gone off the road. He remembers tasting blood in his mouth and he felt a single line of blood dripping. His head was pounding and he couldn't hear much. He turned his head and saw Jules. She was covered in blood but alive. She tried to frantically look in the backseat. Morgan quick spun his head around to see if his son was hurt. The car seat was empty.

Morgan faintly remembered the sound of another car pulling up. Through a high-pitched noise that kept circulating in his head, Morgan could hear a man asking if he was okay. He couldn't speak. He could barely keep his eyes open. The man had called 911. Morgan remembers hearing the man tell the operator that the car was hugging a tree, like "a half moon on a horrid night."

Morgan and Jules had survived but they were unable to get out of the car. It wasn't until an hour later that police revealed that their son had been hurled out of the vehicle and had slammed into a tree. His little body couldn't handle the impact and his back was broken instantly. He hadn't survived.

Morgan blamed himself. He blamed his emotions. He had let his feelings show and now he was being punished. What a role model he was.

The following months were spent in the hospital. Jules had broken her legs and Morgan had suffered a broken collarbone. Both had serious concussions, but doctors were hopeful that both would walk away with no noticeable brain or head damage. Miraculously, they were fine other than that. But the emotional scars were just starting to show. He blamed himself for the crash. He was driving the car. He had one beer. Jules tried to comfort him, saying that he wasn't to blame. But Morgan had pulled away. It had been too much for him to handle. Within a year, he was a full-fledged alcoholic. It was the only way to numb the pain.

Jules had also struggled with depression after the crash. She had felt guilty as a mother and felt like a failure as she was unable to protect her son when he needed it most. But unlike Morgan, Jules had gotten professional help and she was coping with her emotions after the accident. She still had some physical scars from the crash, but she was thriving with hobbies and friends. Morgan was surviving with the bottle as his friend and the bar as his hobby. It had been 20 years - she was still thriving and he was still digging himself into a deep hole.

Nothing had really changed over the years. Jules had desperately tried to get him help. The therapy had done wonders for her and she wanted him to get help so they could enjoy the time they had together. Now that he was retiring they could start doing things together. Perhaps she was wasting her time, but at least she was trying. Morgan loved his wife dearly. She had been there through everything. But he couldn't love her unconditionally. He couldn't love her fully until he learned how to love himself. And who could ever learn to love a baby killer?

- CHAPTER 9 -

It was still freezing outside, even though the temperatures had warmed slightly. Noles had received the keys to the police truck parked outside, the same truck that Morgan had used earlier. It smelled like alcohol and she wondered whether it was Morgan's personal scent or if the car just smelled like alcohol in general. She didn't want to jump to conclusions or judge someone who she had just met. Plus, she remembered how many drunken men she had transported when she worked in the city and she imagined that he could have been busy booking people just the night before.

She started the car and waited for the heat to blast through the vents on the dashboard. Noles thought about what she was about to do. Morgan had asked her to go out to Maple's trailer to tell her that her daughter had been found. Even though this was Noles' first case, she couldn't find reason or logic in this decision.

When he had asked her, Noles had rolled her eyes. He had gotten Christina to give her a note with the request. It's possible he couldn't face her again after yelling at her. Or maybe he just wanted to throw her into his crazy theory that this mother was a killer. Either way, it was shoddy police work and Noles was ready to fight him the whole way.

All Morgan had for evidence were pictures of a little girl wearing yellow pajamas with unicorns on them, possibly similar in appearance to the missing girl. As far as she was concerned, you never tell someone that a child has been found murdered unless you can absolutely confirm it to be true. It was simply bad police work. No matter what happened today, Noles wouldn't confirm or deny that it was Anna's body that had been discovered, as she simply didn't have the proof.

In her many years with the police, she had never been the bearer of bad news. And today wouldn't be that day – at least not if she could help it. Morgan could just be trying to give her more responsibility and throw her into the heartbreaking world of detective work. But he could also be passing on this daunting task, simply because he didn't want to do it. Noles didn't mind. Now she could talk to Maple herself and see if she was really a cold-blooded killer.

While driving through the fields to the trailer park, Noles tried to think about the case – or cases – she had been told about this morning. A girl had gone missing. The mother was distraught. Detective Morgan was convinced she was guilty based on a single conversation – and past criminal patterns that had nothing to do with Maple. Then, there was a body in the woods out at Lander's Lake.

Morgan had asked her to keep an eye out for anything that could provide a motive or any evidence that could give them what they needed to arrest her. But for Noles, it wasn't about finding a connection – it was about finding Anna. This was her chance. This was her chance to solve a case. She pressed her foot down on the gas a bit more before seeing the trailer park on the horizon. She was going to do this her way.

It didn't take long before Noles found Maple's trailer. It stood by itself up on a hill and looked plain. It wanted to disappear into the landscape surrounding it, being the perfect camouflage for the depressing trailer. Nothing had been done to the outside and there was no cozy fire pit where they could roast marshmallows. Many of the other trailers had been designed with an outdoor space in mind and Noles took note of how many of the owners had decorations in the windows and how some people had used their fire pits the night before. There were toy bikes and toboggans outside, indicating a neighborhood with kids. It wasn't the cold drug pit that Morgan had described to her on the way out the door.

But Maple's trailer was dark. The lights were off in the rooms facing the front, there were no toys, and it didn't look like there had been any activity outside for months. The curtains looked old with cobwebs in the corners. Noles shut off the truck and took a deep breath before grabbing her bag with her notes about the case. Maybe Morgan was right. This particular trailer stood out and not in a good way.

Softly, Noles knocked three times and she heard someone get up from a chair. The door was ripped open and Noles noticed the sense of disappointment on the woman's face when she didn't have a little girl with her.

"Who are you?" the woman asked, holding the door in her hand, ready to shut it quickly.

"I'm Noles," she replied. "I work with Detective Morgan."

The woman opened her door and Noles walked in. Despite the cold exterior of the trailer, the interior was warm and inviting. It didn't take Noles long to realize that a little girl lived there. There were drawings on every wall and there were some toys in the hallway.

"I had asked for someone different than Detective Morgan," Maple started the conversation.

"Oh," Noles said, a bit startled at the comment.

"I can't take his attitude. He accused me of hurting my daughter. I would never hurt a single strand of hair on her head."

Noles could see her hands shaking and the tears in her eyes. She knew immediately that she had nothing to do with the case. Her heart dropped.

"I wanted to ask you a few questions about your daughter that I don't think Detective Morgan got to ask," Noles began. "Do you remember what your daughter was wearing when she disappeared?"

"Pajamas, yellow pajamas with these pink and blue unicorns. It was the only set she had," Maple described.

Noles nodded as she swallowed hard. She thought about the pictures she had seen on Morgan's phone of the little girl near the pond at Lander's Lake.

"And do you have a photo of her I could see?"

Maple got up and grabbed the photo of Anna. She handed it to Noles, who examined it. The little girl from the woods definitely had similarities to Anna, but without conclusive evidence, Noles couldn't be sure.

"What has Morgan been working on since he was last here? Are there any leads?" Maple asked, clearly wanting to know where her daughter was, so she could get her home.

Without thinking, Noles answered as truthfully.

"A body was found this morning..." Noles started, but cut her sentence short when she saw Maple's reaction.

The cries were faint, but were followed by screams. Maple fell to the floor, shaking as she tried to comprehend the situation. Noles felt helpless. Even though she knew she had to stay professional, she couldn't help but hug Maple as she lay crying on the floor. Noles could feel her pain. Even though she hadn't said anything about Anna being found, Maple was smart. She knew that children don't go missing here in Beaverville and bodies don't just show up regularly.

Noles imagined what it would be like to lose everything she loved, what it would be like to lose Sam. She imagined losing the baby they had talked about for so many months. He wanted a baby, but she wanted her career first. She had promised him they would start soon. And yet, Noles loved this idea of a baby to the point where she felt physical pain. She felt herself choke up as she continued to hold Maple.

"I can't tell you whether or not it's Anna," Noles began, trying to console her. "I simply don't have the proof that it is your daughter."

Noles realized that she should have been more careful about the information she had on hand. In the city, bodies were found daily and detectives would talk about deceased people all the time. She hadn't realized that she was no longer in that setting. Things were different out here.

"We will find her," she said to Maple, as she continued to cry. "It's going to be okay. I'm going to help you."

Maple struggled to breathe as her entire body shook. Noles knew that she was going into shock. This wasn't going as she expected, but she had no idea how Maple felt. Her whole world had just crashed down on top of her and she had nothing left. As Noles hugged her, she looked around the trailer to see if anything looked out of place. She took note of the newspaper, the coffee mug and the drawings hanging on the trailer walls. A little girl called this place home. The drawings were simple, but they added innocence to this poor trailer. It screamed poverty and yet, this innocence provided warmth, love and a sense of hope.

"Look at me," Noles said suddenly, realizing that Maple had no one on her side.

Maple looked at her through her tears. Her lips were shaking, her hands grabbed Noles' arm for support, and Noles could tell she was trying to say something but couldn't get the words out.

"Where was the body found?" Maple managed to utter softly, not using Anna to describe the deceased person.

"A wooded area on the other side of town, Lander's Lake. Have you heard of it?" Noles asked, trying to see how much she knew.

Maple shook her head, wiping the tears away from her face.

"I'm here to listen to your side of the story. I'm going to help you. But to figure out what happened to your daughter, I'm going to need your help," Noles said, looking deep into Maple's eyes.

Maybe she felt that she was giving Maple a purpose. She wanted her to feel like this was going to get solved, not leave a mother behind with nothing to live for. Maple gave her a weak nod, and she pulled her up. She placed the heartbroken mother on a chair and gave her some space to calm down. Noles looked around and spotted the coffee machine. Within minutes, fresh coffee was brewing with the little coffee that was left.

Maple had calmed down, but her face was red and swollen from the crying. Noles placed the coffee in front of Maple and she took a sip. Noles did the same but immediately made a face, something Maple took notice of.

"Yeah sorry, I should have warned you. The coffee is shit around here," she said, adding a slight moment of comic relief to a rather horrible scene.

"Oh no, it's fine."

"I'm going to get more when I can afford it."

Instead of dwelling on Maple's financial situation, Noles tried to get the conversation back on track.

"Okay, I'm here for you and I want to know everything so I can find whoever is responsible for taking your daughter. But I need you to tell me everything you know," Noles said, grabbing a pen.

She was ready to write and Maple slowly started telling her story. Noles found herself amazed by every word coming out of her mouth, and at times, she forgot to write things down. She had to interrupt Maple a few times and ask her to repeat information. Noles was heartbroken for her. Maple had been a victim all of her life and now she had lost her daughter.

"Do you think that he could have found you?" Noles asked, curious to see if Maple had any theories as to how her ex-boyfriend could have located them.

"I mean, he has friends at that bar. They could have seen me leave. They could have followed me to the train station," Maple said.

"Even if that was the case, how would they know what stop you got off at?" Noles asked to which Maple shrugged.

"Your guess is as good as mine," she said, resting her gaze on Anna's drawings.

"We can't rule him out. That's for sure. He has plenty of motives and he knows how valuable your daughter is to you."

"He knows more than anyone on this planet," Maple pointed out. "He knows that losing Anna will absolutely ruin me. She's my everything."

Noles noticed Maple choking up again.

"My everything."

"I'm going to tell Detective Morgan everything we talked about today," Noles said, closing her notepad and packing her notes away.

"I don't want him working on this case. Do you hear me? He needs to stay away."

Noles looked surprised, but knew that he thought she was guilty. Her expression must have said it all, as Maple started making her case.

"Did you know that he thought I did it?" she asked. "He actually thinks that I could hurt my daughter, my own blood - the little girl that has saved my life again, and again. If it weren't for her, I would be hanging in that noose right now. Do you hear me? She saved me. I owe her everything. I owe her my life. I would never hurt her, abandon her."

Maple was furious, slamming her hand down on the table. She pointed directly at Noles with a faint sense of hope in her eyes.

"I want you to take this case. You trust me. You see things like I see things. I had nothing to do with this."

Noles simply nodded, not knowing if she could actually boot Detective Morgan from the case. But she understood

Maple's point of view. Morgan had been very vocal about his theory, about Maple living in a trailer park that had a bad reputation. But Noles wasn't sure if Morgan had heard the entire story. Surely, if he knew what she knew, he wouldn't pursue Maple as a suspect.

"You have my word. I'm going to leave no stone unturned," Noles said, holding Maple's hands in hers.

Maple smiled and it seemed like this was the first good news she had received in months. Noles got up from her chair and put on her jacket. She handed Maple her phone number and asked her to reach out if she remembered anything else. She noticed that Maple put it on the fridge, visible and readily available. The door opened up and Noles stepped outside, into the freezing weather.

"Do you mind if I just take a walk around the trailer here, just to see if anything looks out of place?"

Maple nodded her head and then closed the door behind her. She heard the three locks being locked as she stepped away from the trailer. As she walked the perimeter of the trailer, she felt a sudden need to solve this case. This wasn't about a title or about having a portfolio of solved cases. This was about a mother, who had lost the only thing she had to live for. Maple had been beaten down so many times, it was a miracle she was still standing strong. If Noles could help give her justice, it would be worth it. She reminded herself that she was still looking for a missing girl, not a killer.

Nothing looked out of place as she walked around the trailer. She stopped at the sliding door and examined the space around it. There were no fingerprints along the sliding door to indicate that anyone had tried to break it open from the outside. There was dirt on the doorframe, but it looked dry as if it had been there for months. Noles took out her phone and took a picture of it – just in case. As she continued to walk around the trailer, her phone rang. It was an unknown number.

"Hello..." Noles answered, stuttering a few moments later, "Detective Watson here."

"Hi, hello Detective Watson. My name is Dr. Weissman. I'm calling from the medical examiner's office. I was told to give you a call about the findings on the girl brought in this morning."

"Ah yes, hello," Noles said, walking away from Maple's trailer just in case she came outside.

"I can't give you a positive ID yet, but we have sent in the dental records in hopes of getting an identity on the girl. We could also present a photo to a relative, which would speed up the process. But in terms of the findings, I can tell you with certainty that this little girl's neck was broken by someone much stronger than her."

Noles stood still in the winter landscape. She was horrified as she listened to his findings. Someone had purposefully wrapped their arms around her neck and pulled her head so fast that her neck had snapped. This little girl didn't have a chance.

"But here's the interesting thing. Her body was completely mutilated. We can't tell for sure, but she was beaten so badly by a large object that she was completely paralyzed. It could be several punches or a single blow with massive force. We can't tell just yet. She has severe nerve damage and her spinal cord is completely severed. From what we can tell, this happened before her neck was broken."

Noles stood silently, trying to comprehend everything. For a brief moment, she questioned whether she could really work homicides. She wasn't sure how to cope with the victims, as she found herself getting emotionally invested. She wasn't sure she could handle seeing a little girl beaten beyond belief – and with her neck snapped. She closed her eyes.

"Could the trauma be caused by a bat or something?" Noles asked, not really sure what else the medical examiner could be referring to.

"Well, you are looking at severe damage. I'm not sure. It could be a car. She could have been thrown from a rooftop. I can't give you a definite answer. That's where my job ends and your job begins."

Noles felt overwhelmed. She turned around to look at Maple inside the trailer. She was crying at the kitchen table, clearly heartbroken at what Noles had accidentally told her. Now, she had the cause of death of the little girl and she felt horrible about knowing this information. But it was best that Maple didn't know anything until she could confirm it was Anna. She knew there would be so many questions she couldn't answer.

However, the arrows were pointing to the fact that it was Anna who had been found in the woods. Noles couldn't tell Maple who had killed Anna or why. What good would it do to tell Anna's mother that her daughter's spinal cord had been smashed to the point where she was rendered completely paralyzed? What good would it do to tell her that her only daughter had her neck snapped after this violent blunt force trauma? It would give her nothing but nightmares. And Noles didn't know Maple. If Maple ended up doing something stupid, she could be dealing with two deaths in one day.

"Thanks for the information," Noles said politely.

She hung up the phone and called Morgan.

"This is a rough one," he said to her, revealing the medical examiner had called him first.

"I'm not going back in to tell Maple what we know. I'm going to wait until we can get some more answers as to what happened to Anna – and get a confirmation from the dental records," Noles told him.

She sensed his anger over the phone, as she had been asked to share the news of Anna in the woods.

"Don't you get emotionally attached," Morgan warned her sternly. "That's not how we solve crimes around here."

Noles took a deep breath before ending the call and getting back into the car. The cold had crept into the car again, as she had been with Maple for a few hours. She turned on the vehicle and heard the heater turn on. She sat for a moment, feeling grateful for the life she had with Sam. He was a successful surgeon, who primarily worked in the ER. Sam had slaved away at medical school and he earned big bucks for his work. But he was also responsible for saving people's lives.

Noles, on the other hand, now solved those deadly crimes. There was one thing connecting them – death. Today had been rough already. But for the first time in her career, she felt like she had a purpose. Anna was her purpose. As the heat started to escape the vents on the dashboard, she looked into the fields behind the trailer in hopes of finding a place to start.

"Oh Anna, what happened to you?"

- CHAPTER 10 -

His office remained the same shade of luminescent yellow. The afternoon sun was started to set and Detective Morgan was still in his office. Given everything that had happened, he hadn't felt overwhelmed. There was something delightful about having Noles work with him. It gave him more time and she could handle the heavy lifting. He had purposefully sent her out to Maple to keep her busy, while he tried to make a case against Maple.

There was something familiar about her case. Not to the point where it was a copycat killing, but just the general scene. Mom is financially broken, daughter is the only value she has left, she's desperate for money, snaps out of anger one day and her daughter ends up dead. Detective Morgan knew that it was mostly boys who had been found dead, but he knew that mothers could snap at their daughters too. He had seen it himself. His mother was no saint.

Over the years, Morgan had seen many cases that reminded him of his past. But he had come to find that the theories about murders held true. People kill for money and sex. In some cases, it's planned and in other cases, it could be in the heat of the moment. It really depended on the desperation of the killer.

Morgan opened a drawer in a filing cabinet and combed through a few file folders. He grabbed four files, each containing a murder case. These cases were parental infanticide cases that had taken place in the state since he started working decades ago. There had only been a few in the past decade, but he had done his research. The drug busts and traffic tickets didn't do it for him when he was in charge. Morgan would examine cases from other counties and treat them as if they were his. He would investigate the case, examine new evidence as it came in, and he had even approached people involved in the cases. One investigator had told Morgan to stay away and mind his business.

Through his investigations, a pattern had emerged. The parents were either mentally ill or they killed their children because they saw no other choice. In a few cases, it had been too expensive to feed everyone in a household and they had exposed of the child. The worst case had been newborn twins, dumped on the train tracks a few years ago.

The station was silent outside of his office. People had gone home to their families at the stroke of 4:30 p.m. and he knew that he needed to go soon. He flipped through the files, examining crime scenes, and suspect profiles. He had a feeling that he could close this case quickly if he could just find supportive evidence that Maple had killed Anna. All he needed was a motive. Why would she kill the daughter she claimed to love? Was it all a lie?

The medical examiner had called him with the details and he had asked Dr. Weissman to call Detective Watson. He wanted Noles to draw her own conclusions from the information Dr. Weissman gave them. Part of him wanted her to learn, but he flashed a smirk at the thought that she would come up with some outlandish theory as to what happened. She couldn't solve this case - even with a team behind her. He hated how she still questioned the identity of the girl in the woods. Why was she being so meticulous?

Morgan closed the file folders and tried to shake the stress out of his body. These old cases were pointless to look at. It was a waste of time. Maple killed Anna. End of story.

His phone vibrated on his desk. It was Detective Watson. Morgan glared at the phone, contemplating whether he should answer, or let it ring, so the machine could get it. On the other hand, he knew he was responsible for her and she could go behind his back. He didn't know her. Maybe she was the type to break the rules.

"Hello," Morgan said, making it sound like a cold greeting rather than a question.

"Yes, hi. It's Noles. I mean, Detective Morgan. I just wanted to let you know that I've wrapped up my meeting with Maple and I'm headed back to the city now."

"Did you find anything at the trailer?"

"No, I walked the perimeter and there was nothing obvious out of place. And if this is Anna, I don't think the killing happened in the trailer or even near the trailer. The crime scene is somewhere else. I mean, the medical examiner said it could have been a fall from several stories up, but the trailer's total height couldn't kill a four-year-old. At least, I don't think so."

Morgan listened to her, as she rambled on about her theories. She had done a great job gathering information, but she needed to be better at putting the pieces together. A suspect wouldn't wait around for an arrest.

"What about a car? He said something about a car," Noles asked.

"Maple doesn't have a car."

"Detective Morgan, pardon my ignorance. But it could have been someone else."

Morgan bit his lower lip in frustration and wanted to hang up the phone. How dare she question his detective work? For a minute, he removed the phone from his ear and he could hear his teeth grinding in anger.

"Sir, are you there?"

"I'm open to hearing your accomplice theory. Maybe you should work on that tonight. Just go home Watson," Morgan said before hanging up the phone, cutting her off.

Morgan knew that the blunt force trauma was so extensive that Maple couldn't have done it alone. With no car in her name, no apartment building nearby and no other heavy machinery nearby to have done the damage, it probably wasn't her alone. But she needed to be locked up for what she had done. If she had hired help or slept her way to a killing, then she needed to be locked up. She was his mission and he wasn't going to let the lack of evidence ruin this final case for him. Maple needed to get locked up. He needed to get justice for Anna.

He sat silently in his office. The days were ticking away and soon, he would have his last day as a detective. Then, he would just become Richard. Nothing more, nothing less. He would become the Richard that drinks all hours of the day, dealing with the losses of the past, and dealing with the inability to move forward with his life. He didn't want an unsolved case attached to his name. Worse, he didn't want a case where the perpetrator went unpunished.

Morgan sat up in his chair and turned on the computer in front of him. It was an old machine. The screen was massive and took up half of his desk. It took a minute to start up and many in his department hated these slow computers. But he liked it. It was reliable. It had helped him investigate all of the cases in the state while he had been working as a detective, and the computer had provided him with a wallpaper of crime scene photos, mug shots, and long police reports.

He opened Google and typed in "types of motives for infanticide." He had hoped to find a solid list with a few different motives. It would have been an easy way to find a motive that fit. He knew that he couldn't build a story around Anna, but he desperately wanted this case to be over quickly, so he could maintain his good name. People make mistakes. This would be his only one if he got caught. He found several articles on postpartum depression, but that reasoning didn't fit with the narrative he wanted to tell. Anna was a child, not a baby. It would be farfetched in court, especially with no other medical records backing him up.

An article popped up from a university about violent women and crimes throughout history. Most of the women highlighted in the article had committed other crimes, such as abuse, theft and assaults before resorting to murder. Maybe he could dig up an old police report with Maple's name on it to prove that she had violent tendencies. Maybe it was just an anger problem and she was hiding it by playing the victim.

Morgan glanced at the corner of the screen where the digital clock was, realizing that it was well past dinner. He had been so intrigued by researching violent women online and digging through old cases that time had escaped him. For a moment, he panicked. He had promised Jules to be home for dinner so they could talk. Then, he felt a sense of hopelessness. He had made a promise that he couldn't keep. He had disappointed her once again. The battle was already lost.

He locked up the office and the station before driving away. As the twilight hours lingered in the distance, he contemplated whether to stop by the liquor store. This could be the night where he needed something to calm him down. It hadn't been the plan this morning, but plans tended to change in his life. Detective Watson had shown up. She had been a pain in the ass since she got here. If it wasn't for her, Morgan could have solved this case quickly and no one would have even known that there was a Maple and an Anna. It was Noles' fault he had been in the office so late, researching old cases. What a bitch.

The road was shining from some light afternoon rain and the streetlights reflected in the water that would soon turn to ice. He drove in the left-hand lane, letting cars pass him by. He could see the orange sign from the liquor store light up from the road, and he swung his car into the parking lot. From his car, he could see the bottles of vodka, tequila and scotch. Today, he didn't care what kind of alcohol it was.

His fingers tapped quickly on the steering wheel as he tried to calm himself down. No one was pushing him to go inside. No one was stopping him either. The tapping became louder and quicker. In a sudden move, he stopped the tapping and left the car. Within minutes, he was back in the car with two bottles of booze. He put the brown paper bag with the bottles down on the passenger seat and looked at them. In an angry rage, he hit the steering wheel repeatedly.

"Goddamn it!"

As quickly as the outburst had come, it left. He quietly turned on the car and backed out of the parking lot. It took another 15 minutes to drive to his house. As he pulled into his driveway, he looked at the bottles once more. He had promised Jules no alcohol tonight. He could still keep that promise. As he removed his seatbelt, he opened the door, leaving them in the passenger's seat.

The door handle to the house was cold. He grabbed it, opening the door slowly. He didn't know what to expect. He removed his shoes and jacket and neatly placed them in their designated spots. No need to cause more damage than necessary tonight. The kitchen was beyond the laundry room where he had entered. Jules had turned off the lights in the kitchen, but he could see her sitting in their kitchen nook. In front of her stood a wine glass with red wine. In his usual spot was an empty chair accompanied by a cold meal on a plate. It looked like a scene from a devastating movie, where Jules had just lost her beloved husband but couldn't quite face the truth and had cooked him a meal out of habit, out of memory, out of grief. He sensed he had to ease into this one.

"I'm so sorry I'm late."

Jules didn't turn around to face him. She continued to stare into their backyard. The twilight sky was turning dark and the black trees stood out against the fading blue sky.

"I tried to leave early. I did. But a body was found. A little girl. It's bad timing with retirement and all, but I'm sure it won't take long."

Jules didn't flinch. Her hand had been resting on the foot of the wine glass and she slowly started moving the glass around in circles, swirling the wine. She looked at him, nodding her head at his plate of food. He wasn't hungry. It didn't look appetizing either.

Without hesitation, he took the plate and placed it into the microwave. Without a word, he heated up the food, placed it back on the table and sat down in front of his wife. He chose water over wine. He was trying. He really was.

"Did you drink today?" Jules asked suddenly.

Morgan looked up with a sense of shock and disgust on his face.

"Is that what you think of me? A functioning alcoholic who can't get through his day without a drink?"

She looked at him. She wanted an admission. He knew what she wanted. She wasn't getting it.

"I haven't had a drink in weeks."

He was lying. She knew it. Suddenly, he didn't care about those efforts.

"If we are going to talk about things, we need to be honest. You drink and I know it. Who do you think cleans up your bottles every week? The garbage man?"

Morgan pushed aside his plate of food. She looked down at the food. He had barely touched it.

"Not good enough?"

"Look, we just found a body of a little girl. A little girl Jules! That's hard for me, okay?"

He slammed his hand down on the table.

"Don't you use that as an excuse again," Jules said angrily back. "We've been doing this for years and you haven't changed."

He looked down, scratching his head. A part of him wanted to yell at Jules, get all of his frustrations out. She had done nothing wrong and she was getting the blame. But she was frustrating the hell out of him. Jules and Detective Watson. Both of them in one day.

"Look, I'm a failure, okay? I admit that I'm not perfect," he said suddenly. "I get up, I go to work, I deal with crimes all day, and when things get rough for me, I drink."

"I can't live with an alcoholic."

"I'm not an alcoholic Jules. I can cope without alcohol."

She slowly closed her eyes. He had given her that promise many times before.

"This case is just - a child's killing. I just keep seeing him."

Jules shed a tear. He could see it roll down her cheek. He knew it wasn't fair to bring up their son in relation to his drinking. While his death had started it, his sobriety was overdue.

"There's always an excuse," Jules muttered, her voice changing slightly.

Morgan knew she was right. He had nothing to add.

"You need help. I can't do this anymore."

She got up from the table and walked up the stairs. He heard her go into their bedroom and slowly close the door. This didn't go as expected. He knew her pleas for sobriety would surface, but he had hoped to skirt over his issues once again, buying him more time to deal with them. Time was up.

How could he cope without Jules in his life? How dare she threaten to leave him? They have years of history. They had a son together. Goddammit, she chose him. Morgan felt the anger building inside of him. No one left him behind, not Jules. He was about to retire from a glorious career. Maple needed to be convicted. Jules needed to stay. And Noles needed to stay the hell out of his way.

The dinner plate flew across the room thanks to his strong throw, hitting the wall. It was silent in the kitchen, as Morgan got up. He had no desire to clean up the mess he had made. He slipped into his shoes and got into the car. In a quick swoop, he removed to cap from the bottle of vodka and chugged it. He immediately regretted his decision. A failure again.

He couldn't hold back. The tears came suddenly as he sat in his car in his dark driveway. Outside the car, the trees waved slowly as the frost started to set in for the night.

- CHAPTER 11 -

The gas pedal hit the floor as she left the little town of Beaverville behind. The town disappeared in her rear view mirror and there was nothing but cornfields around her. The landscape was massive and she imagined it stretching for hundreds of miles. It was a soulless landscape out here. She parked the car on the side of the road and stepped outside as the cold wind started to pick up. Looking ahead, all she could hear were the dry leaves from the corn bashing in the wind. Even if someone screamed out here, it would be impossible to locate the origin of the scream. There was something peaceful, yet scary about this place.

Noles got back in her car and turned on the heat. Her body hadn't been prepared for this shift in temperature. Just last week, it had been the perfect autumn day where she could wear a short sleeve during the day and bundle up as the cooler night weather approached. Now, she felt she needed several layers just to keep her body temperature steady. She hoped she wouldn't get sick, as her body couldn't handle these sudden drops in temperature.

It was time to go home to Sam. She pushed her foot down a bit more on the gas when she got back on the road. Usually, she and Sam would touch base throughout the day, but Noles hadn't checked her phone at all. The only time she had used her phone was when the medical examiner had given her a call. The details of the little girl's death had put her in a fog, and she had put her phone in her pocket without checking it. Maybe Sam was right. Maybe this job wasn't the ideal one for her. Seeing a dead body on television was one thing, but being responsible for solving a little girl's death was already taking a toll on her.

As she was driving, she wondered whether she should call him to let him know she was on her way home. Surely, he would enjoy knowing where she was and that she was okay. On the other hand, it would be nice to surprise Sam by showing up in time for them to eat together. She was planning on cooking him dinner but all she had was some leftover chicken in the fridge. The dinner would already be a horrible display of her homemaker skills. Sam was the chef in the home, no doubt.

For years, Magnolia had tried to be a good housewife, but there was something about it that just didn't appeal to her. She had washed Sam's white button-down shirts with a red sock once, and she had burned dinner numerous times. When grocery shopping, she would always get the wrong kind of lettuce or Sam would just shake his head and giggle when she unpacked the groceries. She knew she was a hopeless housewife, so she let Sam do most of it. He had a certain way of wanting things done, so she let him do it. It was one thing they never argued about. He ran things at home like he did in the emergency room: clean, organized and he always had things ready to go as he needed them. While Noles enjoyed this kind of living, she could never keep up with his standards.

Noles' phone buzzed as she continued to race down the small country road. She knew it was Sam, but she let it ring. She smiled, knowing he would be surprised to see her home so soon. Since it was her first day at work, Noles had hinted that he shouldn't wait for her, as she wanted to be the last person to leave the station. It was all about showing people dedication and motivation. Needless to say, that plan didn't work out today. She hadn't expected Detective Morgan's attitude, Maple's grief, or the hunt for a killer.

For about an hour, Noles cruised along the country roads, as she thought about her first case. There was something about Morgan's theory that just didn't fit. Maple could have snapped her daughter's neck in the woods, but the motive didn't fit. Why would she harm the daughter that kept her strong through one of the darkest periods of her life? If Morgan's theory was true, then there had to be something else. There had to be a reason as to why Maple wanted her daughter gone. Surely, a mother simply doesn't snap her daughter's neck because she's poor. As Noles thought about Maple's story again, the clouds started to gather above her. A snowstorm was coming in and it was headed right for the city.

By the time Noles reached the outskirts of the city, she felt transported back to her old job. It was another mindset. Her thoughts became dark, depressive, and aggressive. She always felt she had to fight for herself, for opportunities and to be noticed. It was a depressing way to live, which is why she was happy she got out. The town of Beaverville had been a savior. Plus, the city was predictable. It was busy, dark, boring, and common. Noles was now in a different world. Nothing could compare her old professional life with that of Anna's case and the old-school attitudes that Morgan represented so well.

The door opened to the parking garage of Noles and Sam's apartment building. It was still as cold in the garage as outside. She spotted his black car in its usual spot and knew he was home. He probably had a short day since he had been on the job for almost 24 hours the day before. The car shut off as she turned the key and she felt the cold air stream through her car as she opened her door. The snow was starting to come down and she managed to get a glimpse of it as the garage door closed after her.

The smell of green beans, baked potatoes, and charbroiled steaks filled the hallway, as she walked towards their apartment door. Simply by the aromas in the shared hallway, she knew Sam had outdone himself. She expected a glass of wine waiting for her as she walked in the door, and he would encourage her to take a hot shower and get comfortable after a long day at work. He had done this many times before and she didn't think today would be any different.

As she opened their front door, she immediately saw Sam in the kitchen, chopping up some vegetables for a salad. As expected, the wine was ready on the kitchen island. He swung around as he heard the door open and flashed her a big smile as he laid his eyes on her.

"Hey, beautiful. Welcome home!"

She smiled at him, as she dropped her bag on the floor. In a swift move, she removed her jacket and hung it up on the rack. Her shoes quickly flew off as well, and she took a deep breath as she let herself sit on one of the bar stools by the kitchen island.

"How was your first day of work? Lots of paperwork?" Sam asked with a smile.

"You have no idea," Noles said while looking at him with tired eyes.

"You know, I thought about making you dinner tonight as thanks for getting up with me this morning," she added.

Sam looked at her with questionable eyes that only meant one thing. Forget it. He wasn't going to eat whatever rice or pasta dish she would throw together. He had told her too many times that her pasta was overcooked. He would rather chow down a fast food burger and sloppy fries than eat her food.

"You let me handle the cooking," he said while pointing at their bathroom with the knife in his hand. "Why don't you go take a shower and then come back out for a glass of wine? I can imagine you want to unwind tonight."

She smiled at him and nodded. It did sound like a great suggestion – as it had been every other day she had come home late. As she walked into their bedroom, she unbuttoned her uniform. Without thinking about it, she got undressed and threw it on the floor. She had longed for the hot shower all day, especially after visiting Maple's trailer. There was something unforgiving about that cold landscape and lackluster trailer park.

It didn't take long for the hot water to steam up the bathroom once again and Noles jumped right in. The water hit her skin, slowly providing the warmth she had desired for hours. As the water hit her hair and shoulders, she thought about Anna. She thought about her role as a detective in the two cases – the death of a child and the case of a missing girl. She needed to solve them to prove herself to Morgan and to the town. She needed a strategy. Perhaps Morgan was right about Maple. Even though it didn't match her gut feeling, Magnolia knew that Morgan may know Maple and may know the community better than her. Perhaps she needed to listen to him and take his theory into account instead of starting from scratch.

She tilted her head back and closed her eyes. The warm water ran down her face as she tried to relax. She wondered how she would tell Sam about Anna and the body in the woods. She heard him from the other room, shouting that dinner was ready. Turning around, she shut off the hot water and grabbed a towel without coming up with an answer.

As she stepped into their bedroom to grab her pajamas for the night in with Sam, she spotted her uniform on the floor. It had been left in a pile, abandoned by her desire to take a hot bath. For a moment, she felt a tremendous amount of guilt. Maple's emotional breakdown from earlier today came rushing back and Noles' heart physically hurt. While Maple sat alone tonight in a trailer in the middle of nowhere, grieving the possible death of her daughter, here she was with a hot shower, supportive husband, and a charbroiled steak waiting for her.

Noles sat down on the bed, grabbed her uniform and looked at it with an intensity that can only be described as heartwrenching. Magnolia felt she was grieving her own child. She remembered what Morgan had told her about getting too attached to these cases, and to the people involved. How could he be so distant? Noles had held onto Maple as she cried and screamed after learning that a body had been found. It was gut-wrenching.

Guilt. Shame. Awfulness.

Noles felt horrible all of a sudden, as she compared her life to Maple's. Her life had been fairly easy, no major hurdles. A part of her knew it was wrong to compare, but she also felt a sense of pride in being able to help Maple. Maple should be eating that delicious dinner that Sam had cooked and drinking the wine.

"Are you okay?"

Sam was standing in the doorway, looking at her holding her uniform.

"Yeah sorry, I heard you before, but I just got distracted."

She smiled at him, nodding towards the kitchen.

"I'll be right out."

He turned around to walk away, leaving Noles behind again with her thoughts. She needed to find whoever had taken Anna away from her mother. There was nothing more important right now than justice.

"Come sit," Sam said as Noles walked back into the kitchen, pulling out a chair for her.

"Thanks babe."

"You seem so distant now. What happened in the shower?"

"Just a long day," Noles said, as Sam placed a perfect meal in front of her, the beans placed neatly on top of the steak. It looked like a magnificent dining experience, something that would easily cost more than an average dinner for two.

"Nightmares about the paperwork?" Sam joked, clearly trying to lighten the mood.

"No, actually, believe it or not - a little girl has been killed. Four years old. Dumped in the woods by some coward.

In addition, a little girl has been taken from her home, leaving her mother completely devastated. So no, no paperwork today."

Sam sat quietly, staring at Noles as she told him about her day. His mouth was open, as he appeared to be struggling to find his words. She knew that the word "killed" had rattled him to the core. Noles was working on the cases, and there was no mention of paperwork. Yes, she had just admitted to lying to him about her work description but she hoped he could forgive and forget.

"The same girl?" Sam asked.

"Very possible, but nothing confirmed yet," Noles pointed out.

"Wait! A body? I thought you were working in the office."

"I know, but they needed extra help in the field," Noles said, trying to normalize the conversation and divert from her lie.

"Did you see the girl?"

Noles shook her head, as she took a big bite out of her steak.

"Just in pictures, but I was told she had a broken neck, and had been killed by massive blunt force trauma."

Sam looked like he had seen a ghost, and Noles knew she was in trouble. She knew that he wanted to protect her. He had seen enough horrible things in his career, and he didn't want her seeing these things as well. Sam sat quietly and she knew he was trying to find the words.

"Yes, I may have stretched the truth a bit," Noles said, wanting to explain herself before he got too caught up in everything. "You know this is my dream. You know I've been studying for this. I didn't know they would find a dead body on my first day of work and I certainly wasn't prepared to talk to the mother of a missing child. But you know what? I'm excited to assist in the investigations and I'm excited that I could possibly help his mother find some justice. You should be supportive of that."

Her tone wasn't harsh. It was calming and friendly. Sam, still in shock, started to calm down a bit, nodding as she spoke. They sat in silence for a bit and Sam nodded once before opening his mouth.

"You are right, I'm so sorry."

He looked down at his plate. Noles quickly interjected.

"Hey…look at me. It's okay. I get you are scared. It's a scary industry. I know. I'm dealing with a killer here."

As soon as she said it, she wanted to take her words back. Sam looked worried, but when she smiled at him, he calmed down. After a few seconds, he looked more relaxed, his jaw less tense.

"So, how are you going to find this mysterious killer? DNA? Fingerprints? Any of your CSI material giving you any ideas?"

Sam was referring to Noles' marathon Sundays, where she would watch crime shows and the occasional documentary.

"Ha-ha," she said mockingly, and he smiled at her.

"I don't know if Detective Morgan knows more than I do, but I know very little. I'm guessing canvassing the trailer park and doing some interviews will be the next step. The medical examiner is looking at the body for any evidence we can use. But I'm not sure of any procedures Morgan follows," Noles said, while cutting her steak and loading some beans onto her fork.

"Do you have a suspect in mind?" Sam asked.

"Morgan thinks that the mother did it, but my heart and mind tell me no."

"Why's that?"

"Because she's a mother. I can't go into detail, but she's had it rough. That little girl was everything to her. She would never kill her. I'm pretty sure that she's innocent and that Morgan is just trying to nail this on her."

Sam drank from his wine glass.

"Well, maybe you should listen to him. I mean, isn't he a seasoned detective?" Sam asked.

"Trust me on this one. She didn't do anything."

They continued to eat their dinner in silence, and Noles knew that Sam didn't know what to say about the entire situation. She had been busted in a lie and he was trying to be supportive. He was avoiding eye contact and she knew he wouldn't want to snuggle her later. It was a loss she was willing to take.

"So, what's the plan for tomorrow then?" Sam finally asked, breaking the silence between them.

"I need to talk to Morgan about finding the girls' killer. We must find some more evidence. And it would be nice if we could find the girl's identity to see if it matches Anna.

"Was that her name? Anna?" Sam asked quietly, to which Noles nodded.

"Anna," Sam said quietly, as Noles hoped he would see things from her perspective.

- CHAPTER 12 -

The yellow moon lit up an otherwise black night sky and Maple sat quietly in her trailer, watching it. She studied every single aspect of it, including the dark shades, the beaming light coming from it, and how it illuminated the landscape below. If she didn't focus on one thing continuously, she felt she was losing her mind.

In the snow in front of the trailer, she could see that a snow bunny had jumped around, leaving small footprints in the snow. She thought about the animal jumping away, seeking shelter in the winter landscape. The cold weather was a challenge for the bunnies as well, as there wasn't much shelter for them out here in the cornfields. They rarely came out here, but when they did, they usually brought trouble with them. Garbage cans would be flipped upside down, and flowerpots left out for the winter would be tipped over.

Her thoughts were drawn to her missing daughter, and how Detective Watson had mentioned another person finding a resting place in the woods on the other side of town. What if that was Anna? If so, she had been far away from her home. How did she get there?

The space heater was going at full blast. The temperature outside dropped at night. It was just after 2 am but Maple couldn't sleep. She hadn't tried to sleep, but she knew that if she went to bed, she would just end up staring at the wall. Her body was tired, but her mind was awake. There was no way she could sleep. There was a big possibility that she had lost her daughter, because someone decided to take her life. She felt completely helpless.

The police station had sent out an incredibly incompetent old detective, who judged her and tried to get her to confess to killing Anna out of anger. She knew that if she said the wrong thing, he would probably arrest her and tell everyone that she had admitted to the murder. But if she could just prove that she had been in her trailer all night and day, surely he would see that she was innocent. That alibi would be tough to prove as she kept to herself. Everyone wanted to be alone out here.

Her eyes had been filled with tears for hours. Detective Morgan had made her feel completely hopeless. She had felt like an incompetent mother, who couldn't even keep an eye out for her daughter. Morgan had judged her and it was clearly an investigative tactic. Without sounding cliché, he had made her cry because he was a bully. He wanted to be right and he didn't care what he said or did to make her feel horrible. It was just the way he was raised and the way he lived his life. Of that she was sure.

Detective Watson had been much better for her. She listened, at least. She hugged her. But Detective Watson didn't seem like she had solved a lot of murders. There was something innocent about her. Maple rubbed her eyes, realizing that perhaps she was more tired than she thought. But this was about Anna. She wanted to find whoever did this to her, and since Detective Morgan wasn't out interviewing people about Anna, she needed to do something. She needed to find out what had happened to her daughter. Maybe she wasn't even dead.

Maple grabbed a piece of paper and one of Anna's crayons. She made two columns and wrote "Willy" on top of the one column and "Beaverville" on top of the other. She wrote fast. There was no time to spare.

"Okay Willy, where are you hiding?"

Willy – or William – was the name of her ex-boyfriend. All of his friends called him Willy. It was a friendly nickname for the otherwise sophisticated birth name of William. He had previously told Maple that William was the name he would use when he got a job, possibly a career. It was an adult name. Willy was the fun name, the party name – a name that carried no responsibilities and no accountability.

Willy didn't know his father and he didn't have the best relationship with his mother. Perhaps she had beaten him when he was little, because he didn't have much respect for her or for the other women in his life. He was simply a rude and dangerous person with some great looks. Sadly, Maple wasn't strong enough to say no to him when he began pursuing her.

He wasn't Anna's biological father, which is why he wouldn't flinch an eye when it came to taking Anna and even killing her. Willy never saw Anna as his own daughter and she was nothing but an extra person who lived with him. She was Maple's baggage.

She had often thought about calling him William in a fight, just to see his reaction. She knew that he refused to answer to William, almost as if he wanted nothing that Willy was doing to be associated with the William he wanted to become one day. For him, they were two different people with two different personalities. But she was scared of the consequences. It was a fine line to straddle and she didn't want to put herself in a dangerous situation. Now that she knew he wanted to kill her, she could have been six feet under by now. And his behavior was all the more reason why he would come after Anna. She was a precious pawn he could easily use to get what he wanted.

He was a scary person, no doubt about it. While she had once loved him, she now knew him as the dangerous person he had always been. Her life was in danger. If he hadn't been so extreme, she would have proudly walked out on him when he was awake and sober. She ran away at night to save her life.

In the column for Willy, Maple tried to come up with every likely scenario that he knew where she was. He noticed they were gone and learned from someone at the bar where they had gone. Someone had followed them on the train. Someone had been following her all along. He had gotten to her friend, who had been forced to reveal the train station where she got off. He had asked around with a picture of them in his hand. He had placed an ad in the newspaper. He had contacted the police and Morgan had found them. Everything could be a scenario she had to explore. Maybe he was watching her right now, waiting for the perfect time to kill her. Or maybe he wanted to leave her be for now, watch her struggle as she learned that he had killed Anna. Emotional torture was his middle name.

In the other column, she wrote down scenarios where Willy was innocent. Not much came to mind at first. As much as she wanted to find him guilty and put him away for murder, there was the slight chance that she had outsmarted him. She wanted to give herself that credit. She had planned everything behind his back. There was the chance that she had escaped him and he had no idea where she was hiding. A part of her felt confident in the fact that she could have fooled him. With that said, it was hard to come up with other scenarios because she didn't know anyone around here. Who could hate her so much that taking her daughter would justify that anger?

Maple didn't know her neighbors. She had no other leads or any other ideas for suspects. A random person could have walked up and taken Anna. Maple found herself grinding her teeth in frustration. The crayon hovered over the damn column but she couldn't get herself to write anything. Anyone could have taken her.

She got up from her chair, pushing it back out in a swift move. She looked out the window again, seeing if she could see something. Maybe someone was watching her trailer. The neighboring trailer was dark. The man who lived next door had gone to sleep. It could be him. He could have taken Anna. She looked at another trailer, where a family lived. Maybe someone from the family had taken her. Maybe it was a friend of the family, who had stopped by that early morning. Maybe it was a drunk person who had taken her.

A light sensor went off on another trailer in the park. Maple's gaze quickly changed, looking at the light. It could be a person in that trailer as well. Her body was tense as she tried to search for an answer. And just as she had been hopeful in her brainstorming, her body went limp. She took a big breath, realizing that she was starting to point fingers in hopes of finding any sort of resolution. It didn't work. It was hopeless.

The column remained empty on her piece of paper. It stood out like a sore thumb. Willy looked like an obvious suspect. The more she thought about it, the more she was confident that she had covered her tracks. There was no way he could know where she was.

Pulling out the chair once again, she slowly sat down and tried to think about random perpetrators. Who would just take a little girl? Did they know she was here? Was it a robbery gone wrong?

"Sexual predators, sex offenders, child rapists, drug dealers for ransom money, robbers," Maple mumbled to herself, as she started a list of possible suspects, writing down every new idea with the crayon.

A physical pain developed in her chest, as she imagined her daughter being the victim of a horrible crime. Her eyes were watering as she imagined a man forcing her daughter to do horrible things.

There was also something oddly painful about her writing out these criminals with her own daughter's crayons. Maple let out a devastating scream as she cried loudly. Regardless of what happened to her daughter, there was a big possibility that she was now dead, possibly at the hands of someone who wanted to hurt or assault her. The realization hit her like a ton of bricks.

She put her head down on the table, sobbing in loneliness. It was a horrible feeling and Maple felt her insides hurting. She remembered how she had carried Anna into her friend's car that night, thinking that she was removing her from a horrible situation. The weight of Anna that night felt good, like a hopeful journey, but now that same feeling was too much. For a brief moment, she had felt a glimmer of hope that she could give Anna a future. She could go to school, come home happy, and have a safe place to live. She could have friends and be proud of her family. But all Maple could offer was a cold trailer for a home and possibly a dark forest as a gravesite. Her cries slowed down and she felt herself relax for the first time since Anna disappeared. Exhaustion was setting in.

In a sudden jolt, Maple sat up in her chair. Her eyes were dry and her skin was sticky. She had fallen asleep on her kitchen table. The clock in the kitchen read 4:54 am. It had been a few hours since she started writing her list of potential suspects. With tired eyes, Maple looked at the document, remembering what she had written down before she fell asleep. She closed her eyes and wiped her face clean, trying to erase the thoughts from earlier that night.

The thought of a sex offender taking Anna was enough to make her nauseous. While Maple wanted to know what happened to her daughter, she had her limits. In this neighborhood, a drug dealer stealing a child as a form of payment to someone who he owed money was much more plausible. While a sex offender taking Anna for thrills and then killing her was horrible, knowing that she may have been part of a transaction was different. She hadn't been the object of someone's sick affection. She had merely been a pawn in a horrible exchange.

The early morning sun was starting to rise and Maple noticed how the landscape slowly came alive. The trees stood still tall as the long shadows began dancing on the ground. She thought about what Anna must have seen as she was taken from the trailer. Did she get to see the sun come up? Was she taken just before the sun arrived? And if Anna was the girl in the woods, was she killed as the sun's rays warmed her body while the snow was pressed firmly against her back?

She didn't want to think of her daughter as a murder victim, but Detective Watson's comments had made her cautious. She wanted to be optimistic, but prepared for the worst. Maple imagined her daughter's death in a poetic and romantic way. The sun had kept her warm, her beloved bunnies had kept her company, and her killer had quickly disappeared. Anna had rested in peace and felt no pain.

The clock read 6:37 am. It was too early to call Detective Watson with her list of suspects. She needed to wait at least another two hours before she would get into the station.

With her hand, she combed through her hair. She needed to shower. Badly. With nothing else to do, she got up and headed to the bathroom. She turned on the water and felt the icy liquid hit her hand. It would take a few minutes before the water would get warmer. When fog from the water started to build in the little bathroom, she removed her clothes and stepped into the shower. The water and soap hugged her body and she felt a sense of relief. The past 24 hours had been pure hell. For now, she could do nothing more than to let the warm water rinse her clean. It was liberating and it was needed.

- CHAPTER 13 -

The sun slowly crept up from the horizon and hit Noles' face. It was the same routine every morning with Noles waking up with the sun. But this morning, she was already awake. She hadn't slept much. Sam had woken up a few times, catching her laying awake with her large eyes staring at the ceiling. He kept telling her that he forgave her for not being completely truthful about her work description and while she was thankful for that, it was Anna that kept her awake. Or it was actually Maple.

Every time Sam had woken up, he had tried to hug her and calm her down. It was irritating, as he would always interrupt her thinking. She would reassure him that she was fine, asking him to go back to sleep. To ensure he would sleep, she would remind him of his upcoming shift.

At 5:27, she was already in deep thought. She couldn't shake the feeling that Maple had nothing to do with the disappearance of Anna. But her mind was consumed with the notion of getting a motive for the body in the woods. If she could find a motive, she could find the killer.

She noticed her phone light up. She had missed a call and there was a voicemail waiting for her. Grabbing the phone, she wondered whether it was work-related. The message was from the medical examiner's office, apologizing for calling so early. The assistant seemed a bit nervous about calling, but eventually confirmed what she already knew. The body at Lander's Lake was indeed Anna.

Sam's alarm clock started buzzing, sending shockwaves through Magnolia. She had been so deep in thought about a killer that she forgot she was in bed with her husband. He reached out for the alarm clock, surprised to see Noles awake.

"Hi beautiful, did you get some sleep?" he asked her.

"Ah, not really. A lot on my mind I guess."

"Hey, look at me. You are forgiven for last night. You lied to protect your career. I get it. I'm not pleased, but it's nothing that can't be fixed with dinner later."

He smiled at her and she knew she had to take the bait.

"Okay, I look forward to that," she replied, smiling before kissing him good morning.

In an instant swoop, he rolled out of bed and headed straight for the bathroom. In the doorway to their en-suite bathroom, Sam stopped and removed his boxer shorts.

"Sure you don't want to join me?" he asked, looking back at her.

Noles sat in their king size bed, looking at her husband. She knew him well enough to know that if she said no, she would need to explain why. It wasn't him. She needed to get to work. Without saying a word, she crept out of bed and stepped out of her pajamas.

The warm water hit her shoulders as she felt Sam's hands all over her body. Her back was turned to him as she held her hands on the wall in front of her. While she was usually a passionate type, she preferred to look at the wall today. She could think about the case, and not about the sex.

Sam moaned as he finished and Noles turned around to give him the affection that he so eagerly wanted. He felt energized as he stepped out of the shower.

"Now I feel ready for the day ahead," he said, while brushing his hair. "You want eggs and bacon today?"

"Ah, actually, I'm in a rush," Noles lied. "I should have been out of here an hour ago to get cracking on the case. But I couldn't resist a little time with you."

She knew her comment would gain points with Sam and he flashed a big smile. Sucking up never hurt.

"Don't let me be in your way Detective," Sam said as he smiled and left the bathroom.

Noles turned the water to hot and let the steam fill up the bathroom. It was the way she liked her showers and there was something relaxing about the steam. She closed her eyes as she let herself drift away for a moment, imagining Anna lying in the forest. The crime scene photos that Morgan had shown her helped her create the scene in her mind. She could hear the water of the pond, splashing against her toes. She could hear the morning birds, singing in the background as the sun began to rise. She could see her broken neck, bones sticking out of her body, protruding underneath the skin.

In a sudden moment, Magnolia snapped out of it. She shut off the shower and grabbed a towel. She needed to get back to Beaverville.

"Do you want a coffee for the road?" Sam asked her as she rushed through the kitchen, grabbing her bag.

"No thanks," Noles said quickly while trying to put her jacket on. "No time today."

"But it's ready for you…"

Before Sam could finish his sentence, the door shut behind her.

Noles didn't mean to stand him up for breakfast, but she had an idea. Since Beaverville was still unknown territory for her, she had an idea as to how she could get more information that could potentially help her with Anna's murder.

While driving back to the city the day before, she had noticed a small diner sitting right beside a gas station. It was a diner that catered to the truckers that drove through on the nearby interstate, so it was most likely packed with people from out of town. But the employees had to be locals. And since they worked in the restaurant industry, there was a chance they were chatty.

The landscape looked different this morning. There was no frost, but everything that had been green and alive just a few days prior was starting to look sad, brown and rotten. The saddened landscape set the tone for the news she would have to break to Maple later. It was indeed her daughter that had been killed and dumped in the woods.

About 45 minutes later, Noles turned off the highway and parked her car in the diner's parking lot. The sign that spelled out the diner's name flickered. For only a few seconds at a time, the sign would spell out "Betty's Diner." It seemed like a friendly place, a place where locals would discuss their lives over black coffee and scrambled eggs. The exterior didn't look inviting at all, but the interior lighting was warm and cozy. She shut off the car, embracing herself for the cool morning weather. While the frost had disappeared from yesterday, the temperature was still chilly. Plus, this new uniform didn't exactly keep her warm.

The exterior of the diner was turquoise and a faded pink. It looked like something that had survived decades of hungry people, who stopped at nothing to get their hands on breakfasts, lunches and dinners. As she grabbed the door handle to the restaurant, she noticed that the place was open 24 hours a day. The poor diner didn't get a chance to rest.

The smell of bacon and fresh coffee hit her when she walked in. On both sides of the door were booths along the windows. In the middle of the diner, there were tables seating either two or four people. The diner's service counter was straight ahead. It was long, reaching almost the entire width of the establishment. Along the counter sat a few truck drivers, sipping on some coffee and reading the newspaper. They seemed like the kinds of drivers, who enjoyed a random conversation with the server while in town. Noles took a few steps, trying to find the best place to set.

"Good morning sunshine. You hungry?" a voice said from behind the counter.

"Ah yes, very much so."

"Please, sit down here at the counter and I'll get you something right way."

Noles sat down, reading the lady's name tag.

"Thank you Myrtle," she said with a crooked smile.

"Anytime my dear."

Myrtle placed a menu in front of Noles and grabbed a mug from a tall stack. She looked at Noles while holding a pot of black coffee with an inquisitive face. Magnolia nodded and Myrtle started pouring the coffee into the mug. She placed cream, milk and sugar in front of Noles.

The menu looked straightforward. A trucker's breakfast with three eggs, toast, bacon, sausages and potatoes was a fan favorite, but Betty's Diner also offered more delicacies, such as eggs benedict, waffles and pancakes. It seemed to be a family-friendly place, despite it being populated with tired-looking men who ate alone. While she waited for Myrtle to return to take her order, Noles looked around to take in the ambiance of the place. Even though it was the ideal truck stop diner, she scouted people who looked like locals. A couple to the right of her looked like they had stepped right out of their home and into the diner, with the man wearing a button-down shirt, some dirty jeans with suspenders and slip-on shoes that could have been mistaken for slippers. He looked right at home.

Another dining guest ordered "the usual" when he walked in, sitting down to read the newspaper as if this was his daily routine. One man looked at Noles in her uniform like he was trying to make sense of her presence in the diner. Perhaps people recognized the uniform as being the same as Detective Morgan's and they wondered why she would be here. Perhaps one detective was enough in Beaverville.

To avoid looking suspicious, Noles turned her attention to Myrtle. She was a great multitasker, chatting it up with diners while making coffee, writing down orders and cashing out customers, who were ready to leave. Despite being in a deep conversation with a diner sitting at the service counter, she would keep an eye out for the kitchen window, so the fresh food was delivered quickly. It was clear she had been working this job for some time.

Myrtle seemed to blend into the atmosphere of the diner. While small, it boasted a big personality. The turquoise elements from the exterior continued inside, and the faded pink was present in the leather seating found in the booths. The tables and chairs looked like they had been purchased for a 1950s diner. While sturdy, the furniture surely didn't look new. Myrtle had a similar feel to her. Since she was in full control of everything inside the diner, she looked like she could be Betty. She appeared proud of the work she did and she spoke with all the guests. It was clear that people not only came for the good food, but also for the excellent service and the friendly conversation.

Myrtle returned to the service counter to take Noles' order. She walked over with a smile while holding a fresh pot of coffee in her hand. Without asking, Myrtle topped up Noles' cup.

"Anything catch your eye?" she asked while nodding her head at the menu in front of Noles.

"The pancakes with light syrup, please."

"Coming right up."

Noles studied Myrtle as she placed the order with the kitchen. Myrtle used a computer to enter the order, while checking with the kitchen to see that the cooks started the pancakes. Once the order was placed, Myrtle grabbed a set of utensils and napkins for Noles. As she walked over, Noles realized that Myrtle knew she was being watched.

"No matter how much you look you won't find any mistakes, Detective…" she said, leaving the sentence hanging for Noles to finish it.

"Watson. Detective Watson."

"Well, it's nice to meet you."

"How did you know I was a detective?"

"You wear the exact same uniform as Detective Morgan and everyone knows he's set to retire. Plus, Christina, the police station secretary, is in here on Sundays with her husband after church and she mentioned that a young detective would be joining the team. The town isn't that big. People notice."

Noles nodded without saying anything. Of course, the small town community, she hadn't thought of that. She should have known that she would stand out like a sore thumb. Before she could respond, Myrtle started speaking again.

"Are you working on finding that little girl's killer?"

Noles looked surprised. With wide eyes and her mouth slightly opened, she struggled to find the words.

"Word spreads fast in this town."

"I can see that," Noles replied, worried she would say too much about the case.

"But yes, that is something I'm working on. Did you know her or her mother?"

Myrtle shook her head.

"I didn't know them personally. They were in here once before, a few months ago. They didn't have much money and the only thing they could afford was a side of toast."

As Myrtle spoke, she leaned in close to Noles.

"I felt bad for them. I sent out a stack of pancakes for the little girl and told her mother not to worry about it. There's no worse feeling than being a mother, who is incapable of providing for her child."

Noles smiled as Myrtle shared her story about the nice gesture. Myrtle was clearly a caring person who didn't want to highlight Maple's lack of money in front of her own daughter. Instead, it seemed like Maple wanted to protect Anna from the harsh reality of her life. She was growing up in a trailer park with no money, no school nearby, on the run from a dangerous man and little hope for a productive and wealthy future.

"When she was in here, did the mother act aggressively towards her daughter? Did you see anything that made you wonder about her as a parent?"

Myrtle gave Noles a crooked smile.

"That mother loved her child. And let me tell you something. It's clear from your questions that you don't have children, but a mother is a fierce protector of her offspring. It doesn't matter whether there's no money, no hope or no future. A mother's bond with a child is almighty and nothing – nothing – can break that."

Myrtle winked her eye. The message was clear. Maple didn't hurt her daughter. While Myrtle hadn't spent time with Maple one-on-one, it was still useful information. She was one of the only witnesses who had seen the mother-daughter duo together, interacting before the murder investigation began.

Myrtle walked back to the kitchen, leaving Noles alone at the bar counter, waiting for her pancakes. She could see into the kitchen, and the chef was flipping the pancakes. The airborne grease from the stovetop was visible from where she was sitting and the pancakes were a perfect shade of golden-brown. All of the butter on the stove would make them crispy once they arrived.

To the left of Noles lay a stack of newspapers from the city. She grabbed a copy and started flipping through the pages to see if anything stood out. The weather would be warmer today than previous days, the local basketball team would be meeting the top team in the league, which could result in some fighting between the fans after the game, and stocks were down again. As Noles flipped through the pages, she noticed Sam on page 16. It was a photo from the night of the accident, where he had helped out. He was standing with a group of doctors, trying to tie a patient to a stretcher. The patient had a neck brace on. Seeing him live in action gave her a chill. While he had told her about the accident, it was something else to see him out there in the middle of the night, saving lives.

The accident looked horrible too. Some of the cars were completely totaled and it was clear that only some had survived the crash. While she felt a sense of sadness for the people who had been in the crash and for the individuals who would not be getting their loved ones home, she also felt a sense of pride and honor to even know Sam. The world could be a cruel place, but at least he was trying to make it better, one life at a time.

"Pretty horrible crash that one there," Myrtle said as she brought over the pancakes.

"Yeah, tell me about it."

"And here's your syrup. We don't add it for you as a light serving in my world would probably be a double in yours," Myrtle said with a smirk, placing a bottle of syrup next to her.

"Thank you, I appreciate it."

As Noles poured the syrup over the pancakes, the surface of the pancakes didn't cave. The surface was hard, as she had suspected given the amount of butter on the stove. As she cut the first pancake with her knife, the surface flaked and made a sound loud enough for the guy down the service bar to look up at her. Crispy, that's for sure.

But the taste of the syrup, the butter and the doughy pancake was heavenly. With every bite, Noles wished she had another three large pancakes on the plate. The world around her disappeared, as she consumed her breakfast. For a brief moment, she didn't think about the case, about Anna, about Sam or about her working relationship with Detective Morgan.

Things simply disappeared, as the taste of the pancakes took her away to a world where everything was peaceful. The coffee was delicious too, and Noles kept nodding every time Myrtle stopped by to top off her mug.

"Those were the best pancakes I've ever had," Noles said to Myrtle as she stopped by to pick up her empty plate.

"I hear that a lot."

"Just amazing. Can I get the recipe or something?"

"Sorry, I would be breaking the law if I gave it out. You know, family recipe and all," Myrtle joked.

"Fair enough, I wouldn't want you to get into trouble."

As Noles folded the newspaper, she removed her wallet from her pant pocket.

"How much do I owe you for that lovely breakfast?"

"Let's see here," Myrtle said quietly, as she looked at the bill. "3 dollars and 42 cents."

"That's the best deal I've received in a while," Noles said, while pulling a 10-dollar bill from her wallet. "Keep the changes and thanks for your help."

"Anytime my dear."

Noles walked out of the diner and headed straight to her car. Even though it was supposed to be warmer today, there was still an unpleasant wind chill. Her car was freezing cold and it took a while before the heat started to come through the vents on the dashboard. She rubbed her hands together and blew air on them to warm them up. The clock read 8:47 am and it was time to head to the station.

As she was about the put the car in drive, her cell phone started buzzing. She didn't recognize the number, but she decided to answer anyways.

"Hello, Detective Watson here."

"Hi, Detective Watson. It's Maple here. I have a few suggestions we should look at. Maybe we can find out who took Anna."

Noles hadn't prepared what she would tell Maple about the conclusion from the medical examiner's office. However, she had already dropped the bomb on her yesterday about the body, so Maple had probably gone through every scenario in her head.

"Listen, Maple. I got a call this morning from the medical examiner's office."

Maple was silent on the other end, clearly waiting for Noles to deliver the news.

"I don't know how to tell you this other than to just say it. The body found at Lander's Lake yesterday…"

Silence again.

"It's Anna. I'm so sorry."

Noles waited for Maple to reply, but she just heard silence. Then, the silence was broken by her cries.

- CHAPTER 14 -

The headache from the booze had resulted in little sleep. Morgan had stayed in his car for a few hours, contemplating how to handle the drama with Jules before re-entering the dark house. He remembered walking back into the house but he didn't remember cleaning up the food he had thrown across the kitchen and he wasn't quite sure whether he was sleeping in his bed or on the couch.

Morgan slowly opened one eye and the bright light was enough for him to shut it again. He was in his bedroom and the curtains had been pulled aside once again. This meant that he was in his bed and Jules had already gotten up. She had made her side of the bed and pulled aside the curtains, showered, and had probably already started her day. Once again, he had disappointed her.

He started to wiggle his feet. He hadn't moved at all since he woke up and his body was stiff. He almost felt dead lying in his bed. The alcohol was slowly killing his body and he only had so much energy left to deal with these hangovers. He hated them, Jules hated them even more, and surely, his colleagues were wondering why he always smelt like booze and why Jules was never around anymore.

After losing her son, Jules had continued to stop by the station with baked goods whenever they were working late to solve a crime or get an arrest warrant. She would always support the entire team at the station, not just him. But after he started drinking and she took notice of people's reactions to him smelling like booze, she stopped coming around. He was an embarrassment to her.

One eyelid opened slightly and he felt unprepared for the sunlight that hit his face. It was already a bright day outside and Jules made sure he got all of the sunlight in his face. He groaned a bit before rolling over to his side. He was exhausted but he knew he couldn't skip out on work. A sick day did sound nice though.

Morgan rolled out of bed and sat on the edge for a minute. His head was spinning from the drinking. The exhaustion of dealing with Jules was partially to blame. He sighed loudly and gathered enough courage to stand up to face the day. The hot water in the shower only made him queasy and out of frustration, he aggressive turned on the cold water.

Jules wasn't in the house. The food he had thrown into the cupboard the night before was gone and the cupboard showed no signs of dried food or permanent damage. He didn't try to call out Jules' name, but noticed that her car keys were gone and that her shoes were missing. He hadn't heard her, but she was out living her life.

At times, Morgan had wondered whether she was cheating on him. She could easily be hiding a lover from him, as they rarely saw one another. Her lover could be a morning person, someone who took her to brunch and catered to her needs when Morgan was at work. Then, she would stop whatever she was doing with him and come home to listen to Morgan beat himself down over his lack of desire to stop drinking. But deep inside, Morgan told himself she wasn't. She couldn't betray him like that after losing their son together the way they did. She knew that if she left him, he would die. She was his lifeline, but kept her distance when she could.

The bright sunshine didn't bother him as he drove to the station. He wore his sunglasses along with his policing uniform cap. With his eyes hidden, no one could see his tired baggy eyes and the tears he had cried in frustration the night before. As he drove through town, he thought about the case and tried to get back into the mindset of being a detective.

The station seemed lively today and Noles was already there. When he walked into the station, she looked up at him as if she had been waiting for him. He glanced at her while keeping his pace steady, then looked away as if he didn't want to talk. He walked into his office and put his jacket away. He left the door open as an invitation.

"You got a minute?" Noles asked as she appeared in his doorway.

He looked at her while sitting down in his chair, turning on the computer in the same motion. No words were uttered. Her face smirked for a second but she took the hint and sat down.

"Did you hear about Anna? They confirmed it was her through dental records."

He nodded before reminding her that he had already told her this when the body was found.

"I think we need to talk to the locals around town to see if they know something," she suggested.

Morgan found himself squinting his eyes, wondering how she managed to come up with that option considering he asked her to look at Maple as a suspect.

"I had breakfast at the diner this morning and I talked to the server there. She had seen Maple and Anna together having breakfast. Maybe we can find someone who saw them together or knew of their situation in hopes of getting a lead."

Morgan continued to sit in silence, watching her come up with more suggestions to make her case. He almost wanted to let her talk until she had nothing more to say, and then shut her down with a simple "no."

"Maybe someone had talked to Anna in these past few days. Maybe she revealed something to someone…" Noles added, her thoughts seemingly fading along with the volume of her voice.

"Look, I appreciate your efforts, but I think we should go back to the trailer and find some kind of physical evidence against her. Maybe there's blood somewhere in the trailer. Maybe there are hairs or footprints in the area surrounding the trailer," Morgan began. "I think there's a lot more to Maple than we know and we've just begun to scratch the surface."

That was a long "no," a bit longer than he had hoped.

"So that was a no, in case you were wondering. No to the interviews, yes to the trailer investigation," he added.

Detective Watson sat in silence. It looked as if she was thinking about something. He couldn't quite make it out, but hopefully, she was listening to what he was saying. After about a minute of silence, she spoke.

"She called me this morning with a suspects list."

Morgan looked at her and she stared right back. Was she trying to challenge him in how he investigated crimes? Was she trying to get the upper hand in this investigation by going behind his back to do interviews? Was she trying to play hardball?

"I talked to her too," he replied coldly, lying to her face. "I don't find the suspect list believable."

He didn't flinch. He played his poker face, hoping she would be caught off-guard. She looked stone cold.

"You don't think a sex offender sounds possible given where she lives?" Noles asked him without removing his gaze from him.

"I've already talked to people," he said, lying once again. "I was out all last night talking to the locals about Maple and there's a general belief that she's guilty."

"I think there's cause for concern and I think there's reasonable doubt here. We need to look at the sex offenders in this town and rule them out," Noles said firmly.

"There are no sex offenders in the trailer park," Morgan responded, knowing he was making random statements without any evidence to back up his claims.

"There are indeed, three of them."

Noles placed three file folders on his desk.

"Age, sex, location, past crimes, registration information, family backgrounds and everything else you may be wondering about – photos included," Noles said, pointing her finger at the files.

Morgan sat still, looking straight at Noles. He licked his lips in hopes of calming himself down. He could feel his shoulders rising to his ears and he was holding his breath. His tongue kept circulating behind his teeth, as he continued to grind them. He thought about throwing her out of his office.

Send her back where she came from. She interrupted him in his thoughts.

"Look, I'm not questioning your authority. I just want to do a thorough job here."

She looked at him, changing her voice to a softer tone.

"I want to explore these options with your blessing. While I agree that we should also look at Maple, I think it's important we don't get too narrow-minded with her. As I said earlier, I spoke to someone this morning that had seen her and Anna together. She doesn't believe Maple could kill her child – or any mother for that matter…"

"Then you haven't been a detective for very long," he interrupted her, pointing around the room.

He thought about his own history and how he had been responsible for his own child's death. While not on purpose, she didn't know what she was talking about. Anyone could kill.

"Fair enough," Noles replied, continuing with her argument. "All I'm saying is let's do our job and investigate all possible scenarios before we settle on a possible suspect."

Morgan leaned back in his chair, folding his hands on top of his belly. Noles sat quietly on the other side of his desk, clearly waiting for him to speak. He tried to hold her in suspense, as he started rocking back and forth. She started to lose her grip on the situation and her eyes began to shift a bit. He was irritating the hell out of her and he enjoyed seeing her squirm. For a moment, he felt euphoric for having all of the control and power in the room. He called the shots and she had to beg for space and resources to work.

"What's your plan, detective?" he asked her, curious if she had thought ahead.

"I'm going to find these individuals, ask them about alibies. Where were they the night Anna went missing?"

"And if none of those alibies match our case?"

"Then we start looking elsewhere, possibly dig into her ex-boyfriend and other people in the trailer park who could have taken Anna…" Noles explained, adding after a brief pause, "…including Maple."

Morgan smiled. He wanted her to remember Maple as a suspect. He was only concerned with building a case against her. Maybe he could get Noles off his back while he looked for a motive. Maybe her playing cop with the sex offenders could be a good thing.

Morgan sat up in his chair and started playing with the computer mouse. As he looked at the screen, he gave his orders.

"Okay, go explore these individuals and see what you can find out. When you are out there, stop by the trailer to see what Maple has to say about these people. Maybe she knew some of them personally."

Noles lit up as if she had been told she was getting free reigns to do as she pleased.

"Awesome, thank you!" she said eagerly, grabbing the files.

"But Watson," Morgan began. "Don't waste valuable resources on this. You can go play detective this once, but we have to find a motive for Maple and that should be your top priority when you aren't working directly with me. You can close the door on your way out."

He saw the hope disappear from her face, as she closed his office door. Just as he had built her up, he had ripped her to

shreds and brought her down. No one said detective work
would be fun.

- CHAPTER 15 -

With a sense of defeat and some heavy steps, Noles left the police station. She went into the police car that had been parked in the parking lot all morning. For a minute, she contemplated going to the station to get a blanket for the cold leather seat, but decided against it, as she didn't want to run into Detective Morgan again. She didn't want him to change his mind about giving her free reigns, as it had almost seemed like a favor.

She put the key in the ignition and turned on the car. It rattled a bit as it started and she patted the dashboard. Noles had a feeling that the car had an old soul and had been of great service for years.

"It's okay old lady," she said quickly. "I'll take it easy on you today."

This time, she didn't wait for the car to warm up. She just wanted to leave so she could get some time to think. The meeting with Morgan had been exactly what she had hoped for, except for his attitude. What an asshole. She would have to fight for Anna and Maple if he wasn't going to. She needed to talk to Sam. She needed to get her frustrations out.

As she drove down the main stretch of Beaverville, she took notice of some of the amenities around. The liquor store stood out with its big orange sign near the road. Even though it wasn't lit up, it was dominant on this small stretch of road. She also spotted a grocery store with a few cars in the parking lot and a local postal office.

She turned the vehicle into the grocery store parking lot and put the car in park. Her phone was cold as she started calling Sam. It took a few rings before he picked up.

"Hey you, what's going on?"

"Hey, not too much. Just wanted to hear your voice."

"Oh, well you caught me at a good time. I'm just having a cup of coffee here in the cafeteria. I'm going into surgery all afternoon, so I'm just relaxing now."

"Oh, well that's good they are keeping you busy. Shotgun wound?"

"Actually no. Traffic accident. Nothing major. Not urgent enough to move another surgery apparently. But you know, patient confidentiality and all."

She could hear him smile through the phone.

"At least you are having a better day than me. So Morgan is convinced Maple killed her daughter. It's very frustrating."

"Honey, you have to give him some credit. Maybe he knows more about the locals than you. Perhaps you should listen to him."

Noles was taken aback.

"Wait, what? I thought you were on my side in this."

"I am, I am," he assured her. "And I want you to follow your heart and do what you think is right. All I'm asking you is to listen to him – just once in a while. Give him some credit. I mean, how would you feel if someone younger came to work with you and doubted everything you said, especially right before retirement?"

"You mean, respect the hierarchy."

"I mean, I don't think it will hurt you," he said quietly. "I think it's about picking your battles wisely and you don't need to waste your energy on this guy."

She felt her eyes close as she hung her head down. She knew he was right. Morgan was taking up so much of her energy because he was telling her what to do. And despite giving her free reigns to pursue the leads she had found, she still let him control her.

"Are you there honey?"

"Ah yeah, yes. I was just listening to what you were saying. You are right, I need to let go a bit. Maybe I should spend more time out of the office."

"Well, if you do, make sure you wear a warm coat. Don't want to see you in here with frostbites young lady," he joked, causing them both to laugh softly.

"I appreciate you, you know that?" Noles told Sam, who had the same reply to her. "But not as much as I appreciate you."

"I'll call you later," she said before hanging up.

The phone was quickly out of her hands and she took a deep breath. Time to hit the reset button and start over. Rather than let Morgan influence her work, she would try to work this case as if she was the only detective available. Sam believed she could do it, as long as she did it with respect and dignity –

and didn't downplay Morgan's theories. While she would keep her eyes open while visiting Maple, she did think that talking to Maple about her theories would yield better results. She wasn't in the profession to judge people. She worked to solve puzzles and one puzzle would be to find out what happened to Anna.

As soon as she stepped out of the car, she felt the icy cold wind. It hit her face as a gust of wind swirled around in the parking lost, making a plastic bag dance in the wind. It was beautiful and somewhat poetic, even though it was just a piece of plastic. The bag caught Noles' attention and she found herself drawn by its beauty, motions and dance. Her head started to move with the bag with the car door still open. Her brief moment of dreaming was interrupted by a car honking its horn. She snapped out of it and closed the door.

The grocery store wasn't as big as she had anticipated. It was quiet and she could hear music playing. However, it was so faint that she heard someone drop an item in an aisle. There was also a cough from the lady at the checkout counter. Noles moved softly, scared to make a commotion. It was daytime and yet, the grocery store here seemed abandoned.

Within a few minutes, she had picked up a few snacks for later, just in case she had to work late. As she walked towards the cash register, she spotted some coffee and tea. She paused as she saw a big tub of coffee. There was enough coffee in this tub for a month – at least. She looked around to see if anyone was looking at her, as she contemplated whether to buy it. Buying the coffee would help out Maple who didn't have any. But buying it would also be a friendly gesture, something Morgan surely wouldn't appreciate. As long as he didn't see her buy it, it wouldn't hurt.

She rolled her eyes and grabbed the coffee. He wasn't going to decide how she treated Maple. Last time she checked, Maple was innocent until proven guilty.

The lady at the cash register looked tired. The bright blue eyeshadow and bright pink lipstick didn't help her worn-out appearance. When Noles put her items down on the counter, the lady didn't move. She looked at Noles with a stare that frightened her a bit.

"Just these things, that will do," Noles said, trying to break the ice and avoid her gaze.

The lady continued to stand firm, reaching one hand out to grab an item and scanned it. She would slowly register all of the items but she didn't drop her stare once.

"You aren't from around here," the lady said, her tone firm and certain.

"No, you are right about that."

She continued to scan her items and then packed them slowly into a plastic bag.

"Why are you here?"

The questioned stunned Noles. Myrtle had been so friendly at the diner earlier this morning. Now, she was seeing another side of town, a less inviting side.

"I work here now," Noles said firmly back, wanting to prove that she deserved to be here. "I'm the new detective in town. Who knows, maybe you'll need my help one day."

She saw that her total was $12.86 and she put $13 on the counter. Grabbing her bag, she walked out of the store without saying a word. There was no respect for those in uniform. She pondered if Morgan's drinking could have anything to do with the way he had been treated throughout the years – and the way he had treated people.

Noles didn't look back as she entered her car, turned the keys and drove out of the parking lot. Unfortunately, this was the only grocery store in town. She would have to come back to get snacks unless she prepared well and got some snacks over the weekend when she and Sam would go shopping together. She rolled her eyes as she drove away from the main stretch of town.

The sun was bright as she put her foot on the gas. She needed to get out of town and think about the case. And there was only place where she could think about going.

It only took a few minutes to get there, but the diner looked the same as it had this morning. The faded pink and turquoise features beamed in the sunlight as she stepped out of the car. It had been a few hours since she was there for breakfast, but Betty's Diner was a place where she thought she could get some help from the locals without the attitude.

As she opened the door to the diner, a small bell rang above it. She looked straight ahead, hoping Myrtle would still be working. The diner was half-full with truckers chowing down on sandwiches, fries and milkshakes. Noles looked around, but only spotted a frail-looking server, writing down an order at a booth with four large men.

"Add two fries to the order," said a voice from the kitchen.

The voice belonged to Myrtle. Noles smiled and approached the service counter, found a spot and sat down. She folded her hands, waiting patiently for Myrtle to come out from the kitchen. The door swung open and there she was, carrying three plates with steaming hot foods. She spotted Noles immediately and flashed her a smile.

"One second dear and I'm all yours," she said.

Myrtle walked over to a booth with a family, putting down the food in a cheerful manner. It didn't seem like she knew the family and Noles wondered how many people she would meet during a single week. The diner was placed strategically near the interstate, so truckers, road trippers or families heading on vacation would stop by for food, snacks and a restroom break.

Myrtle was quickly back again, grabbing a lunch menu on her way over to Noles.

"Now, if you are hungry, I highly suggest our burger. We make it here in-house and the secret sauce is what has people coming back for more. And the fries are spectacular. But if you're still a bit full from breakfast, I would go with the French Onion soup…unless, of course, you are here on official business."

Noles opened her mouth and was about to say something, but held her breath. She relaxed her shoulders and simply uttered, "The burger with fries sounds delicious."

Myrtle winked at her and made a nod at the files Noles had with her. The two women looked at one another and there was a mutual understanding. She would give Noles the answers she was looking for.

"When the burger arrives…" Myrtle noted and walked away.

Within 10 minutes, the most delicious and juicy burger stood in front of Noles. The bun was freshly baked, the lettuce, tomato and red onion rings looked crisp, and the cheese was still bubbling on the patty. And on the top bun, the most delicious secret sauce was spread out, oozing out of the burger as Noles stacked it and got it ready.

"Oh, that's delicious," she said after the first bite and she wasn't even lying to boost Myrtle's confidence in her choices. It truly was the best burger she had ever tried.

"Told ya," Myrtle said. "Next time, get the kale Caesar salad instead. It has a bite. So much garlic in there."

"Deal."

"So, what can I help you with?"

Noles put the burger down and while she continued chewing the massive bite she had just taken, she got the list of sex offenders out from her folder.

"Can you tell me something about these three men?"

Myrtle studied the men and it was clear that she had seen them before.

"This fellow right here," Myrtle said, pointing to the first man on the list, "He left town. He's not around here anymore. I heard he was arrested in California on some pretty serious charges, so I doubt he's even on the streets. I think a simple Internet search could give you more information as to where he's locked up and why."

Myrtle moved her finger to the next man on the list.

"And this man right here, he's dead. He committed suicide a few months ago. Jumped out from the bridge in Clearwater County. Apparently, he had sexually assaulted a family member, a little girl, and the girl's father wanted to kill him. After he disappeared, people actually thought the father was responsible, but they found a suicide note and the body in the river. Apparently, the father's alibi held up."

"Okay," Noles said, writing down the key facts Myrtle was giving her, just for verification.

"But this one right here, he's still around. He doesn't come in here, possibly because he's not allowed to be around children. But the last I heard, he was living in the trailer park outside of town. Do you know where that is?"

"Yes, I've been out there once and I'm planning on stopping by this afternoon. Do you happen to know where in the trailer park?"

"No," Myrtle answered. "That's just the last I've heard and that was a while ago. I used to see him at the grocery store and liquor store, picking up food and supplies for the week but it has been ages."

"Okay," Noles said softly, noting the last few things that Myrtle remembered. "Thank you for this."

"Sorry I couldn't help more, but people tend to leave this place. I bet I don't have to tell you why."

"You've helped more than plenty. It can be tough to be new in town, especially when you have to be so nosey and ask people uncomfortable questions."

"It happens sometimes," Myrtle pointed out. "Sometimes we have to fake confidence until we have that confidence. But don't worry. I think you are as confident as you need to be. It's a friendly approach that I find appealing... unlike what we are used to in town."

Without saying his name, Noles knew that Myrtle was referring to Detective Morgan. The bad attitude she had seen wasn't just her being insensitive or inexperienced. He really was a rude guy, who didn't leave the best impressions around town.

"Well, thanks. I hope to keep it up," Noles said, trying to steer the conversation in a different direction. "What's the story with these guys? I mean, are their crimes well documented here in town or do they go largely unnoticed? I'm curious about the fellow you say is possibly still around here."

"Well, I can tell you that it involved child pornography. I don't recall there ever being an incident of a child being molested. But he is deemed a danger to society and he did serve time. I don't know if he's under house arrest or doing community service, but he keeps to himself – well, so much so that I haven't seen him around."

It wasn't the answer she had hoped for. A better answer would have been him living in the area, stopping by the diner for daily lunches, and perhaps even being chatty with his neighbors. But working to find and investigate a recluse from afar wasn't what she had hoped for.

"I'll let you know if I see anyone on the list come in here. But for now, please enjoy your burger," Myrtle said, ending the conversation so she could get back to work.

Noles nodded and thanked her once again for her help. When she had come into town this morning, she wasn't quite sure what to work on. Now she had a person of interest, someone who would have something to gain by taking Anna. If everything worked out, she could have a potential suspect.

Based on the menu price of the burger, she knew that she owed no more than $13. She put a $20 down on the counter, as she finished off the remaining fries. The information provided by Myrtle was helpful and it had fueled the fire that Noles had for the case. For once, she felt there was something to work on. And there was only one person who could help her.

- CHAPTER 16 -

The clock indicated that it was early afternoon. The sun was starting to shift as it had already peaked in the sky. Maple had been awake for hours and the shower this morning had been the only break for her. She had spent the last few hours, flipping through old newspapers to find any stories about sex offenders, robberies, or any other crime-related story that could possibly be linked to a little girl going missing and being killed. Nothing had surfaced.

She looked at the clock again. Detective Watson had promised to stop by today so they could continue to explore some possible theories as to what happened. Deep inside, Maple knew that Watson would listen to her theories about Willy, but also come up with possible suspects if he had a strong alibi. She was open to ideas, unlike Detective Morgan.

For the past 24 hours, Maple had barely slept. Her body wasn't reacting as it had a few days ago and she struggled to keep her eyes open. The exhaustion was hard to fight. The mirror told her that she was tired and she couldn't deny the bags under her eyes. Her body was telling her to sleep, but she was scared to let herself rest. What if Anna's killer came back while she was sleeping? What if Willy was coming back for her? What if she missed a clue that could help solve her daughter's murder? She needed to be ready and sleep would only make her vulnerable.

Maple started to pace around the trailer. She had closed the door to Anna's bedroom, knowing that someone may have been in there. Maybe Detective Watson would examine the room for evidence even though there hadn't been a sign of anyone breaking into the trailer. The pacing kept her awake and kept her blood circulating. She was starting to get hungry. For once in the past 24 hours, her body was screaming for food to refuel. No food and little rest meant that her body was starting to come unglued. Her mental state was frail. One mention of Anna and she would burst into tears.

Despite the cold temperatures outside, Maple had opened the window in the kitchen. The cold air was refreshing as it hit her bare skin. She could hear a few birds sing outside. They provided a soundtrack for her day. With their chirping, she didn't feel alone. She looked at the clock again. 10 minutes had passed.

A car slowly drove into the trailer park. She could hear the engine in the distance, even though several trailers hid most of the sound. Maple's trailer was in the back of the park, so she often didn't hear vehicles approaching until they had passed the trailer just in front of hers. But today, she was on edge and she paid attention to the smallest thing that appeared to be out of order. Every person who walked her way, every car that came too close, and every sound from the landscape surrounding her were under examination.

The car slowly came around the corner and Maple realized it was a police car. She felt the excitement building in her body, as she was finally getting a chance to find Anna's killer. Through the window, she tried to see who was driving the vehicle. She hoped it wasn't Detective Morgan. With little sleep and nothing to eat, Detective Morgan wouldn't be happy with her snappy attitude and her drive to find the person who had taken Anna away from her.

The car parked right outside of her trailer. For a few seconds, nothing happened. The person inside didn't get out. Because the sun was shining from behind the vehicle, Maple couldn't make out who was driving the car. In suspense, she waited for the person to make an exit. She could see movement inside the car and when the door opened, Detective Watson got out.

Maple was flooded with a sense of relief. Her hopes had been high and she almost broke into tears after seeing Noles get out of the car. The young detective had promised she would stop by and she had kept her promise. Maple's story had clearly made an impact with her. She was willing to hear about her list of suspects.

It took a minute for Noles to reach her front door, as she was carrying two bags. Maple opened the door to greet her and when she saw her, the detective handed her the two bags.

"For you."

Without checking to see the bags' content, Maple said thank you and let Watson into the trailer. The ladies sat down and Maple looked in the bags. She pulled out a burger and a side of fries packaged in a box.

"I thought you could use a bite to eat. It's from Betty's Diner by the interstate. They say they have the best burgers in the world and I do believe it's true," Noles said while Maple seemed shocked and surprised.

"Thank you…really," Maple replied.

"Don't forget to look in the other bag. I got you some coffee, should last you a month or so."

"Really, thank you. You don't know how much this means to me."

Noles appeared surprised when Maple reached out for a hug. There was no time to react but Noles seemed to accept the fact that she needed to be close to someone. She had lost her daughter and had no one else to talk to. Noles bringing her the burger was a big gesture for her.

It didn't take long for Maple to chow down on the burger. As she ate, she noticed Noles looking at her. Perhaps she could tell that Maple hadn't eaten anything since learning her daughter had gone missing. Maybe she guessed that it had been weeks since Maple had a good meal.

There was an awkward silence as she was eating the burger. Noles gave her a nod, indicating that she should eat and finish every French fry, and they could talk afterward. While Maple ate, Noles began unpacking her bag. It was clear that she had a few questions or things she wanted to discuss.

"Thank you, I needed that – without knowing I needed that," Maple said as she removed the remnants of the lunch she had just consumed.

"You have to take care of yourself," Noles explained. "Anna needs you to be the best you can be. That's how we solve this. Just let me know if you need anything. I'm here."

Maple smiled at Noles and put her hands on top of hers.

"From the bottom of my heart, thank you."

Noles smiled back.

"Now, I need your help."

The two women sat at Maple's small kitchen table and looked at files of the sexual offenders living in Beaverville. Even though Myrtle had only seen one of the three men around, Noles knew sex offenders didn't necessarily like walking around in public. People could be harsh in their treatment of sex offenders, and sometimes those situations could become dangerous. There was a big possibility that Maple had seen a few of them around during her time in the trailer park.

"I need you to take a look at these men for me. It's okay if you need time to think but please examine them well."

She placed the three men out on the table in front Maple. She noticed how Maple looked at the first suspect, the one who was supposedly in jail. With her finger, Maple slowly dragged her finger along the side of his face. Her gaze was steady on his face, as she touched his cheeks and lips. She closed her eyes, as if she was trying to imagine an interaction with him. She opened her eyes after a few seconds.

"No, I haven't seen this one."

She repeated her odd ritual with the second man, who Myrtle said committed suicide. Noles wasn't quite sure what Maple was doing, but she was taking her time like she had been asked to do.

"Handsome," she whispered before giving him a critical and judgmental look.

Perhaps she knew what these men had done. Maybe she thought about how these handsome men could manipulate women and children. She looked up at Noles and shook her head.

She slowly pushed the two images out of the way and placed the third photo in front of her. Her facial expression changed as she dragged her finger downward, along his cheek, chin and finally his collarbone. She sat in silence, as she looked right at his eyes. Her lips quivered a bit and Noles noticed that her body started to tighten.

"Blue eyes, brown hair," Maple said softly, while looking at the black and white photo that Noles had been able to print at the station.

"I'm sorry, did you say something?"

Maple spoke softly, and Noles couldn't hear everything. She didn't respond and the ladies once again sat in silence.

"24."

"24? What does that mean? 24."

"Number 24," Maple replied.

She dropped her gaze and looked right at Noles.

"He lives in trailer number 24."

"Are you sure?"

Noles grabbed her notepad and started writing.

"I'm absolutely certain. He has seen Anna and I walk by. He knows where we live. Did he take her?"

Noles realized that Maple was angry, ready to go over to number 24 and literally kill the man.

"No. I don't know," she replied honestly. "I'm providing you with sex offenders in the area based on your suggestions. We are just trying to find some people to talk to so we can find out who took Anna. We are not finding the needle in the haystack. We are trying to locate the haystack."

There was a sense of disappointment in the room. Maple felt frustrated. She had hoped for a guilty person, an open and shut case. But she knew that Noles didn't have the answer. In fact, none of them any clue as to who took Anna.

"So, what happens now?" Maple asked.

"Well, I'm going to look for more information about his man. All I really know is that his name is Mr. Donald Sukuti and he is a registered sex offender. I also know that you believe he lives in trailer number 24."

They would not be knocking on Sukuti's door this afternoon. She glanced at Anna's bedroom door, realizing that her trailer was also considered a place of interest that needed to be investigated as per Morgan's orders.

"I'm going to send some crime scene investigators out here tomorrow. They are going to take some fingerprint samples and collect evidence from your doors and windows. It's just routine, just to see who may have been in here."

"That's fine, I'll be here."

Noles started to gather her papers together, including the photo of the three men. Maple was rattled after identifying Donald Sukuti. She saw it as a big leap forward, but she couldn't read Noles' thoughts about the case. Detective Watson had been stoic through this whole thing, including when she interviewed Maple the first time. Noles seemed to distance herself from the case. Maybe she hadn't experienced this kind of loss. She probably hadn't lost her parents and never given birth to a child. As Noles packed her bag and got ready to leave, Maple shed a tear.

"Are you okay?"

"Yeah," Maple said, fighting back the tears. "It's one thing that she's gone, but it's quite another to possibly be looking at the man that took her."

"I can only imagine what you are going through. Remember, he's just a person of interest. I have no proof that he took Anna or that he was even interested in your daughter.

In fact, I have no proof that she was even the victim of sexual assault."

Maples looked at Noles. Her eyes were filled with tears.

"I take comfort in that fact."

Maple's voice was shaky as she continued to look at Noles, trying to hold her emotions inside.

"Yes, please do. And trust that I'm going to update you with whatever information I do find," Noles added.

She packed the files into her bag and grabbed her jacket from the chair. Before she faced the door, she looked at Maple once again, briefing her on what she knew. Maple was thankful for whatever Noles could tell her.

"So I'm going to ask the crime scene investigators to come by tomorrow, so they can get out of your hairs. If you do see Sukuti around your trailer or looking in your windows, call me – immediately," Noles said while pointing at her business card on Maple's fridge.

"What should I do if I see him?"

"Just ignore him. Act like you normally do."

"But should I…"

Noles interrupted her.

"No, don't do anything. If he realizes that he's one of the primary suspects in a murder case, he may flee. Sex offenders have to register, but if he's running away from a murder charge, chances are he's going to go into hiding. We don't want that if we want justice for Anna."

While Maple understood what Noles was saying, she didn't seem happy with the answer.

"Just give me a few days. Let me get the information from the crime scene investigators' search tomorrow and we can go from there."

"Okay, thank you."

Maple walked Noles through the kitchen and thanked her once again for the coffee and lunch. Maple watched her as she went into the car and fiddled a bit with the heater. As she put the car in reserve, Maple noticed how Noles paused and looked straight at trailer number 24. Maple followed her gaze. It didn't look abandoned but it didn't look like Donald Sukuti was home.

There was something creepy about looking at the home of a sex offender in the dirtiest of trailer parks. There was something disturbing about her bringing Anna here, but she could justify her decision when she thought about Willy. She was a mother, running for her life with her daughter on her arm. Now her daughter was gone, possibly because of a man's crazy lust for young girls.

She noticed Noles putting her face in her hands. It looked like she was crying. Maybe she did feel something. Maybe she could feel the pinch in her heart when she thought about a little girl being brutally murdered. Maple noticed Noles wiping tears from her eyes and slowly driving out of the trailer park. Noles was present. She was here. She was invested.

- CHAPTER 17 -

"So, you presented her with the photo of Donald Sukuti and she told you where he lived?" Morgan asked Noles in hopes of getting clarification.

"Yes, number 24. He's the only one who she remembers seeing in the trailer park of the photos I brought out there."

Morgan leaned back in his chair in his small office. Noles stood in the doorframe. She hadn't asked to come in and made no effort to sit down. Her body language told him that she didn't really want to be there. He sensed that she didn't respect him the way he wanted to be respected.

He wasn't surprised. For years, his co-workers at the station had slowly distanced themselves from him. Deep inside, the drinking had been the reason. It was hard for them to communicate with him, as his short fuse was prevalent when he was hung over. If one person pissed him off, the entire station would know about it.

Over time, people had stopped coming to him with evidence, information or work. They had quickly learned that he would come in late, and possibly be under the influence of alcohol, so it was much easier to leave things on his desk with a note. His co-workers wouldn't even leave a name with the note. Half the time, he had no idea who had placed things on his desk. It was only Christina who would leave notes with her name on them.

But Noles had been quick to distance herself. He felt it. She hadn't engaged herself in the work like he had expected. Maybe he had hoped that she would look at him like a mentor and use his office as an inspirational tool to do her investigations. He had hoped to mold her into the detective he wanted her to be, as she took over for him. But that hadn't been the case. He knew that she had sensed the drinking and possibly saw it as a flaw. He knew that he had lost her respect and there was no turning back.

"Did you see anything in the trailer that looked suspicious?"

"No, not on the surface. But we have crime scene investigators looking at the trailer tomorrow, so maybe they will have something for us in a few days," Noles replied.

He smiled at the news. He had forgotten about the crime scene unit coming out to look at Maple's trailer. It had been his request to get them to look at her home, as he was convinced that something had happened there. While Morgan didn't think the death happened there, he does think that Anna was taken from there against her will, even if it was by the hands of her mother. An altercation could have happened, including Anna trying to fight off her attacker. He was convinced that Maple hadn't done it herself, so a strong person, such as a man, must have helped her out. Even though Anna was only four years old, someone must have carried her into the woods and snapped her neck. That takes strength and Maple looked weak.

Hopefully, the crime scene investigators could find something in her trailer. Anna's hair mingled together with a stranger's hair, DNA, sweat from an unidentified person – anything that could prove that Maple was lying about who had been in the trailer the night Anna went missing.

"What time are they expected to be out there?"

"I'm not sure. Maybe around noon," Noles mumbled.

Morgan wanted to be there when they went through the trailer, but he didn't want Noles there. She had grown close to Maple and she couldn't see the possibility of Maple having something to do with the crime. She couldn't see the case with a critical eye and he questioned whether she was truly the right person to take over for him.

On the other hand, she wasn't a complete lost cause. She could use her experience to nail Donald Sukuti on his behalf. There was nothing exciting about having a sex offender on the streets of Beaverville. Plus, with her out of the way, he could work on building his case against Maple. He fiddled with a pen before he made up his mind.

"I want you to work on Sukuti."

"What do you have in mind?" she asked.

"Find out whatever you can about him, and find out what he did that night when Anna disappeared. We need an alibi to completely rule him out."

Noles nodded. Her face became less tense. It was clearly the reaction she had hoped for, as she could dig deep into a suspect without thinking about building a case against Maple. He wondered if she could even see Maple as a cold-blooded killer.

"You can leave now," he said, making a gesture towards the door she was standing nearby.

"Keep in touch," she said before turning her back to him.

When Noles was out of view, he rubbed his face and his eyes. He was exhausted and it wasn't even work-related. He had been so caught up in his feelings and arguments with Jules that his stress and anxiety were starting to spill over into work. He had hoped that his slow-moving police career would continue to slow down as he wrapped up work before retirement, but then Maple had come along, Anna had been killed and now, Donald Sukuti had come back into his life.

The walls surrounding him told many stories with articles, crime scene pictures, and that insignificant red string that hung on the wall with pushpins. Somewhere on the wall was the story of Sukuti. It was six years ago that Morgan learned about a sting operation that had found Sukuti's IP address as one of many involved in a child pornography group. Because of the location of Sukuti, Morgan had been responsible for building a case against him. The list of people had been massive and it had been much more work than investigators had expected. Instead of charging everyone involved, investigators responsible for the sting operation had asked local enforcement to investigate and charge these men as they saw appropriate given the evidence they had.

When Detective Morgan had learned about Sukuti's activities, he was disgusted. While he wanted him off the streets, he had also seen this as his chance to really have a big success in his portfolio as a detective.

Without doing any further digging into Sukuti's past, Morgan had taken the IP address and gone out to the trailer. After a tough confrontation, he had arrested Donald Sukuti on child pornography charges. He had been proud of himself even though the lead was handed to him. Sukuti was in his jail and he saw it as a victory.

For weeks, Morgan kept him locked up in his little jail cell at the station. For him, Sukuti was guilty, so he wasn't going anywhere. For days in a row, he would withhold food in hopes that Donald would crack and admit to his crimes. While they waited for a court date, he could do whatever he wanted to get a confession.

The IP address had given him a search warrant for the trailer, but he wasn't able to find anything. The computer had been wiped clean and had nothing on it except a few documents, including a personal budget. Morgan had torn the trailer apart in hopes of finding a single picture, a digital conversation or an external hard drive.

After five weeks in the local jail, a judge set a date to hear the evidence against Sukuti. Morgan had hoped for an open-and-shut case as he felt that an IP address had been as good as DNA. But the judge didn't see it that way. He decided to let Sukuti go with time served and he had warned Morgan about locking people up on suspicion alone.

"What evidence do you present?" the judge had asked Morgan, who had looked confident in court.

"It's all in the file."

"Do you mean to tell me that your evidence is an IP address?" the judge had inquired.

Morgan had been taken aback as he was convinced that the IP address given to him had been enough to charge him with child pornography.

"Well, yes. And you see the content he was looking at."

The judge had looked at Morgan, removing his glasses slowly.

"Detective Morgan. Do you know how many people work at your station?"

"I believe around 15."

"15 people. Of those people, how many of those are computer savvy?" the judged asked.

"Well, probably a few of them. But I don't see how…"

The judge had cut him off.

"Do you know how easy it is to change an IP address these days, Detective Morgan?"

Morgan felt nervous all of a sudden. He hadn't educated himself on IP addresses. He knew that a single IP address was linked to a device, but he thought it was an identification staple. He thought it was a device's DNA, something that couldn't be changed. He swallowed loudly before speaking to the judge.

"I received the evidence from an operation sting that had been watching Sukuti from afar. I received this information from other investigators," Morgan told the judge, trying to shift the blame a bit.

He didn't want to come across as someone who didn't know how to do his job. The judge was making him look bad in front of a man that he wanted to be charged and locked up.

"Do you have anything else to support your case?"

Morgan had scrambled with his papers, something he regretted doing because it made him look weak and disorganized.

"I mean…"

"Do you, or do you not, have anything else to support your case that Mr. Sukuti should go to jail for child pornography?"

Morgan looked at the judge and swallowed before shaking his head.

"I'm going to need a vocal answer for the record."

"No, your honor."

"The case against Mr. Donald Sukuti is hereby dismissed."

When the judge's gavel hit the stand in front of him, the sound resulted in an echo in the courtroom. It was a large room and it was only Sukuti, Morgan and the judge in the room. Sukuti didn't have a lawyer present as Morgan had broken a few rules and regulations to get him behind bars. One of those regulations included getting him legal representation.

When the echo vanished, Morgan looked back at Sukuti and he gave him a guilty smile. They both knew that he was guilty, but Morgan had clearly messed up in this case. The judge noticed the tension between the two and called out Morgan's name.

"Detective Morgan!"

Morgan looked back at the judge, not realizing that he had been trying to get his attention several times.

"You need to let him go. The charges are dropped and he is a free man. Please free him from the handcuffs."

Morgan released Sukuti from the cuffs, and Sukuti got right in his face in a gentle way. He didn't say anything, but smiled in such a way that Morgan felt defeat.

"Detective Morgan, please come see me," the judge said as Donald walked out of the courtroom.

"Next time you want to find someone guilty of a crime, you better have the evidence to back it up. Keeping someone locked up for weeks without a solid case is against the law. If I find out you have done this before or again, it will be you behind bars. Do we have an understanding?"

Morgan didn't answer.

In the weeks following Sukuti's release, the entire case had been dismissed. Even though Sukuti had been a registered sex offender from a previous offense, there was no evidence to lock him up this time. This had been an important case for Morgan, but had turned out to be a major embarrassment for him. He had been proud to be in law enforcement, but a judge had overruled the IP address evidence, arguing that anyone coming and going from the trailer could have used the computer. Anyone could also have wiped the computer clean. There was enough reasonable doubt.

As he sat in his office thinking about Maple and Noles, he cocked his head. Maybe Noles could build a case against Sukuti that included framing him for the murder. While he wanted to nail Maple, he realized that he couldn't just put her away for murder without evidence. If Maple didn't work out as a viable suspect, he could always use Sukuti as a backup. Regardless, the case would be closed by the time he retired and should it be reopened, Noles would be the one to take the fall for it.

The office had gone quiet over the past couple of minutes. Morgan poked his head out the door and looked in both directions. No one was in sight. In the back of his office stood a tall filing cabinet. He slowly walked over to the cabinet and pulled out the third drawer. Near the middle of the drawer was a folder with the label, "Sukuti, Donald."

The folder was thin. He had never made an effort to build a case against Sukuti. If he had, Sukuti could be in jail and his folder would be packed with evidence against him. He took the folder out and opened it at his desk.

Photos of his trailer, documents about the IP address, and some of the websites that had been visited were in the folder. He could give this folder to Noles to help build a case against him. But he questioned whether she would truly use the information within to solve the murder of Anna.

Morgan opened a browser window on his computer and found several pictures of little girls that looked like Anna. He downloaded the photos to the computer and put them into an official police folder that he used to document evidence. He changed the date to reflect his case from six years ago and printed the photos for his folder. The content he had just printed were neatly put in a paperclip and stacked near the back of his filing cabinet.

While he hoped to nail Maple for the crime, it didn't hurt to have enough evidence against Sukuti to finally put him away for good. And while he knew what he was doing was illegal, his career would soon be over. If he could prove that Sukuti had been looking at photos of young girls that looked like Anna, a judge would possibly see that he needed to be locked up for life. A judge had already deemed him a danger to society based on a previous conviction for a sexual offense, but Morgan wanted to lock him up for good. He wanted to finish what he was unable to finish years ago, and he was ready to step beyond the law to do it.

He closed the filing cabinet once again and looked down the hall to ensure no one had seen him. He would check the documents daily to ensure no one caught him. His plan was to burn the documents once the case wrapped up so no one would ever know that he planted evidence to win a case.

- CHAPTER 18 -

It had been days since Noles visited Maple in her trailer. Noles felt a sense of failure within because she wasn't able to provide an arrest. Despite having Donald Sukuti on her desk as a potential suspect, she hadn't gone to talk to him. Morgan had asked her to dig deeper into his past in hopes of finding a link or pattern between his previous crimes and the disappearance of Anna.

Since she last saw Maple, Noles had spent hours making phone calls, getting arrest reports, checking local jails, and browsing through old news stories in hopes of getting a larger picture of who Sukuti was. Unfortunately, she could only find things that had been documented in the media or in police reports – things she already knew. Since it was such a small town, she would have to go knock on doors to get more.

The crime scene investigators had found absolutely nothing at Maple's trailer. The only thing they could match were fingerprints to Maple. They had also identified smaller prints, but since Anna's fingerprints were not on record, they couldn't be sure. It didn't help them at all.

Sitting in her small office at the station, she looked at the clock. It was inching closer to the day's end and she could soon go back home to Sam. Over the past few days, she had driven back and forth between their apartment in the city and her job at the station. She had only spent time inside, doing research. While she realized that her job required research, Noles felt like she was disappointing Maple as she hadn't talked to Sukuti. She hadn't moved the case forward. And the more time she spent behind her desk, the more frustrated Maple would get. Before long, Maple could take things into her own hands and pursue Sukuti herself.

"How are things coming along?"

Morgan stood in the doorway to her office, leaning up against the doorframe with a cup of coffee in his hand.

"Well, I'm not finding much. What would help is knowing his alibi for the night and morning Anna went missing."

Morgan nodded while sipping his coffee.

"Do you think we are ready to go talk to him?" Noles asked.

Morgan stood still, before nodding his head.

"But just you. He's not fond of me and I may make him clam up."

Noles looked at the stack of papers she had on her desk from all the research.

"Speaking of that," Noles began while grabbing some papers from her desk. "I found some information about Sukuti that involves you. It says here you tried to bust him for child pornography but was unable to nail him due to insufficient evidence."

His expression changed from friendly to defensive. She knew she had brought up a sore subject, as this was an example of Morgan's previous failures.

"It wasn't my fault. The evidence given to me from a sting operation didn't hold up in court."

"It also says that you held him in custody without his will while you waited for a court date."

Morgan closed his eyes slowly, trying to maintain calm in the workplace. Noles could see him struggling before interrupting the silence.

"I mean…if Donald Sukuti is guilty, could he have killed Anna to get some sort of revenge or reaction out of you? Do you think he used Anna as a pawn to get to you?"

It was a far-out theory, but not impossible. Noles knew that people could do crazy things, including using a little girl as a pawn in some insane plot to get revenge on a man, who may have made a mistake. She knew the pressures of performing and a part of her understood why Morgan had kept Sukuti in custody while searching for evidence to convict him. But she didn't understand why he would break the law and keep him confined at the station.

Morgan listened to her theory but eventually shrugged it off.

"If anyone is going after anyone, it's me who is going after him. I want you to go talk to him now."

Noles looked at the clock. Morgan noticed that she was looking at the time, thinking it was almost time to go home. It was Friday afternoon and she had hoped to go home early to relax a bit. She had spent hours in front of the computer and she was mentally drained. The office work that Sam had joked about with her had worn her out.

"Don't even think about going home. You are going out to Sukuti now. Do you want another child to go missing?"

Morgan's tone sounded demeaning and she realized he was issuing an order. He didn't move as he stood in the doorframe with the coffee mug in his hand. Noles stood up, grabbed her jacket and car keys and walked past him. She didn't say a word to him, hoping he would see just how insensitive he was being.

The sky was changing color as she got into the police cruiser. She let Sam know that she was working late and headed towards the trailer park. As she drove through the main stretch of the town, she noticed the many pickup trucks and vans lined up outside of the liquor store. The locals rushed to the store before it closed down to get the weekend's booze.

Without the alcohol, it would be hard to survive out here for someone with little to live for. Noles swung the car into the parking lot next to the store and watched as the regulars stopped by to get alcohol. Each of them walked out with two or more brown bags of beer or hard liquor. She could tell by the size of the bag what kind of alcohol was inside. She didn't recognize any of the locals. In her hand, she held a photo of Donald Sukuti from her research. Hopefully, he would show up to get some alcohol and she could see what kind of man he was prior to visiting him. She had no idea how he had evolved over the past couple of years. While Morgan was able to lock him up, she was scared that he could overpower her with her tiny frame.

He didn't show up. The sun was starting to go down and a twilight setting was slowly growing on the horizon. Noles put the car in drive and headed back out on the main strip of town. As she hit the outskirts of Beaverville, she put her foot on the gas and sped off. She wanted this interview to be done quickly, so she could go home to Sam. She didn't understand why it couldn't wait until Monday. Sukuti had no idea they were on his trail or that he was even being considered as a suspect. But like Morgan, she didn't want another child to go missing. She couldn't live with herself if another child was killed and she had been too lazy to interview a potential suspect.

There was something innocent about a child. While she didn't grow up with a younger sibling, she had often talked about having a child. For years, Sam had begged her to have a baby. His life was complete and structured. From an early age, he had known that he wanted to work in the hospital. The pace of the emergency room excited him and he loved being the person people would call for assistance. He had studied hard in medical school and he knew everything when it came to being an emergency doctor. So after having worked for a few years, he was ready to settle down.

But Noles had been gaining traction in her own career over a longer period of time. Sam was ahead of her in many ways. While he had worked hard, Magnolia had taken time off after school to travel. She wanted to experience the culture of Spain, the pasta and fresh tomatoes of Italy, and the heart of Amsterdam. She knew her career would be waiting for her when she came home.

Sam hadn't taken time to travel. He had been a dedicated student because he knew what he wanted. And now he wanted a family. For two years, Noles had avoided the conversation, begging him to give her time to advance her career. For years, she was stuck doing petty crime. Now, she finally had a chance to solve a murder and she realized that she couldn't place herself in Maple's shoes. She knew that losing a child was horrible, but she couldn't relate to Maple's heartbreaking pain, her anger building within, and her desire to go confront Sukuti right now and possibly hurt him.

The trailer park looked dark from the main country road. A few lights lit up as its residents began having dinner, hiding out in the dark from the residents of Beaverville. But for the most part, one could have sped right by it without noticing the many trailers stacked away in the field. She pulled into the park and drove slowly through, trying not to draw too much attention to herself. From the car, she could hear the gravel underneath the tires as she approached Donald's trailer. He hadn't heard her coming. There was a light on inside the trailer, but he hadn't peaked out of the window facing the front. She could also see someone moving inside. The car came to a slow stop in front of his home and she shut off the engine. She quietly got out of the car and walked along his trailer to the edge of his property. From here, she could see Maple's trailer. Anna's bedroom window was facing away from Sukuti, but he would be able to see her front door, her kitchen window and her bathroom.

It was silent in the trailer park. She could hear the wind pick up and the trees surrounding the lot were swaying. The branches and the remaining leaves on the trees provided a soundtrack to the scene. There was something eerie about being outside, walking around between these trailers. She was well aware that criminals came out here to hide. Approaching Sukuti's front door, Noles took a deep breath and gathered some courage. She knocked three times.

Silence.

She watched the window beside the front door. If his trailer layout was the same as Maple's, it would be his kitchen window. She spotted someone moving around inside, as the brightness of the light changed with a figure moving around. Someone was inside, avoiding her knocks. She knocked again, and told him that she was with the police.

The front door slowly opened, and it was just enough for him to look out with a single eye. Noles hadn't expected the first time encounter to be so spooky, so she took a step back.

"What do you want?"

"Mr. Sukuti? Mr. Donald Sukuti?"

"Who is asking?"

"I'm Detective Watson. I work in Beaverville and I'm in the trailer park, investigating the disappearance of a little girl. She lives in the park. I would like to speak to you about the case."

The single eye she could see through the crack of the door looked her up and down. He opened the door a bit more and she could now see his full face. He matched the image she had in her car, just a bit more aged. He looked frail. His thin hair barely covered his head, his face was long as if he was sick, and it was clear that he hadn't eaten much. He looked skinny, weak, and downright bland. Four fingers surfaced from behind the door, as he grabbed the door in an effort to open it more. His fingernails were long and she noticed that there was dirt underneath every single one of them. She thought about Anna in the woods. Chills went down her spine, but she tried to keep calm.

"Do you mind if we speak for a minute?"

Donald looked her up and down again.

"Are you working for Detective Morgan?"

"Well, we are at the same station, but I'm taking the lead here. I'm aware of your past and I know you've been wronged so I'm here to have an honest and fair conversation with you. You are not a suspect," Noles explained, stretching the truth slightly to ease him into a conversation.

Sukuti didn't say anything as he continued to stare down Noles. After a few moments of silence, he slowly opened the door and invited Noles inside. She felt the heat from the trailer immediately as he had cranked up the temperature. Perhaps it was the lack of fat on his body that made him cold during these freezing nights. When she stepped inside, she immediately removed her jacket. The heat didn't help her anxiety in the situation.

The layout of the kitchen was identical to Maple's trailer. His kitchen table was in the same spot, but his trailer didn't have that comforting feeling that she had experienced in Maple's home. There was no sense of innocence in his trailer, and it was dirty. There were plastic bags on the floor, dust in the corners and all of his furnishings were brown, torn and worn out. His home looked like a place where he slept at night, not a place he would come for comfort or security.

The kitchen table seated two. It was old with scratches and cuts on the surface. It looked like a hand-me-down table and when she sat down on the chair he had pulled out for her, she felt herself losing her balance slightly. Both the table and her chair rocked, showing how poorly he cared for his furnishings. He sat down in front of her and waited for her to speak.

"So, as mentioned before, I'm here about a little girl that went missing. Are you aware of any children living in the trailer park?"

"No."

Noles was stunned by the short answer, as he sat coyly in front of her.

"Have you seen this little girl?" she asked, as she put a photo of Anna in front of him, a picture she had borrowed from Maple.

"No."

"I find that odd to believe. She is your neighbor. She lives right there," Noles said, pointing in the direction of Maple's trailer.

"Oh."

He crossed his legs at the table, grabbing a pack of cigarettes. He lit a cigarette with a lighter and placed the lighter gently down on the table as he inhaled. He watched Noles as he blew out the smoke, tapping his foot lightly as if to intimate her. Without saying much, he was playing with her emotions. The tension in the room was clear. He didn't respect her because of her uniform and he didn't take her seriously. Sukuti had been locked up against his will, so she knew he was strong.

"What were you doing the night and morning of the 17th of last month?" Noles asked him, hoping to get his story of the night and morning Anna went missing.

"I don't recall."

He tapped his cigarette and let the ashes fall down in an ashtray on the table. The kitchen started to smell like cigarette smoke and Noles felt uncomfortable. The more she could smell the stench of cigarettes, the more she wanted to get out of there. It was still hot and the smoke was beginning to choke her.

"I see here that you are a registered sex offender and you were almost caught a second time. Tell me why we shouldn't be looking at you for the death of Anna, who we found in the woods east of town a few weeks ago."

Her tone was firm and he seemed surprised that he was a suspect in the case.

"She's dead?"

"Yes, someone killed her."

"Well, I surely didn't kill anyone. It's not in my DNA to do that."

"But it is in your DNA to molest a child?"

He tapped his cigarette again and inhaled as he continued to smoke.

"I see you have done your research."

"I'm not here to judge you based on your previous crimes. I'm here to figure out where you were the night and morning hours of the 17th, as Anna disappeared from her trailer and was later found dead."

He nodded slowly, looking at Noles as he appeared to be contemplating his next move.

"Whatever you think about me, you are wrong. I'm innocent. I didn't kill that little girl. While I may do horrible things to children, I'm no killer. In that sense, consider me a coward."

"Can someone provide a corroborate your story?"

Donald looked around his trailer and used his arms to gesture that she could pick from any of his belongings.

"I was here. The walls will tell you."

There was an awkward silence while Noles looked around. She didn't have a warrant for the trailer, so she couldn't go digging for information or possible evidence. It also scared her that she didn't know what she would potentially find. His home was creepy and she imagined finding everything from child pornography to drugs around the trailer, hidden in every drawer.

"How did she die?"

His way of breaking the silence was eerie and Noles slowly turned her head to face him.

"Someone snapped her neck. Major blunt force trauma."

As odd as it was inappropriate, Sukuti let out a small laugh.

"Now, you see - that's all you need. Look at me. Do you think I'd be strong enough to break someone's neck? I have cancer. I'm dying. And I'm not getting any treatment to save my life. I can barely get food for myself in town."

He leaned forward in his chair, so he was halfway across the table before continuing.

"How do you expect to prove that I killed a little girl given my condition?"

His face looked frail in the little light that came from above them. He looked like he wanted to hide here, die out in the backroom somewhere and hope that no one ever found him. It was sad to see a man this way. She had to keep reminding herself that he was a child molester and a registered sex offender. But his physical appearance did hold up with his word. He couldn't possibly have taken her out to the woods. His body wouldn't allow him to carry her, even if she was already dead or just unconscious.

"I think you are looking in the wrong direction," he said suddenly, trying to get out of the chair.

She observed him as he got up to grab a cup from the cupboard. He wanted some water and he started coughing aggressively from the cigarette smoke. He was weak and he struggled to keep his balance when taking just a few steps.

"Tell me more."

He didn't say anything as he poured himself some water and sat down.

"Have you looked at Barnes?"

"I'm sorry, who?"

"Michael Barnes. He lives over in 57. Well, I mean - he used to live there. His mother kicked him out when he tried to choke her. Now, he tends to bounce around on people's couches, but he has been known to keep an eye out on people, rob them for cash and valuables, peek through people's windows."

Noles scribbled down what Sukuti was telling her. Perhaps Morgan knew about him or had a history with him. But a part of her also had her guard up. Maybe Sukuti was lying about the cancer and playing weak tonight in hopes she would look elsewhere. She couldn't ignore the obvious connection and the proximity of the two trailers.

"I'm not going to bother you more tonight, but I am going to see if we can speak more at a later time, should I have any more questions for you. See if you can find someone who can corroborate your alibi for the night and morning in question."

Noles got up from her chair and grabbed her jacket. He slowly nodded and he continued to sit in his kitchen chair, grabbing yet another cigarette. He smoked a lot considering he said he had cancer, but she felt it wasn't her place to dictate or question his decisions. As she started to open the front door, he shared his last words of the night with her.

"Be careful with Barnes. He's been known to be - well, you know – not fond of women."

Noles didn't care to shut the door lightly behind her. Sukuti was playing her, questioning her authority and her stamina. While she didn't want to let him go as a suspect, she did have another potential lead. Michael Barnes.

As she slowly drove through the trailer park, she located number 57. It was rundown, the siding was coming off and the eavestroughs were separating from the roof. No one was taking care of the property and no one really seemed to care about the appearance of the home. The light was off inside, but she sensed a shadow was lurking behind the trailer. She wasn't carrying a weapon and there was a frightening sense of discomfort in her stomach. She quickly locked all the doors in her car and left the trailer park.

- CHAPTER 19 -

The liquor store sign hung over the main strip of the road, as it had done every other night for the many years Morgan had been a customer. It was Friday night, Noles was out of his hair, and Jules was out of town with a girlfriend. He had the whole house to himself. Things were going well at work too. Even though Noles had been a pain in the ass when she first started, she was now doing a lot of the heavy lifting. Despite not listening to his orders about Maple, she was magically going after his loose ends. Maybe he could get a conviction before retirement, even if it wasn't for Anna's murder.

For a few minutes, Morgan contemplated whether it was worth it to go into the liquor store. He could take the night off from drinking now that Jules wasn't home, but on the other hand, she wasn't there to judge. He found himself opening the car door. Within seconds, he was browsing the aisles in the store, looking at bottles of vodka, whiskey and bourbon. On bad days, he would go for the strong stuff. He would go for the large bottles so he could drown his sorrows. But he felt positive and celebratory today. He could just go for the beer.

"Hello Detective Morgan," the cashier said as she scanned his three beers and a single bottle of bourbon.

He nodded, hoping he wouldn't have to start a conversation.

"Find the killer yet?"

"You know I can't talk about the case," Morgan said, quickly paying his bill in cash.

"Who do you think done it?"

Before she could finish the sentence, he had walked out the front door. The pressure was big for him to solve this case. This wasn't just a murder. This was a little girl, who had been dumped in the woods by someone who had broken her neck. He knew how serious this was for Beaverville - and for his career. While no one really knew about him keeping Sukuti against his will, people do remember him not being able to keep a child molester off the streets.

The brown paper bag with the alcohol rested on the passenger seat, as he started the car. As he was about to drive home, his phone rang. He struggled to get the phone out of his jacket pocket and worried that Jules was calling him. Perhaps she had spotted him at the liquor store or maybe she had come home early tonight, and she was waiting for him at home. But to his surprise, it was Detective Watson.

"Detective Morgan here," he responded as he answered the phone trying to sound official.

"Ah hi, yes, it's me. I just left the trailer park behind so I thought I'd give you an update. My gut feeling tells me it's not him."

"Don't let him fool you."

"Yeah, I kept that in mind, but he's sick. Did you know he has cancer? He looks frail, tired, weak. There's no way he could carry her into the woods alone."

There was a silence in Morgan's car as he learned about Sukuti's illness. Underneath his breath, he whispered "dammit," as he had hoped he would be their lead suspect. He closed his eyes and stretched out his neck.

"Did he say anything else?"

"I told him to get his alibi in order and find someone who could corroborate the fact that he was home the night of Anna's murder. Also, he brought up some disturbing things about a man named Michael Barnes."

Morgan sighed in the car as he heard the name. Michael was no stranger to the police force in Beaverville and Morgan had repeatedly asked him to play nice to avoid being arrested.

"Do you know him?"

"Yes, he's a local criminal. Don't pursue him Noles. He's dangerous."

"I stopped by his trailer…" Noles began, but was interrupted by Morgan.

"No, you cannot go see him. He's dangerous and I don't want you near him."

In a calm voice, Noles laughed a bit.

"Don't worry, Morgan. I'm in my car, safe and sound on the way home. I just wanted to see what his home looked like so I knew what I was dealing with."

Morgan let out a sigh of relief. He didn't want to go out to the trailer park and bring home an officer, who was in danger thanks to Barnes. Barnes had already caused too many issues for the police department in Beaverville. For two months straight, Morgan's budget had been stretched because he had to have officers ready all the time due to the number of break-and-enters he had caused. Sometimes, there would be families home and Michael would barge in, beating parents in front of their children.

"Let's talk about it on Monday," he said before hanging up the phone.

With Noles going home, he now had Beaverville to himself. The town was his to patrol and keep safe. As long as nothing major happened over the weekend, it could wait until Monday. He put the car in drive and headed home.

His house was dark and uninviting when he finally rolled up. It was so late that Jules was either still out with her friend, or had gone to bed. When she was out with her friends, she would sometime come home late at night as they would go see a late-night movie or hang out over drinks at the local bars in the city. She would then share a cab with a girlfriend back to Beaverville. If she weren't in bed already, it would be hours before she would come through the door.

The house was empty. She hadn't returned yet. He turned on the lights and noticed a spotless kitchen. She hadn't left any food for him and it appeared that she had cleaned the house earlier. He opened the fridge, realizing that there was little food there. Maybe she had thought that he would eat on his way home, as he had done before. He picked up the house phone and called the local pizzeria.

"Hi Moe, I'll get a large pepperoni pizza. When can you get here?"

A few minutes later, he had the money ready by the kitchen counter and he was ready to drink some beer with the pizza. He removed his uniform shirt, revealing a white t-shirt underneath. His uniform pants had become his daily pants and he often wore them until he passed out. Unlike the official shirt, the pants had become rather comfortable throughout the years. When Jules would wash them, they would shrink a bit and they would be uncomfortable for a few days. However, he preferred them this way. He didn't care that they smelled like the station or the police truck.

The doorbell rang after about half an hour, and a young man stood outside the door with his pizza in hand. Without saying much, Morgan grabbed the pizza box and gave the young man the $20 bucks. He didn't recognize him, despite knowing many people in town. After he closed the door, he went to the nearest window and watched him get into his car. He didn't recognize the car either. The pizza delivery guy started a long string of thoughts that kept him at the window, staring him down until he was out of sight. A stranger in town could have killed Anna. There was nothing that could prevent him, the pizza delivery guy, from pulling up to Maple's trailer, enter the premises and take the little girl.

It didn't matter about motive either. He could be a thrill seeker. Morgan experienced a moment of clarity, thinking about the possibility that a complete stranger had entered his town and committed this murder. Was the killer taunting him by delivering pizza to him? Morgan grabbed the phone.

"Who is your new delivery guy, Moe?"

"Oh, he's my nephew. Visiting from out of town. He's just here for a few days, trying to make a few bucks delivering the pizzas. Is he giving you trouble?"

"When did he get here?"

"Yesterday. Why?"

He sighed on the phone, realizing he may be overreacting. He didn't want to spread panic over the phone with someone who had no connection to the case.

"No worries, Moe. I'll see you later."

Morgan opened the pizza box. The smell of pepperoni and cheese hit him right in the face and he realized how hungry he was. He hadn't thought about dinner all day, but now that he was home, he was ready to relax. He grabbed a slice of pizza and cracked open one of the beers. While Jules loved him eating in the kitchen and keeping the living room clean, she wasn't here to tell him otherwise. With greasy fingers from the pizza, he grappled the remote control, turning on the news.

There wasn't anything worth watching. While eating, he got caught up on the latest political drama playing out in the country. The Democrats were upset with the Republicans once again. It seemed like they were repeating the discussions for the sake of airtime, using the same experts and the same arguments night after night.

Bothered by the news, he got up from the couch and headed to the kitchen. The sound of the bourbon hitting the glass he had gotten from the cupboard sounded lovely. Familiarity rushed over him. It was like his best friend, singing to him, falling asleep in a mother's warm bosoms.

The bourbon felt lukewarm as he took a sip. He felt it go down his throat. It was a feeling that used to be much more intense a few years ago. Now, he couldn't get the same rush anymore, no matter the amount. Sometimes, he convinced himself that he just needed to drink more or find the strongest alcohol at the liquor store. Jules hated when he tried to test these limits, so he often tried at the bar instead.

The pizza was quickly gone as he inhaled the eight slices he had ordered. It was best when it was hot and he didn't mind burning the roof of his mouth. It was a pleasant experience for him, almost as a sense of punishment for hitting the bottle once again. He placed the pizza box on the kitchen counter, knowing he wouldn't be cleaning it up before Jules got home.

The house was empty without Jules. It lacked a sense of love and comfort. There was no warmth in the house and he felt the draft come through the dark living room. The television was still on, as he could faintly hear the news anchor, discussing the political landscape and a state election that would soon take place. He took another sip of the bourbon and got an urge to reflect and relive the past.

Years ago, he and Jules had been the perfect couple. The loss of their son had changed that. Tonight, as he was home alone, he thought about what life would be like if his son had been here. His son would be greeting him at the door, asking if they could order pizza together. He imagined what it would have been like to go to soccer practice with him on the weekends, and taking him to the playground when he was a child. He imagined how he would be so proud of his son going to college. He wouldn't be drinking. He would be sober and Jules would love to see her boys together, bonding over swimming, soccer, and movies.

Jules had packed all memories of their son away a few years after the accident. She needed to remove the memories of him to heal properly. Now, she could look at photos of him and smile. Morgan couldn't look at a photo of his son without breaking into tears. Despite putting on a rough exterior, he hadn't dealt with his feelings. He hadn't truly grieved the loss of his son. The daily intake of alcohol helped numb the pain, but in reality, he was scared to feel his own emotions.

Without alcohol, he would be forced to deal with his issues. And he was scared that he wouldn't be able to pick himself up again. His son's death had rattled something within him - a disconnect he was unable to fix.

He chugged the bourbon in his glass, as he headed straight for the attic. Jules had hidden the photos of their son as a way to move on, but Morgan was convinced that she had hidden the photos to protect him, so he could grieve on his own time.

The attic was dark and the cobwebs lit up as he turned on the single bulb hanging from the roof of their house. Jules had organized all of their belongings in the attic and labeled the boxes based on what was within. He looked through all of them, searching for labels that told him what was inside. Easter and Christmas decorations took up most of the boxes, and he found a few boxes of old clothing. A small box stood near the end of the attic. Just by looking at it, he knew what it was.

Without breaking his line of sight, he walked straight over to the box and brought it back to the light. It wasn't very heavy, as they hadn't been able to save a lot after his death. Slowly, he opened the box. Immediately, he regretted leaving the bourbon downstairs. Just by lifting one flap of the box, he could see his son's beautiful face. Jules had truly saved the best photos of their son. He was giggling in this one photo. He seemed so happy, and then thanks to his dad, he was slammed against a tree. Morgan broke down crying, letting his feelings take over. He continued to look through the photos, reliving all of the memories.

The box also contained a few body stockings, including the one he had worn on the day the nurses revealed he was ready to go home from the hospital. He had been so small and Morgan remembers driving very carefully as they took him home from the city. It had been a long drive, but their son had been sleeping so peacefully in his car seat. Jules had been beside him in the backseat, singing to him while she stroked his little head.

Morgan knew these things had been put aside, but there was one more item in the box. It was a picture frame. He pulled it out and saw that the frame read, "Best Father – First Father's Day." In the frame was a photo of Morgan holding his son. He had never seen this before. Jules had prepared this gift for him for his first Father's Day, but she had never given it to him. Father's Day was just one week after the accident.

Morgan completely lost control, sobbing and screaming. The alcohol fueled his feelings and he allowed himself to feel. It hurt inside, but he couldn't keep it in anymore. His heart literally hurt as he relived all the happy moments with his wife and his son. He had never been happier than those times, and if he had received this frame when his son was alive, it would have been his favorite. He closed his eyes, imagining the frame placed on his office desk at the station.

He imagined his son coming to visit him, telling the other police officers at the station that Morgan was his father and he was catching all the bad guys. He imagined the role model he had wanted to be for so long.

The accident came into view. Morgan grabbed one of the baby body stockings and covered his face with it as he continued to sob. Perhaps it was the alcohol playing tricks on him, but for a moment, he felt like he could smell his son. He felt his son close to him, almost as if he was there again. In his mind, faint babies cries came from his old nursery downstairs. He was dealing. He was grieving. For once, he was letting go.

- CHAPTER 20 -

The sun didn't shine through Noles' large apartment windows on this particular weekend. The weather had been horrible and they had been living in a gloomy and cloudy city, where the rain had turned to snow and then back to rain. On an autumn weekend, Noles and Sam would bundle up and head down to the farmer's market by the river. During the winter, they would explore the Christmas decorations and get some hot chocolate for the walk home. When the summer arrived, they would get some fresh vegetables and meat, and have a long day of relaxing followed by cooking at night.

But this weekend, nothing had been the same. Sam had been called into work Friday night and constant overcast had kept them inside all of Saturday. Noles couldn't sleep at night. She couldn't get her conversation with Sukuti out of her head. As she lay in bed, she thought about what had transpired just 36 hours prior.

His trailer had felt creepy. She could still smell the disgusting stench of the trailer not being cleaned regularly, and she could feel the warmth from the heaters. It would make her skin itch, just by the thought.

Sam rolled over in bed and hugged her. When she didn't hug him back, he opened his eyes.

"How long have you been awake?" he asked, mumbling a bit as he struggled to keep his eyes open.

"Not long, just can't sleep."

"Work?"

"Yeah, just thinking about the case."

Sam pulled her closer to him, trying to get her thoughts on other things. However, Noles was not in the mood to be a loving spouse right now. Her mind kept circulating around the idea that Michael Barnes, not Sukuti, was responsible for Anna's murder. There were many puzzle pieces that had to fit, and as she lay in bed this Sunday morning, she tried to make the story reasonable.

When Sam was called into work Friday night, Noles had spent the night researching Barnes. She had hoped Morgan could answer a few questions, but she had been unable to reach him and he didn't call back on the Saturday either. From what she could understand, Michael had been the type of guy who had escalated his crimes over time. There was nothing about murder, but he had been busted for break-and-enters and a few assault charges. In that particular case, he had served a lengthier prison sentence for beating a man with a bat.

"What do you say we make some eggs and bacon?" Sam suggested, continuing to snuggle her with his eyes closed.

"Actually, I was thinking about going back to Beaverville today. I think I may have an idea."

Sam opened his eyes, seemingly surprised that she would willingly work on a day off. Plus, this was only one of two days they had together for a while, so she knew he had hoped to spend it with her.

"How about this?" she suggested before he could object to her plans. "I hurry out to Beaverville, talk to the person I need to talk to, and then get back here as soon as I can. I'll aim for early afternoon. Then, I'm all yours."

Sam looked at the windows, realizing that it would be another gloomy day outside. He nodded as Noles crept out of bed. She hopped in the shower and this morning, she didn't care to wait for the water to heat up. She didn't have time to relax. Beaverville could some answers that she wanted, so she could narrow down the suspect pool. And since Morgan wasn't answering his phone, she only had one other idea in mind. After her shower, she quickly grabbed some clothes from her closet.

"Are you sure you don't want some breakfast before you leave?" he asked through a sizzling sound.

Sam was flipping bacon on the stove. The eggs were standing next to him on the kitchen counter. He was clearly trying to make her stick around or possibly even change her mind.

"Sorry, I need to do this. I'll be back after lunch. Promise."

His scruffy face scratched her, as she kissed him on the cheek. Within seconds, she had grabbed her purse, her car keys and a jacket. She also took a mug shot of Michael Barnes she had printed out. As she walked down the hallway of their apartment building, she could smell the bacon. There was something familiar about the bacon that almost had her turn around. It would be nice to spend time with Sam now that they finally had some time off. On the other hand, Anna was on her mind.

The cornfields looked calm as she sped past them. She spotted no other vehicles on her drive out to Beaverville. The weekends seemed even slower out here in the country. There were no trucks hauling freight, and there were no locals going to work in the city. Other than the wind hitting the car, Noles was driving in complete silence.

Her conversation with Sukuti had scared her a bit. There was something creepy about him. She couldn't get him out of her head. If he could simply provide an alibi that he was home the night of Anna's disappearance, she could clear him. But him saying he was home wasn't enough. While she explored Michael Barnes, both men would be on the persons of interest list.

After an hour, she started to see the outskirts of Beaverville. She knew that no one would be at the station this weekend, so she didn't bother going into town. The last thing she wanted was to talk to the odd lady at the grocery store again. Instead, Noles turned off near the interstate and headed out to the diner where she had always felt welcome. It was a bit of a stretch, but she hoped Myrtle also worked on Sunday mornings.

The diner wasn't too busy considering it was Sunday. For some reason, Noles had expected that she wouldn't have an easy time talking to Myrtle. With hungry families and couples coming home from road trips, Magnolia had expected to wait for hours to get Myrtle to herself. As she stood in the door, she saw that the service counter was empty. A young woman stood behind it, making a new pot of coffee. Only two other parties were in the diner, but no Myrtle. Noles approached the young server and caught the eye of the young server.

"Good morning. How can I help you?"

"A menu would be good – and coffee."

"Sure thing, coming right up."

Noles watched her as she poured a cup of the freshly made coffee and handed her a menu. The young woman smiled. She looked like a small-town girl, so Noles had no doubt that she lived in Beaverville.

"Is Myrtle here today?"

The young girl shook her head.

"Just Monday through Friday."

"Do you know where I would be able to find her?"

The young woman looked surprised. Noles could see that she wasn't expecting to answer questions about her co-worker, especially give out personal information such as a phone number or an address. She was clearly protective of Myrtle.

"I'm sorry, do you know her? Are you a relative or something?"

"Detective," Noles said, showing the young woman her badge.

"Oh, I'm so sorry. I didn't realize," she said, as she made a gesture towards Noles' outfit.

Watson was wearing skinny jeans, a grey t-shirt, an army green jacket, and a pair of white Converse shoes. There was nothing official about her outfit.

"That's okay."

"Let me see what I can do. What's your name?"

"Detective Watson. She'll know who I am."

The young girl disappeared from the service counter and went into the diner's office in the back. She was gone for a few minutes and Noles looked at the other patrons while she waited. The coffee was great when it was this fresh and before the young woman could return, Noles had already consumed the whole cup. She surfaced from the office and walked straight over to Noles.

"She said she'd be right over. You can take a seat in a booth to wait if you want. It provides a bit more privacy than the service bar. She also said to serve you our pancakes – light syrup."

"Light syrup sounds good."

The server topped up her cup of coffee, and Noles got up from the service bar and found herself a cozy spot in a booth. She placed herself so she faced away from the front door. In return, she got herself a nice view of the cornfields that ran for miles. The diner was situated on a hill, so she could see Beaverville. She could spot the wooded area where Anna had been found and some local farms out in the distance. She recognized the entire layout based on the maps at the station.

As she drank her coffee, she thought about Anna and the distance between the trailer park and Lander's Lake where she had been found. From where she was sitting, she couldn't see the trailer park or the city where she had come from this morning. From up here, she could sense how far Lander's Lake was from where the trailer park was. A little girl couldn't walk that by herself. Even if it had been summer, her little feet couldn't handle the rough roads. The morning she had gone missing, the ground would have been ice cold. The ice must have burned her skin with every step.

Someone took her to Lander's Lake. It was remote. No one could hear her scream. Maybe no one heard her scream because she wasn't killed there. Or maybe she didn't scream because she knew her killer. Maybe she trusted him or her, and didn't suspect any danger.

Her train of thought was disrupted. Someone had placed a hand on her shoulder. She jumped slightly and the familiar voice apologized.

"I'm so sorry dear. Didn't mean to scare you."

Myrtle stood next to her and waited for Noles to gesture for her to sit down. The young lady behind the service counter noticed Myrtle had walked in and was already on her way over with a cup of black coffee for her co-worker.

"Just something to help get the day started," she said as she placed the cup in front of Myrtle.

"Such a darling," she replied.

Sitting across from one another, Noles smiled as she began to speak.

"Thanks for meeting me. I know it's your day off and all."

"Don't worry about it sweetie. I assume I'm here on official police business."

"Well, yes – I did some digging and I pursued Mr. Sukuti. Did you know that he is sick with cancer?"

Myrtle shook her head slightly but then stopped.

"Well, actually – now that you mention it. A few months ago, a friend of mine claims she saw him. He looked awfully weak, but she didn't realize he was sick. Months have passed now, so he could be worse now. I mean anything is possible. That's just hearsay though."

"He struggled to get out of his chair when I was there talking to him," Noles pointed out.

Myrtle looked a bit sad at the news, even though she clearly condemned sexual predators.

"Cancer is a bitch," she said, taking a huge gulp of coffee.

"Personally, I'm uncertain that he was capable of doing this – at least on his own. He pointed me to another possible suspect and I'm wondering if you could tell me a bit about him. His name is Mr. Michael Barnes."

Noles put a picture of Barnes from a previous arrest in front of Myrtle and she raised her eyebrows.

"Yes, I know him," she said in a calm voice. "I went to public school with him years ago, just outside of Beaverville. He was a troublemaker back then."

She picked up the photo and studied it closely.

"So sad how he continued to spiral out of control. No family structure either."

"What can you tell me about him?"

Before Myrtle could start, the young lady from the service bar came over with her pancakes. Before leaving, she asked if they wanted anything else, but Myrtle sent her on her way again.

"When we were in the seventh grade, he killed a squirrel with a hammer. He decided to bring it to school and he hid it in the teacher's drawer in her desk. When she pulled open the drawer, she got squirrels' blood on her. She wasn't happy about it. He was expelled after that."

"Just the squirrel?"

"No, from what I understand, that was just the beginning."

Noles got out a notepad and a pen, ready to write some notes. She also pulled out Barnes' arrest record to see if she could match Myrtle's story with her records.

"There was a period of about six months where people's dogs would go missing around here. It remains a mystery to this day, but Barnes was suspected of killing them and burying them in the cornfields. When we were in middle school, he often begged for a dog, possibly because he didn't have any siblings, you see. He also had no real friends."

Myrtle took a sip of coffee before continuing.

"Some people suspected he killed the dogs because he couldn't have one himself."

Noles had no record for that behaviour.

"So the behaviour escalated…"

"For sure," Myrtle said. "He seemed to be getting worse, I think just because no one told him no. There was no discipline for him."

"I have a charge here of break-and-enter with an assault charge," Noles pointed out, wanting to hear if Myrtle knew anything about it.

"Oh yes, poor Marge."

Noles put down her pen, wanting to listen to the story. It sounded like Myrtle knew Marge personally.

"You see…Marge was a regular in here. She would stop by for morning coffee and read the paper. One night, she was at home watching television when Michael broke into her house. He tied her up and stole all of her belongings. He would beat her if she didn't tell him where her valuables and cash were hidden. He beat her so badly she had a fracture in her skull. He broke her legs and she's now struggling to walk. She can't drive her car over here anymore. She's essentially a prisoner in her own home."

Noles looked at her list of charges and then back at Myrtle.

"He should be behind bars for this. What happened?"

Myrtle leaned in.

"Honestly? Shitty police work."

Noles' faced changed. She knew Myrtle was talking about Morgan. Apparently, Sukuti wasn't the only person who Morgan had rubbed the wrong way. She started to wonder if Detective Morgan really was on anyone's good side.

"Morgan?"

"Yup. He seemed more interested in using him for inside information than getting him behind bars. Michael is an interesting fella. He could possibly provide many names, but he's also a danger to society. Detective Morgan chose to put his own work status over the lives of Beaverville."

"Interesting."

Noles hadn't heard this story yet and she questioned whether it would be wise to talk to him about it. As she continued to chow down on pancakes, she wondered what Barnes could tell her about Morgan. Given what he had done to Sukuti, it's possible that Barnes had a few stories about Morgan. Noles leaned towards Myrtle to avoid causing concern.

"Do you think he's capable of killing someone? A child?"

"I think anything is possible."

"No sexual predator tendencies you know of?"

"No. But I do know that he doesn't like women. He's had some mommy issues and I think he takes it out on women. That's just my personal theory, but he has lashed out at any woman he's ever had to answer to."

Noles nodded as she wrote down what Myrtle was telling her. As she was writing, she felt Myrtle's hands on hers.

"You should be careful dear. He could really hurt you."

For a moment, Noles hoped she didn't have to speak to Barnes on his turf.

- CHAPTER 21 -

Maple didn't know whether it was Wednesday, Friday or the weekend. All she knew for sure was that Anna was gone and she wasn't coming back. Her body was starting to send her some signals, including hunger. She had her appetite back now that the shock was starting to wear off and she had been sleeping a bit again. The exhaustion had been extreme and while her mind wanted to keep going, her body had given in to sleep. She felt guilty for sleeping but she was getting to the point where she couldn't function without some rest.

Before Anna went missing, Maple was very cautious of their surroundings. She overanalyzed the placement of the newspaper outside of her trailer, she always made sure to lock all of the locks on the doors and windows to keep them safe, and she would always look around when they went into town. Now that Anna was gone, she felt like she hadn't done her job as a mother.

There was something that had died within her when Anna was found in the woods. She had failed as a parent so she didn't feel she could use the label "mother" anymore. That title was diminished. It was tarnished. She would never be a mother again. A voice within was telling her that she didn't deserve it. But the caring and loving side of her had also died. The days were strung together and Maple didn't wake up with motivation in her heart. She wanted Detective Watson to show up with the news that they had arrested the person who had killed her little girl.

Willy was the last person she wanted to see, but if he shot her from a distance when getting the paper, she would see her daughter again. Both living and dying had pros and cons.

Sometimes, she found herself looking out the window, waiting for him to walk up and confront her. She imagined him confessing his crime to her, telling her that he only took her to spread anger, panic and utter heartbreak. But he was coming back for her. His plan was to cause inexplicable pain to Maple and let her live a miserable life before coming back for her, putting her through a slow death.

But every morning Maple woke up, she told herself that he hadn't found her new home yet. He hadn't made his move. Now, she found herself looking out the window again, waiting for someone to pull up to the trailer. A bird outside the window surprised her and she snapped out of it. She blinked and wet her lips. She had been thinking for quite some time and had been staring out the window for several minutes.

The heater was still going on full blast, as the temperature was still chilly outside. The newspaper was on the road outside but she only spotted it now. She had been so deep in thought that she hadn't even seen the paper rolled up on the ground. All of a sudden, there was an urge to get the paper inside and read every page. Maybe there was a clue about Anna.

The pink-faded housecoat hung on the kitchen chair. She had worn it almost every day, but had removed it this morning to take a shower. Now, she wanted to get the paper so she threw it over her shoulders to keep her warm as she headed outside.

It was eerily silent outside. She could hear the door creak as she took a step outside of the trailer and the door's sound almost echoed in the woods surrounding the trailer park. For a moment, she stopped and looked around to see if she could spot unusual movement. The only movements she could see were the trees and a few birds flying around, possibly trying to find something edible.

Maple convinced herself that no one was around and she took a few steps, reaching the halfway point to the newspaper. She looked up and saw a man looking at her from inside a trailer. The face was the same as the man, who she had seen in the photo when Detective Watson had been there. Donald Sukuti. He looked at her as she grabbed the paper. She turned around and rushed back into her trailer, turning around to face the window as she closed the door. He was gone.

Maple could feel her heart beating fast as she stood inside her kitchen. Panic started to spread as she thought about him taking Anna. She wondered whether Anna had been watched for days before she disappeared. Slowly, she looked out her kitchen window to see if he was back. His embroidered window cover hung completely still, as if he had never been there.

Maple looked at Noles' business card on her fridge, wondering whether to call her. If she spotted him again, she would call for help. What if he was coming after her now that the police had him on their suspect list? What did he have to lose by killing her too?

An hour passed as Maple simply sat in her kitchen chair, anxiously smoking several cigarettes. The incident with Sukuti had freaked her out and she didn't know what to do. The smokes had calmed her down and she decided that she would tell Noles about the incident, just in case something was to happen to her. She got up from the chair and decided to put on a pot of coffee now that she had some good coffee from town. As the coffee was brewing, Maple opened the paper and started browsing through the articles. There was nothing new about the case other than a discussion piece from a random writer, questioning how a mother couldn't have known anything about her daughter going missing.

In frustration, she threw the paper into the garbage can. She couldn't use judgmental articles written by people who knew nothing about the case. It was pointless. She looked in a shoebox that was on the kitchen table, which stored all of the articles written about Anna. They all held some clues as to what happened that night. She just needed to put them together and solve the mystery.

The sun was shining brightly and her kitchen lit up. It was a beautiful day outside, but also very quiet. She guessed it was the weekend simply because of the silence in the trailer park. No one left on the weekends, as they wanted to stay in hiding. Sometimes, people would walk around, soak in the sun and get some fresh air. But if more than a few people were out at a time, people tended to wait until they were alone to venture outside.

A car started to pull into the trailer park and the sound of the engine was loud. It crushed the silence in the park. The car rolled slowly through and stopped outside of her trailer. She didn't recognize the car or the person inside. For a moment, she panicked a bit. While keeping an eye on the car, she locked her door and pulled the curtains together. If someone was coming to see her, she didn't want to be home.

A woman stepped out of the car. Immediately, Maple felt a sigh of relief. She hadn't recognized Noles. Even on weekends, Noles was keeping her in her thoughts. She quickly undid the locks and opened the door to welcome Noles inside.

"To what do I owe the pleasure?" she asked with a smile as Noles entered the trailer with a simple wave.

Maple felt the atmosphere in the trailer had changed. An hour prior, she had been terrified of the weak and frail sex offender living next door. Now, she had Detective Watson in her trailer, ready to lay down the law. It was hope. And she felt hopeful that Watson had good news about Sukuti.

"Well, tell me what's new," Maple said, shaking a bit from the excitement in her body, while grabbing a cigarette to help calm her nerves.

"I'm not sure I have good news."

Maple tapped her cigarette, the blood draining from her face.

"Just tell me."

Noles sighed before speaking.

"I talked to Sukuti. My gut feeling tells me he didn't do it."

Maple bit her fingernail as she looked out the window, directly at his trailer. She was tapping her foot in frustration and took another hit of her smoke.

"I don't understand…"

"He's weak. He has cancer. He couldn't even get up when I went to visit him. There's no physical way that he could have carried her into the woods, let alone into a waiting car."

Maple shook her head a bit.

"So, now what?"

"Have you eaten?"

Maple turned to face Noles.

"What does that matter?"

"Here," Noles said, giving her a bag with a container inside. "Eggs and bacon from the diner."

Maple felt a sense of disappointment over her behavior. She felt bad for snapping at Noles because she hadn't arrested Sukuti, and here she was, bringing her food as a peace offering. Given she hadn't eaten in a while, the breakfast was welcomed.

The warm eggs and crispy bacon hit the spot. Her stomach stopped growling and she felt a sense of calmness after eating. Her head was clear and she was less anxious. She knew that her not eating was bad, but a part of her didn't think she deserved to eat. It was a sense of self-punishment for letting Anna out of her sight.

"So, are we back to square one?" Maple asked, breaking the silence after she had eaten the breakfast.

"Well, no – not exactly. While Sukuti may not be our man, he did bring up the name, Michael Barnes."

Noles looked at Maple for a reaction. She could sense it but she didn't know the name. It sounded fairly generic.

"I'm sorry, it doesn't ring a bell."

Noles put a photo of Barnes on the table and Maple recognized him immediately.

"Oh, I've seen him," she said, and then looked up at Watson. "That guy?"

Barnes didn't seem like a threat to her or a little girl. He kept to himself, he didn't look out of his windows, and she had never spotted him around her trailer.

"He has a lengthy history with the police and he hasn't shown much respect for anyone, including women and kids. While there's nothing specific tying him to Anna, we can't rule him out as a suspect either."

Maple nodded a bit, but remembered her interaction with Sukuti earlier. She didn't want to be watched by others. She wanted action, even if it meant getting involved.

"Are you going to wait weeks before approaching him?"

Noles sat quietly. Maple knew she had touched on an interesting topic. While she was happy she had Noles in her corner, she wasn't one to take action right away. Right now, she wished Morgan was in charge, coming out here to arrest Barnes for the murder of her daughter – just as he had been ready to arrest her on the first day. Things were moving too slow.

"I know it's an excuse, but we have to handle this situation with Barnes a little differently. I can't just go talk to him. He hates women."

"Two women at once? During the day?"

Maple wanted to be around when Noles confronted him. She wanted to see what he looked like, how he reacted when he heard about him being a suspect in Anna's murder, and she had become protective of Noles. Even though things weren't moving along as fast as she wanted, Noles was the only one doing something – anything.

Noles was here on a Sunday morning, getting her breakfast and looked out for her as she helped her with the case. She had never experienced a friendship like this before, even though she knew Noles would put her in handcuffs if she was responsible for Anna's death. And yet, confronting Barnes could move the case forward. Plus, what would he seriously do with two women standing firm in front of him?

"I know what you are thinking, but it's not happening. We can't risk our lives. We can't take any chances with this guy. I need to think of a better way to approach him about this case."

"What do you know that I don't?" Maple asked her in a slow and calm voice.

Noles looked directly at her, warning her with the eyes that she didn't want to know the details of his charges.

"Tell me what you know about him," Noles said, requesting information instead.

Maple rubbed her eyes, realizing that while Noles was in her corner in regards to Anna, she wasn't going to break protocol for her. There were details about Barnes that she would never know and she questioned whether she was truly ready to hear about what he had done to other victims. Hearing about Sukuti had freaked her out. Hearing what Barnes may have done out of anger could be even worse. Slowly, she accepted the fact that she was still Anna's mother and that Noles was keeping things from her to protect her. It was sensible and even though she wanted to know everything about Anna, she was grateful that she could be spared the possible circumstances of her daughter's death.

"I've seen him hanging out near a trailer a few rows over."

"How often?"

"Not often. I never noticed him before. Just the tattoo."

"How so?"

"It's big. It takes up his whole arm. And it's ugly."

Maple took another cigarette out of the package and lit it.

"I've seen him get violent with a woman."

She noticed Noles perk up, writing notes as she continued to speak.

"One day, Anna and I were coming back from the town with some groceries. He looked at us walk by. After we had passed them, I heard him yelling at a woman. I looked back and saw him grabbing her arm. When she screamed, he swung his other arm and hit her in the head."

"Do you know this woman?"

Maple shook her head.

"I only saw her that one time."

"Do you remember the number of the trailer?"

A moment of silence passed.

"50-something. It's two rows over."

Noles continued to write information down and Maple studied how she appeared excited about this new suspect. Confronting him would be satisfying, but she didn't want to ruin the investigation. She also didn't want to be his next victim.

"Detective…"

Noles looked up from her notepad, waiting for Maple to say something. She looked a bit uncomfortable, but she clearly wanted an answer.

"When can I have Anna back?"

Noles smiled crookedly.

"Soon. I promise. Just a little while longer."

"I want to give her a funeral."

Noles nodded.

"We will do that."

Noles smiled at her, and she felt that she was being heard. Now that she knew the outcome of Anna's disappearance, she just wanted her girl home.

"What now?" Maple inquired.

"I'm going to speak to Morgan about confronting Barnes together. I think Morgan may be a good person for this task."

Both ladies smiled. The investigation was moving forward and Morgan could handle the dirty work.

- CHAPTER 22 -

She grabbed the handle to the front door and exited the trailer with Maple following her out. With a new person of interest in the case, Noles hoped that she could see that they were moving forward with the case. The last thing she wanted was for Maple to feel that Anna wasn't important. She was important in many ways, both for Noles as her first murder case and for Morgan as his last case. But most of all, Noles wanted justice for both Anna and Maple who had been wronged in so many ways.

She got into her car and started the engine. Instead of driving out of the trailer park, she grabbed her cell phone. She sat silently in her car, watching the trailers around her. There was something eerie, yet peaceful about this place. The clock read past noon. She already knew that she would disappoint Sam. Even if she left the trailer park now, there was no way that she could make it home on time. Her meeting with Maple had lasted over an hour, way longer than she had anticipated. But there was something useful about the meeting. It had been a good morning for Maple, as she had gotten a new person of interest and a warm breakfast. She could see Noles working on the case and that's what mattered right now.

It had been just two days since Noles had been out here by herself. She glanced at Donald Sukuti's trailer, thinking back to the interview she had done with him, where he pointed the finger at someone else. She then turned her head, looking in the direction of Barnes' trailer – number 57. She hadn't confirmed that this was indeed his permanent residence, but it was something to go on.

There was something intriguing about going after Anna's killer on her own. Deep down, she had a feeling that Morgan would take all the credit once the case was solved. She had no interest in doing all the work and him taking credit, especially since he was so hooked on nailing Maple for the crime. She looked at her cell phone and then at the trailer again before calling Morgan. It rang five times before someone answered the phone.

"What?"

The greeting surprised Noles and she couldn't quite make out the voice. She removed the phone from her ear to double-check the phone number. It didn't sound like Morgan.

"Morgan?"

"Yes, who is this?"

The voice was very raspy and she could hear him coughing on the other end. It sounded like he had just woken up or was very sick. But she had a feeling that it was due to alcohol. There was a sense of sadness and disappointment in his voice.

"It's me, Noles. I'm calling you from the trailer park."

She could hear him sigh as he tossed and turned in his bed. She looked at the clock again and felt a sense of helplessness. Morgan had spent the majority of his Sunday morning in bed. Even in the early afternoon hours, he was sleeping off a night of drinking. He was clearly not too happy right now and she could tell that he was upset about the phone call. However, she felt ready to go confront Barnes and she wanted him to know.

"I'm at the trailer park. I'm thinking about confronting Michael Barnes today."

There was silence on the other end. She knew that her words were not what he wanted to hear.

"No, you're not. He doesn't like women and he's dangerous. Let me handle it."

"You are still in bed. You aren't capable of doing this right now," Noles replied, realizing that she may have overstepped her boundaries a bit.

"You shut the fuck up! You hear me? You are nothing without me! You don't do anything without me!"

Noles could sense the saliva coming from his mouth as he yelled. He was spitting and she imagined his hand turning red from gripping the phone so tightly. No one had ever called him out before and she dared to question his abilities as a detective. She dared to question his alcoholism.

"Well, why don't you come join me then?"

She could hear him tossing and turning, possibly thinking that Barnes could be stupid enough to admit to the crime. She imagined that he wouldn't want to miss out on a possible arrest.

"Listen, you can't do this now. We don't have anything concrete on Barnes. All we have is someone who is a suspect, pointing the finger at him to get the heat off himself. And he's pointing at a guy, who we may target because of his past."

As he spoke, Morgan was calming down. Noles knew that she had managed to freak him out and get him very upset because she questioned his authority. She waited for him to gather his thoughts before continuing the conversation.

"I understand what you are saying," Noles began. "But I still don't think it would hurt if we talked to him. Who knows? Maybe us showing interest in him will scare him a bit. If he did indeed do it, he may start acting differently, covering up his tracks."

There was silence on the other end. Then, she heard him move. It sounded like he was getting out of bed and walking around his house. She heard what sounded like a light switch.

"Morgan, are you there?"

"I'm thinking."

The silence continued, as she heard him washing his hands. She wasn't sure what was going on, but she wondered whether he was getting out of bed and getting ready to come meet her at the trailer park. After about a minute of silence, Noles spoke.

"We don't have anything else to go on right now. We are still waiting on the DNA from Anna's body, right?"

"About that…" Morgan began. "I checked in with them last week, they should have the results soon."

The pieces of the puzzle were slowly coming together, but everything was moving very slowly. It wasn't the same pace as the crime scene shows she watched at home on the weekends. It was painfully slow. Morgan wasn't helping the situation either, as he didn't seem as passionate about solving the crime. It was as if he was just waiting for the puzzle pieces to come his way and when he got them all, he would sit down to put them together the best way he knew possible. He never actively looked for the pieces.

For a brief moment, Noles considered reaching out Dr. Weissman herself to get an update. While she trusted that Morgan would follow protocol to some extent, she wondered if he pushed for the results as much as she would.

"Okay," he said suddenly. "I'll come out there and we can go talk to Barnes together. But don't do anything stupid while I'm en route. Just stay in your car and keep a low profile. Are you packing?"

"No, it's a Sunday and I'm off duty. I have no gun, pepper spray, nothing."

"Another reason for you to just hide out. Just wait for me. I'll carry."

Noles could hear him fumble with some drawers and it sounded like he was getting dressed. She looked at the clock, judging him a bit for letting his drinking go so far. While she had never met his wife, she had seen a photo of her in the office. Without saying anything, she questioned whether Morgan was dealing with much more at home than she thought. While she could ask, she also felt that some things were better left alone.

The phone call ended with an agreement for them to meet away from Maple's trailer in a little spot that had previously been a parking area. Here, they could make a plan before approaching Barnes' trailer. Morgan had been very clear in his instructions and Noles didn't want to disobey him. She slowly drove her car over to the spot where they had agreed to meet. But Noles wasn't in uniform so she technically didn't pose a threat to anyone who wanted to avoid the police.

As she sat in the car, she looked around the park. There was something calming about the day today. Her stomach was full from the breakfast, the sky was blue, the birds were singing, and it was warm enough for a light jacket. It had been freezing this morning, but the sun was slowly starting to warm everything outside.

She stepped out of her car silently to avoid drawing attention her way. Leaning up against the car door, she closed it slowly until she heard it click. She looked around, but no one had heard her. If she walked a few hundred feet, she could see Maple's trailer. She imagined that Maple thought she had left the trailer park completely. The last thing she wanted was for Maple to come running out while they were talking to Barnes, getting involved in their investigation. While she understood Maple's desire to be involved in the investigation, she could also hinder it in many ways.

As she stood by her car, Noles began investigating the trailers she could see from her position. Some of them were very neat and tidy, and it was clear that the people who lived within them cared about people's opinions and judgments. Others were far from presentable. Several trailers looked as if they had been completely abandoned. It was heartbreaking to see and Noles thought about her own life with Sam.

Sam had always been a neat freak and he always wanted the best for him and Noles. When they started dating, she would always find herself cleaning up after herself to impress him. If she had left a shirt out somewhere or forgotten to put her socks in the laundry hamper, he would do it for her – even when they were just dating and she lived alone. Sam just liked things to be orderly, clean and perfect. If he knew she was walking around out here, he could possibly lose his mind. He may even demand that she quit her job and find a desk job somewhere.

She checked her phone. No messages and only a few minutes had passed since she talked to Morgan. It would be at least another 20 minutes before he got there. She had promised him she wouldn't go confront Barnes without him, but he hadn't said anything about not wandering through the park, simply to kill time. Putting one foot in front of the other, Noles started to walk through the trailer park, taking in the ambiance of the place. She thought about Anna and how this was her home. Some of the children here may not have known another sense of home, safety or comfort. This may be all their parents could offer them.

The trailers all looked to have the same layout as the ones she had been in. The kitchen was linked up to the front door and stretched to the opposite side of the trailer. The kitchen took up about a quarter of the trailer and was at the end. Then, from the kitchen, a hallway went straight down the middle with a room at the end. This room had a door to the outside. Maple used it as her bedroom, but it could be a living room as well. From the hallway, there were closets. There was also a single bedroom facing away from the front of the trailer – a room that Maple had used as Anna's bedroom. Directly across the hall from this bedroom was a small bathroom. It was big enough to have a shower, a sink, and a toilet, but there wasn't a tub or any additional storage. It was a crammed way to live, but most people out here didn't seem to mind. It wasn't much, but it was home for many, including Maple and Anna.

Suddenly, Maple noticed a trailer that looked like it didn't belong. While the exterior of the trailer looked horrible, it was the tarp covering the windows and the wooden boards that had blocked the backdoor that caught her eye. It looked as if someone was trying to hide something. She looked around, seeing if anyone was looking at her. She also noticed that she had lost her way. She wasn't quite sure where she was or where her car was. Her cell phone told her that she still had about 10 minutes before Morgan was set to arrive, so she had time to walk back.

A piece of tarp got caught in a wind gust and shocked her. It lifted up so a portion of the window appeared. If she got closer, she could see inside the trailer. She took a few steps forward in hopes of being able to see more. With each wind gust, the tarp blew a little higher, exposing the window even more. And with every step, she could see more and more.

She was within arms reach of the window and with one more wind gust, she could see what was inside. Given the rhythm of the wind, she counted down the few seconds before it was set to come. But just before it was set to lift the tarp once again, she heard a click behind her.

She recognized the sound of the click. It was a gun. She stood frozen, realizing that she was trespassing and looking through someone's window. She wasn't wearing a uniform, so it's possible that the person had no idea she was a cop. On the other hand, it could be Morgan, who was pissed off that she didn't listen to his instructions. Adrenaline rushed through her body as she waited for someone to say something. She closed her eyes, hoping the person wouldn't fire, killing her instantly with a bullet to the head.

"Who the fuck are you?"

It was a man's voice. He was clearly angry and she sensed an aggressive in his voice. And it wasn't Morgan.

"I'm sorry," Noles began. "My name is Magnolia and I was just taking a walk."

"Looking through my window?"

"I'm sorry. It wasn't my intention. I was actually looking for someone specific."

"Who?"

Noles didn't respond as she thought about how to answer the question without risking her life.

"Who motherfucker?" he yelled as she felt the gun press on the back of her head.

"Turn around!" he yelled, as he was angry with her for not answering his questions.

As soon as she turned around, she recognized him. It was Barnes, threatening her with a gun. But he seemed to recognize her as well.

"You are that fucking cop!" he said, taking one step closer to her. "I fucking hate cops and I hate women like you. Tell me why I shouldn't blow your fucking head off right now and bury you in the cornfields!"

As he threatened her, he put the gun right to her forehead and pressed so hard that she felt herself losing her balance. He was serious about his threat and she closed her eyes, thinking this was the moment she would die.

- CHAPTER 23 -

He looked in the mirror. It wasn't a good luck. Usually, Morgan didn't take the time to shower but this morning, he felt that a quick shower would only help the situation. He could smell himself. For the first time in a long time, he could smell the alcohol on himself. Jules had been gone since Friday afternoon and he hadn't seen her since Thursday. Even though he had expected her back, she had never come home.

As a good husband, he should have called her and checked in. Before the accident, Morgan would have been worried about her absence and silence. But now, he seemed to be angry with her for not checking in with him. If she was going to be gone for a whole weekend, she could have texted him. She could have left a note.

Because of her absence, Morgan had consumed everything he had brought home from the liquor store. Her absence combined with the items he had found in the attic had resulted in him being an emotional mess. A part of him wished she had been there to pick up the pieces, but he also knew that she had tried to be there for him so many times and he never accepted the fact that she was trying to help him move on. Now that he really needed her, she was gone.

Before going into the shower, he opened his closet and took out a clean t-shirt. The white one he had worn for the past couple of days was completely dirty and yellow. His long drinking binge had resulted in him throwing up on himself. His whole bed had been covered in his vomit and he had spent the night washing the bed sheets. While he had vomited many times before as his body adjusted to the amount of alcohol in his body, it was almost like he had hit rock bottom. Jules wasn't there to help him cope and he was forced to face the demons on his own.

The warm water felt good on his body. His head was pounding, but it was refreshing to feel the water on his skin. All of the drinking had left an emotional toll on him and the alcohol had helped numb his body. The warm water trickling down his skin made him feel a bit more human, a bit more vulnerable, and a bit more awake.

As he stepped out of the bathroom after his shower, he heard someone in the house. He stopped for a minute and listened to the person walking around downstairs. It was silent for about a minute, and then he heard the floors creak. Someone was in the house.

Quietly, Morgan went to the bedroom and quickly put on his clothes. He wanted to confront the person downstairs. His thoughts were running wild as he struggled to put his pants on. Perhaps the pizza delivery guy from Friday night had come back to go through Morgan's belongings. As he slowly crept downstairs without making a sound, Morgan thought about how many times people could have broken into his house while he was passed out upstairs. He wouldn't have heard a sound.

He pulled his gun out, holding it ready by his leg with both hands. If someone was in his home to kill him, he wanted to be ready.

Again, he heard something in the kitchen. He looked up briefly, as if praying for bravery, and then took a step into the kitchen, holding the gun up directly at the intruder.

"Jesus Christ!"

She let out a scream. Jules stood near the sink, slowly washing some fruit. Morgan found himself pointing the gun at his wife, who was shocked to see him. She had yelled out in surprise, perhaps a bit scared that she was facing a hung-over husband who was pointing a gun at her.

"Jules…" he said, lowering his gun, feeling slightly embarrassed at the situation.

He put the gun down on the table next to his jacket, so he didn't forget it on the way out.

"Where have you been?" he asked her quietly, not wanting to stir up the tension even more.

"I was gone for the weekend. You know this. I've told you this."

"I'm not so sure you have," Morgan replied, feeling rather confident in the fact that she had forgotten.

"Who did you go with?"

She turned to look at him, appearing rather upset that he would imply that she hadn't been honest with him. "Seriously?"

"Well, I don't know."

"Come on now."

"You didn't answer the question."

"Does it really matter who I went with? Don't we have some bigger issues to deal with?"

She pointed to the laundry room, where the bed sheets were hung up to dry. While he was a detective, she was very good at spotting stains on the bed sheets and she must have known what had gone on in the home when she wasn't there. Without telling her a word, she already knew that he had been drinking all weekend, risking his life once again. This was a conversation that he had no desire or time to have.

"I'm actually on my way out. A call came in. A potentially dangerous situation."

"Of course you are," Jules uttered under her breath, so Morgan couldn't hear what she was saying.

"What did you say?"

"Nothing."

Morgan stepped over to her, asking her to look at him.

"I've waited for you all weekend so we could talk. I'm trying here and you aren't helping me at all. Now you are home, but I have to work. What more do you want of me?"

"I want you sober."

"Well, here I am!"

Jules shook her head, knowing that he was playing games with her. He realized that his answer wasn't ideal, but he had no other way of venting his frustrations.

"Being sober for three hours isn't being sober!" she yelled, slamming her hands down on the kitchen counter.

He was surprised by her reaction. He had never seen her so sad. She was broken. He had broken her.

"Everybody knows you drink," she cried, her tears starting to roll down her cheeks. "Even your new detective knows. Of course, she knows!"

He rolled his eyes, a bit frustrated that he was going to have this conversation with her now. He wasn't in the mood and he was on a schedule. The thought about Noles being in the trailer park, confronting Barnes on her own, was enough for him to look at the door.

"If you leave right now, I'm leaving for good," Jules said, looking at him glaring at the front door.

"I told you, I have to go somewhere for work."

"There's always an excuse and if you leave now, I'm leaving you for good."

He stood for a while next to her before sitting down at their kitchen table. Surely, Noles could stay in her car and wait a few more minutes as he tried to save his marriage. Jules made herself a cup of tea before sitting down in front of him.

"What do you want to talk about?" he said in a tone that almost mocked the entire situation.

"Why are you meeting her now?" Jules questioned.

"We are confronting a man, who could have something to do with that girl's murder. If it is him, we want him off the streets before he does it again."

Jules took a sip of her tea, looking out the window as if she understood the urgency. Her eyes were glazed over, looking wet from the tears that had been on her cheeks just a minute prior. She looked satisfied, yet exhausted at the same time.

"I love you, you know that, right?" Jules asked, changing her focus from the landscape outside to Morgan.

"Yes," he replied.

"And you are my best friend."

He felt uncomfortable about the conversation. Talking about how they were best friends was just wrong considering they rarely talked. At times, he felt replaced by these girlfriends who she would her spent days with. She was clearly enjoying her life with them and not with her husband, who was supposedly her best friend. He tried to avoid eye contact. He didn't know what to say to her comment. It was silent between them, and they could hear the wind outside.

"I'm seeing someone else."

The statement was damaging. Jules couldn't look him in the eye when she was saying it. He slowly turned his head in shock, hoping she would take the statement back. It had been his biggest fear that she had found someone else, but to hear her say the words was enough for him to lose all sense of time and place. He hadn't expected to hear those words. Even though she had merely admitted to an affair, he saw their entire relationship go down the drain. Their son, their marriage, and their plans for retirement all went away. Now, he was left with anger.

"I was with him this weekend. I feel like you should know."

"How long?"

His voice was calm as he looked down at the table while he asked her.

"Rich…" she began, but he interrupted her.

"How long!" he screamed.

He slammed his hand down on the table in anger, causing her tea to spill out of the cup.

"Three years."

He looked at her in shock, his mouth open and his eyes widening. For three years, she had been seeing another man behind his back. For three years, he had been lied to and fooled by the woman, who he loved. Sure, they had their issues and he had been drinking too much at times, but he would never have guessed that she would betray him by going behind his back.

As he stared at her in disbelief, he shook his head. His stare was vacant, but his mind was running wild with thoughts. All of these years, he thought they were working towards something, a future together. He thought they were working on fixing their issues so they could enjoy retirement together. Now, a man who had his life together had replaced him.

"Who is he?"

Jules tilted her head, knowing she had to ease the blow a bit. He knew she was treading carefully and he wanted her to. If he knew the man, he wasn't sure about holding in his feelings. He didn't want to lose his temper, but as he saw it, he had nothing else to lose.

"It doesn't matter."

"Tell me."

"It doesn't matter. You don't know him. He's not from Beaverville. Nobody knows."

Morgan stretched his neck, almost angry at the fact that Jules had made an effort to keep it all a secret. While there was no joy in her parading around town with another man, he felt like he was losing his grip on her. All of these years, her smiles had been due to another man. Her happiness had been because of another man. Her intimacy had been with another man. Suddenly, Morgan's face got pale.

"Has he been here?"

The question fueled a fire within him. He could picture Jules in bed with her lover. He imagined her naked in bed with the man on top of her. He could see the passion in her face.

"No, of course not!" Jules interrupted, seeming almost offended by the question.

Morgan felt physically ill by the thought of his wife in bed with another man, but he had to know. If she had been with him sexually, the marriage was over. He leaned over the table, and looked her right in the eyes.

"Did you fuck him?"

Jules looked surprised at the question and leaned back.

"You smell like alcohol," she replied, sipping some tea.

"I said - did you fuck him?"

There was silence between them.

"Yes, we've made love."

"Here? In our bed?"

"No, of course not."

"Where?"

"Does it really matter, Rich?"

As she spoke, Jules rolled her eyes. Morgan caught her doing it, as she was about to take another sip of her tea. Her eye rolling was the final straw for him. Throughout the conversation, he had tried to stay calm. He knew Jules was leaving him, but as Noles had angered him with her smart-witted comments and judgmental attitude, Jules was pushing him over the edge. She thought she was better than him. As she pulled the cup to her lips, he raised his arm and slammed the cup out of her hand. She jumped back in surprise, stunned at the cup that flew across the room, shattering on the wall.

"Oh my god!" she screamed, seemingly scared of her own husband.

"You fucking bitch!" he yelled at her, as he jumped out of the chair and hit her on the head with full force.

She fell out of the chair, crying loudly. This wasn't the way he had hoped the conversation would go, but he was losing control. He had lost his son and he was now losing Jules. But he couldn't lose Jules. What would his life be without her?

He was a respected citizen, a police officer, and a detective. But he was also a fraud, a baby killer, and now a wife beater.

Jules. Jules was to blame. If she had just been there for him when their son had been killed, things would have turned out just fine. If she hadn't slept with another man behind his back, things would have been just fine. If she had stayed home and been a housewife, things would have been just fine. Now, his world was unraveling and his wife lay before him, terrified of the husband who had just knocked her to the ground.

"Get up!" he yelled at her, grabbing both of her arms as he pulled her halfway up from the ground.

"You are mine, do you get that?" he yelled, hitting her in the face as she continued to scream.

"Do you think he's a good fuck, huh?" he questioned her, taunting her with his comments.

He started unbuckling his belt and his pants, pushing Jules back down on the ground. Her face was covered in blood and she cried out for him to stop. There was nothing remotely sexual or arousing about the situation, but he couldn't help himself. It was about power and control, and if he didn't take her now, he would never have her again. She continued to beg him to stop, as she held her hands over her face, the blood streaming down her cheeks towards the floor.

He blocked out her cries for him to stop. He could only faintly hear her voice. All he could hear was his own voice, telling himself that this was the last time he would have Jules to himself. This was the last act of intimacy between them. Somehow, he convinced himself that no one could have Jules, at least not at this moment. She cried out as he inserted himself. All he could hear was the sound of his belt buckle hitting the floor as he continued to rape her. Her cries faded out as he took control. She was his and there was nothing she could do. He felt empowered.

Clink. Clink. Clink. The belt buckle hit the floor and she cried out again. He stopped for a moment, slapping her across the face. She passed out from the impact, still breathing. The silence was pleasing to his throbbing headache. She was now unable to defend herself, giving him even more control over the situation.

Clink. Clink. Clink.

- CHAPTER 24 -

The end of the barrel was cold. It pressed hard against her forehead. Noles had never imagined that she would be standing here, facing the bottom of a gun barrel on a regular Sunday afternoon. She thought about Sam, about how she had promised to be home by now. She wondered whether he was worried about her. If he could see this right now, he would be angry with her for risking her life.

"I just want to talk," Noles said quietly, making the gesture for him to put down the gun.

He raised his arm even more, putting his face close to hers while keeping the gun steadily on her forehead.

"I should kill you right now."

"I'm not here for trouble. I just want to talk. Maybe you can help me."

"I don't help women."

"I'm just here about the little girl who was found murdered. She lived here. I just want to know if you know anything about the situation."

He cocked his head and she could tell that he was running various scenarios through his head. Noles wasn't in full uniform, so she thought that perhaps she could fool him by saying she was talking to him as a friend, not as a police officer.

"I knew the little girl," she lied. "I just want to know what happened to her. I'm not here as a police officer. I swear."

He began to shake his head. His pupils were changing, first from very small then to big. His hand was a bit unsteady as he held the gun. Noles looked down his arms. He had needle marks up and down, and he was wearing a white sleeveless wife beater tank top. He had red blemishes on his face and he hadn't shaved in a few days. Despite the temperature outside, he didn't appear to be cold. Perhaps the drugs were tricking him into thinking that his body temperature was warm.

"I don't know her. Never seen her."

"Are you sure?" Noles asked. "Can I show a picture of her?"

He didn't say anything, and Noles wasn't sure if he was starting to believe her. Perhaps he had been a suspect in many cases before and he was used to defending himself. Noles pulled the picture out of her pocket and held it up. He looked at Anna and then at Noles.

"Cute girl. A virgin I bet. Perfect place to bring her, a trailer park full of sex offenders."

As he talked about the park, he used his arms to gesture how big it was, removing the gun from Noles' forehead. Instead, he waved it around as he continued to talk.

"Talk about responsible fucking parenting!"

Noles nodded, trying to show understanding for his point of view. Now that he had lowered the gun it was time to strike up a conversation. Good cop, bad cop scenario.

"I know, and shit happens. I'm just trying to figure out what happened to her, man. I've just heard that you are the guy to talk to."

Noles was trying to butter him up and it seemed to work. He flashed her a smile, almost beaming with pride that he had a reliable network out here.

"Maybe I am."

"So, can you help me?"

"What do you want to know?"

"What happened to Anna?"

"I don't know anything."

He wasn't biting. Maybe he needed a more direct question to jog his memory a bit.

"Where were you the night and morning of the 17th of last month?"

He looked surprised at the question.

"Now you are starting to sound more like a cop, asking me about my alibi. Did they not teach you about this place in detective school?"

He took a step closer to her, resting the gun on her cheek. He placed his face right up against hers, so she could smell his breath. It smelled rotten, as if he hadn't brushed his teeth in weeks. He smelled like cigarettes, and alcohol. She had to hold her breath to avoid throwing up or making a face to tick him off.

"Do you know what we do to people like you out here?" Barnes whispered to Noles.

Without saying anything, Noles waited for him to continue his sentence. He put his mouth right by her ear with the gun in her face. She was scared to move, feeling her heart pound faster and faster.

"Little girls like you aren't safe out here. You'll end up in someone's trailer, bound up, gagged, raped. You'll be sexually assaulted, beaten. If you are lucky, you'll be killed and buried in those fields. That's a much better option than living on, my dear, seeing my face for the rest of your life. Because you will see my face, imprinted in your mind. Scared. Terrified."

He took a step back, nodding his head at the picture of Anna still in her hand.

"And don't think a little girl like that is safe. She's just an easier target than someone like you."

Noles didn't know whether to take his comment as a warning or a threat. While she could charge him with a petty crime, she didn't see the point. Right now, she didn't even have handcuffs on her and it was very doubtful that he would follow her to her car, where Morgan could take over. She noticed Barnes smiling, looking at his gun.

"Those little girls are so easy. You can take them away when they are sleeping."

He chuckled as he smiled, watching her squirm. It was uncomfortable to hear him talk about what he would do to someone like Anna, but he was also taunting her with information that could fit the crime. But she was having a hard time putting everything together, as he kept flaunting the gun in front of her head. She was worried his finger would flick the trigger and go off.

"Did you take her while sleeping?" Noles suddenly asked boldly.

"You would like that, wouldn't you?"

"No, not at all. I would like to clear you."

He moved his head a bit.

"Anyone of these sex offenders could have taken her. She's too young for me. But you," he said, looking her up and down. "I could take you."

While Noles had known that her life was in danger, she hadn't thought about Barnes taking her against her will and possibly assaulting her.

"Did you kill her to hide someone else's crime?"

Noles knew the question was bold. She didn't mean to accuse him of a crime, but she couldn't help but ask him.

"Are you calling me a killer?"

"No, I just want some answers."

Suddenly, his facial expression changed. His eyes got dark and Noles felt uneasy. He wasn't the person she had just talked to and for the first time, she regretted walking away from her car.

"Get inside," he said, flipping the gun to indicate that she should get into his trailer.

"No."

"If you don't get into the trailer, I'm going to shoot you and put you through the wood chipper so no one ever finds you!" he said firmly, close to her face so no one walking past them could hear him.

"Someone is en route. They are going to catch you," Noles said in hopes of scaring him.

"Who? Morgan?" he laughed, frightening Noles.

The one person who could come to her rescue wasn't respected enough in town in terms of authority. While she didn't know Morgan's history with Barnes, it wasn't a comforting feeling that he was laughing simply by the mention of his name, and Morgan feeling the need to bring a gun with him.

"Get inside," he said again.

"Why? Why can't we talk here?"

He started to lift up her shirt.

"I want to see what's under here," he said, licking his lips. "And then I'm going to hurt you because you are a cop, torture you because you are a woman, and put you through the goddamn wood chipper so I never have to see your ugly face again!"

Noles stepped backward as a reflex, wanting to distance herself slightly from this man, who was threatening to kill her. But her reflex was enough to scare him a bit, as he flung the gun at her head. It hit her so hard that she lost her balance. She felt something warm immediately, dripping down her cheek. She opened her eyes. She could hear him laugh at her, as she tried to get up on both feet.

Her head was spinning and she tried to locate Barnes. She could sense where his torso was and his legs, but struggled to accurately locate him. She felt like she was close to passing out, but she refused to fall down and be another one of his victims. She stood up and held herself up with the help of the trailer's exterior wall.

"You like that?" he questioned. "You want more?"

He pulled his arm back with the gun in his hand. He was getting ready to strike again and she knew that if he hit her again, she would be unconscious. She also knew, given his reputation, that it was very possible that no one would ever see her again. The thought of Sam learning about her fate was heartbreaking and she found the strength to get up and start running.

"You bitch, get back here!"

Barnes yelled at her, as she ran without knowing where she was going. She simply ran in the direction where she had come from, zigzagging her way through the trailers. She knew she was trespassing, but she didn't care. Barnes was running after her, but given his intoxicated state, he couldn't get ahead of her. His bad lifestyle choices were helping her out, as he wasn't fit enough to keep up with her, despite her almost passing out.

Suddenly, she was back on the main entry road to the trailer park and she knew if she ran up the road, she would get back to Maple's trailer. From here, she remembered where she parked her car. Barnes was right on her tail, trying to reach her before she got back to her car.

"Get back here," Barnes yelled at her. "You bitch, you aren't getting away from me."

She heard a gunshot being fired, but it didn't hit her. She started to panic, running as fast as she could. Her car stood alone in the parking lot, as Morgan was nowhere to be found. He hadn't come out there as promised and now, she could possibly be killed. She pulled the door handle on the driver's side, but it was locked.

The keys. Where are the goddamn keys? She fumbled with the keys, feeling them in her jacket pocket. Through the vehicle windows, she could see Barnes running towards her, aiming the gun at the car. He fired, shattering the windows on the passenger side. She unlocked the car and got in. She pressed the lock button from the inside, locking all doors. Luckily, Michael had run around the vehicle to get her, not tried to enter from the passenger's side. She turned on the car, putting it in reverse. As she sped off, she heard the sound of gunshots being fired. Her hands were covered in blood, and she couldn't see out of her left eye.

- CHAPTER 25 -

Morgan's body was tense with anger, as Jules slowly started to move her head. He was still on top of her, still inside of her, and still in control of her. She moaned as she struggled to make sense of her pain. She continued to bleed from her head. Even though she was physically hurt, Morgan had no sympathy for her. In his head, she had brought this on herself. There was something eerie about her lying on their floor in a pool of blood, with her husband on top of her. He had just raped her, and yet, photos of their memories together surrounded them, and the furniture they had shopped together stood neatly next to them, and their beautiful country home was still a symbol of the future. They had purchased the house so Jules could watch the deer in the morning, as she had her coffee.

Everything had been planned out. This had been the place where they would grow old together. They had spent more than they should on the house with the sole goal of retiring here. But now, she had someone else and Morgan was left to pick up the pieces.

He crawled off of her, choosing consciously not to look at her as he got up. He took a few steps, turned his back to her, and buttoned his pants. The sound of the belt buckle was loud, as there was nothing but silence between them. He heard her trying to sit up and when he turned around to look at her, she was huddled up against the couch, her legs pulled close to her body.

"You disgust me," he said to her, as she tried to comprehend what had just happened. "You deserved that for walking out on me. Now go be with that piece of shit lover of yours. When I get back, I don't want to see your ugly face here again."

His tone was calm but firm – and he meant every word. The last thing he wanted was to see her again. If he had been under the influence, he was scared of what could have happened. He was scared of himself. He believed he had the strength, anger and motive to kill Jules. The level of anger within him was beyond comprehensible.

On the way out of the house, he grabbed his keys and slammed the door. While he knew that Jules would never forgive him for what just happened, he didn't want her forgiveness. In fact, he wanted nothing at all from her. She had betrayed him, played him like a fool. She had lied to him for three years about an affair, and he couldn't trust her. Cheating was the ultimate betrayal.

During the car ride, he thought about what life would be like now with Jules gone. He knew that she wouldn't stay because of what he had done to her. The marriage was over. She would pack her bags, leave him behind, and a few weeks down the road, he would get divorce papers in the mail. Jules was predictable, and this rape had been his last effort to both control and hurt her.

The cornfields rushed by him as he sped through the countryside. He was headed to the trailer park to confront Barnes and he was under a natural high after what had just happened. As he thought about the way he would confront Barnes given his state, his cell phone buzzed. It was a text message from Noles.

"The station, urgent. 911."

The text message changed his attitude immediately, like a bucket of cold water to the face, and he quickly turned the car around in a U-turn on the country road. He pushed the gas pedal to the floor as he rushed back into town. He looked at the clock and realized that it had been over an hour since he said he would be at the trailer park. Noles couldn't have waited that long to confront Barnes. Or maybe Barnes had found her. The urgency of her text message scared him. It scared him more than losing Jules.

Noles' personal car was parked outside of the station. The windows were smashed in on one side and Morgan noted the bullet holes in the side of the car.

"Fuck," he said softly as he examined the vehicle.

He turned his attention to the station's front doors and rushed inside. There was blood on the floor in the lobby and he found Noles inside, bleeding profusely from a wound on her head.

"Jesus Christ!"

Noles' eye was swollen shut and was turning black and blue. Rattled by the sight of her, he quickly grabbed a Polaroid camera from a storage closet. He needed to document her condition if he was going to pursue Barnes on possible attempted murder charges. Any evidence in this case was good evidence. He asked her to sit up as straight as possible, so he could take a few photos of her. He didn't know what had happened, but getting the photos was a top priority. Once he had enough photos, he grabbed a first-aid kit from the reception desk and started cleaning up her wounds.

She was so beat up that she didn't really flinch when he cleaned the wound with alcohol. The wound continued to bleed, as he got the needle ready. She would need several stitches to close it up.

"Jesus, what happened to you?" he asked without expecting much of an answer.

"This is going to hurt, okay?" he said, warning her about him stitching her up.

She nodded slightly, as he started to stitch her up. He had seen worse, but it worried him that one of his officers had been brutally beaten. Noles didn't seem nervous about him performing the stitching. She appeared to trust him blindly, but he knew what he was doing.

"Did Barnes do this to you?"

Noles nodded slightly.

"With a gun," she managed to say with a slightly mumble.

He sighed loudly, telling himself that Barnes would pay for this.

"Is he still out there in the trailer park?"

She nodded slightly again.

"He threatened to kill me, put me through a wood chipper."

Morgan stopped the stitching and looked at her in disbelief. While he knew Barnes had often threatened people, he didn't question that he meant everything he was saying. She continued to provide a few more details about what had happened, and he soaked it all in. The more he knew, the bigger the case he could build against Barnes to take him down. Barnes had just beaten up a detective and threatened to kill her. He could argue it was attempted murder and put him away for life.

After he had cleaned her up, he put out a cot for her to sleep on. The station had a few of them available, just in case they needed to have someone in custody overnight. He told her to get some rest, while he tried to find some more information about Barnes. He was more convinced than ever that he could nail the murder of Anna on Barnes. While Maple and Sukuti were still on his personal suspect's list, he wanted to close this case up and leave Beaverville behind. With Jules' betrayal, he was eager to sell the house and start over somewhere new.

Morgan sat in his office for a moment, enjoying the silence. It had been an awful day so far. Losing Jules, raping her out of anger, finding his closest colleague beat up by a man who had threatened to kill her, and now he was sitting in his office without any real ideas on how to proceed with the case.

It was Sunday, so he knew many people wouldn't be working. He looked through his Rolodex, questioning who would be picking up the phone on a Sunday. Dr. Weissman could be somewhat reliable on the weekends. He dialed his number and waited for him to pick up the phone.

"Weissman."

"Hey, Dr. Weissman. Detective Morgan here from Beaverville. I have a question about the case of Anna, the young girl."

"I'm busy at the moment, family time."

Morgan rolled his eyes. A child had been killed and given Barnes' aggression, more children could soon be killed. What's more important than that?

"Go on," Weissman said, after realizing that Morgan didn't care about the medical examiner's family time on the weekends.

"Actually, the question is more of a request. The DNA sample you sent in for analysis. We are going to need that result as soon as possible, ideally tomorrow."

"That's impossible. Do you know the wait time for DNA results? We are backed up for months."

"Yes, I'm aware, but the prime suspect in a murder case just beat one of my officers to the brink of death. I'm going to need that result as soon as possible before half the town of Beaverville is killed."

"Oh, an officer was involved? Well, that changes things. Let me see what I can do. I'll get back to you."

Dr. Weissman quickly hung up the phone and Morgan hoped it was because he was rushing to make calls to speed up the process. He knew that when an officer was involved, things were taken seriously. It was the same when an officer had been involved in a shooting or if an officer was hurt. The arrest often happened faster and the sentence was often harsher. There was nothing more powerful against a person than an assault on an officer.

DNA was being handled. Noles was resting. Barnes was looking more like a suspect in Anna's disappearance than Sukuti. While Sukuti had a motive, he didn't have the means. While Barnes had the means, he had no motive. While there was a chance that they killed Anna together, the chance was slim. Why would Barnes risk his freedom so Sukuti could have a night with a young child? Why would Sukuti tell Barnes to kill Anna to avoid being identified, when a sentence for sexual assault was lower than murder?

His thoughts were interrupted by a knock at the front doors. Someone was tapping the glass door, loudly enough for him to hear. As he swung into the hallway, he spotted a young man. He was clean-cut, wearing glasses, jeans, and had brown hair. It was clear that he wasn't from Beaverville. He looked concerned, and he waved to Morgan as he saw him coming. Morgan had never seen him before, but given Noles' condition, his guard was up. Anyone and everyone was a suspect.

"Can I help you?" he asked through the door without unlocking it for him.

"Yes, I'm looking for Magnolia Watson. I'm her husband, Sam Watson."

Morgan looked him up and down, trying to figure out if he had seen him somewhere before. He wasn't going to just open the door and let him in. What if this guy was working with Barnes and was coming into the station to shoot Noles in the head, removing all evidence of the earlier altercation?

"How do I know that?"

Sam appeared surprised that Morgan didn't believe him. He clearly wasn't used to being questioned by a police officer, especially when it came to his relationships. Sam pulled out his phone and started scrolling through some photos. He held his phone up against the glass door, showing a photo of himself and Noles on their wedding day. Morgan looked at the photo and then at Sam again. He couldn't deny that it was Noles in the photo. Morgan slowly unlocked the door and let him inside.

"Where is she?" he said, rather panic-stricken.

"In there," Morgan said, pointing his finger to a room off the main hallway.

Sam rushed inside and let out a faint cry as he saw his wife for the first time. Her swelling hadn't gone down and he grabbed her hand and stroked her face as he tried to talk to her.

"She's resting now. I stitched her up after cleaning her wounds. She will be alright, she just needs to rest."

Sam looked at Morgan.

"Thank you."

Morgan nodded and left the room. Within a few minutes, Sam followed him into the hallway.

"I made some coffee if you want," Morgan said, nodding his head towards the coffee machine.

"What the hell happened to her?" Sam questioned as he grabbed a cup from the machine.

"She went to go confront a suspect on her own, even though I told her to wait. Apparently, he recognized her and he knew she was a cop. He doesn't like cops or women, so Noles got beat up – pretty badly too. He beat her with his gun, threatened to kill her, held a gun to her forehead, and told her he was going to put her through his wood chipper so no one could find her."

Sam stood in shock with the cup in his hand. He looked like he had only taken the coffee out of respect for Morgan and he only wanted to hear about Noles. His jaw dropped and his eyes were wide, almost as if he was imaging his wife going through the wood chipper. Morgan found some joy in rattling her husband. Clearly, Noles was stronger when it came to this kind of work.

"Wait, let me get this straight. He was going to kill her?"

Sam looked concerned for his wife and Morgan found it irritating. Sam was exhibiting the kinds of feelings that he once had for Jules. It was irritating that Noles had that kind of relationship, and he had a wife, who had hidden her indiscretions for years. Everything Sam and Noles had together was everything he hated at that moment.

"Well, yes. He probably could have. But she got away." Morgan's answer was calm and certain, and he knew that Sam was rattled by his response.

"How are you not concerned about this? Is he coming after her?" Sam asked, stepping forward as he asked the question.

"Easy there," Morgan said, gesturing for Sam to step back.

Sam shook his head as if to snap out of his anger. It was clear that he loved Noles and didn't want anything to happen to her. But he was rattled by the thought that she could have been gone thanks to some lousy criminal who just wanted to piss off a detective like Morgan.

"Sam?"

The voice came from the room where Noles was. She had gotten out of the cot and was standing in the doorway, leaning her head on the doorframe.

"Honey," he said, walking quickly over to her to assist her. "How are you feeling? I hear you got beat up pretty badly."

"I'm okay. Thanks for coming."

Morgan could see how Sam was caring for her, caressing her face where she wasn't swollen. He was studying her face and her eye, which was swollen shut. She had clearly reached out to him when it happened, asking him to come to Beaverville.

"I have some treatment for that at home," Sam told her quietly.

"Hey listen," Morgan said, interrupting their conversation. "I think you should take some time off, get well, heal yourself. I'll handle the DNA results, and I'll keep you posted."

Noles stood silently, looking at Sam and then directing her stare to Morgan. She nodded without saying much and Morgan felt that perhaps she was only agreeing for the sake of Sam. He appeared to be very protective of her, so maybe he didn't want her rushing back to work.

"I'll call for someone to tow your car," Sam said, stepping away from her. "You guys can talk about work for a second."

Sam called a towing service and scheduled an appointment to get Noles' car windows replaced. Morgan took a few steps towards Noles, asking if she was okay. He promised that he would keep her updated, but he wondered whether this was a good idea. Now that she was resting at home, he had a week or two to solve this case by himself and take credit.

As Sam helped Noles into his car, Morgan was thankful that he had nothing to worry about. With Noles at home and Jules out of his life, he could focus all of his energy on work.

- CHAPTER 26 -

It had been a few days since Sam had picked up Noles at the police station. She had spent the days in bed, feeling her head pounding as she recovered from the Barnes confrontation. She really wanted to get back to work, but Sam had taken time off from work to care for her. He had been her nurse, as he had cared for her, cleaned her wounds, given her silence to sleep, cooked her meals, and even assisted her when it was time to bathe. She was forever thankful for his help, but she was eager to get out of bed and be useful.

After a few days at home, Sam felt confident in leaving Noles at home by herself. She had convinced him that she just wanted to sleep and watch crime shows. Before he went back to work, he had stocked the fridge and freezer with her favorite foods, including her two favorite ice cream flavors. He had done everything to ensure she was comfortable.

"You just call me if you need anything. I don't think I have any surgeries coming up, so I can come home anytime," he said, as he was getting ready for work.

She nodded at him, resting her eyes, as he got dressed. She wanted him to feel that he was in full control of the situation and she didn't want him to worry about her. He appeared calm and didn't seem to question his decision to go back to work. Before he left, he kissed her forehead and encouraged her to rest up so they could go on vacation soon. Noles smiled at him, turning over in the bed as he walked out of the apartment.

But Noles didn't have plans to stay in bed all day. In fact, within the hour, she had plans to go back to Beaverville. She knew Morgan would have an opinion about her going back to work, so the plan was to avoid the police station altogether. She already felt she had enough information about the case and she didn't need to go to the station. As long as Morgan and Sam thought she was in bed, her plan was working.

As she tried to pull herself out of the bed, she realized just how weak she was. Her head started spinning and she questioned whether it was a good idea to get in the car and drive for an hour. However, she felt a responsibility to solve this case for both Anna and Maple. Now that she was injured, she felt that Barnes needed to be removed from the streets.

She sat on the bed, waiting for the spinning to stop. While the swelling around her eye had gone down, her vision was still very limited. She could see fine from the other eye, but everything hurt. If she needed to squint, she would squeal.

The hot water quickly began to cloud the mirror in the bathroom as she stripped down. Despite the pain, it was relaxing to stand in the shower and think about how she was going to get through the day. She needed to be back in the city and back in her bed by mid-afternoon. If Sam came home early, she needed to be home. He would be furious with her and she didn't want to deal with an upset husband.

The confrontation with Michael Barnes had taught her that it didn't matter whether she was in uniform or her weekend clothes. People in Beaverville knew she was a cop, and this black eye was going to stand out like a sore thumb. In her closet, Noles found a big sweater with a hood, a pair of jeans, and a baseball cap. The cap would hopefully help cover her eye. She also put on a pair of sunglasses in hopes that no one would recognize her.

Before leaving her apartment, she looked in the mirror. She looked like a mess and Sam would have walked right by her on the street. He wouldn't recognize her. While Noles wasn't the kind of person to wear lots of makeup and spend hours on her hair, she didn't hide either. Now that she was injured, she had a natural hunch as well, as she instinctively tried to protect her face.

Even though Sam wanted her in bed, he had made every effort to fix her car since the incident with Barnes. Her car was in her parking spot in the garage. While the car was still riddled with gun holes, the windows had been replaced. After Sam had picked her up at the station, he had called for her car to get towed. Within two days, the windows had been replaced but she would need to put the car in the shop for days to fix the bullet holes.

The sun was covered by the clouds this morning and the grey skies hinted that rain was to come. It wasn't too cold today, so the drive out to Beaverville was a pleasant one. She hadn't been able to sleep the night before because she knew Sam was going back to work. Throughout the night, she had been planning what to do the few hours she could escape her bed. Sam couldn't know and Morgan couldn't spot her in town. There was only place she could go and stay out of their way.

Betty's Diner hadn't changed at all. The last time she had been here, Myrtle had warned her about approaching Michael Barnes, as he hated cops and women. And here she was, just days after he had completely beaten her and threatened her life. A part of her wanted to speak to Myrtle, but another part of her just hoped that Myrtle could help get her mind back on track.

Morgan's focus had changed from Maple to Barnes shortly after the attack on her. He had pushed for the DNA results, he had kept track on Barnes himself, and she suspected that he had stopped looking into Maple's past. At times, it seemed like he just wanted to arrest someone for Anna's murder, and ideally the person who easily fit the profile. Maybe a conversation with Myrtle could help her get back on track and get her thinking about Anna again.

Noles opened the door to the diner, stopping at the front door to scout out the place. Myrtle was working behind the service counter, making a fresh pot of coffee. When Noles walked through the door, Myrtle looked up and came to a halt when she saw her. Watson had no doubt that Myrtle recognized her and caught her subtle message with her attire. Myrtle nodded at a booth on the left-hand side of the restaurant and Noles took her cue.

She sat in silence for about 10 minutes before Myrtle came over to the booth. She was carrying a stack of pancakes with light syrup and a cup of coffee. Noles smiled to the best of her ability, but it was clear to Myrtle that it was painful.

"Don't worry about it sweetheart," she said, placing a small plate of bacon down on the table in front of her.

Noles slowly removed the glasses to properly say thanks to Myrtle, but when Myrtle saw her face, her expression changed.

"Did he do this?" she asked and Noles nodded.

"When did this happen?"

"A few days ago."

"What happened?"

"I went for a walk in the trailer park where he lives. As it turns out, he knew who I was and decided to threaten me. He tried to get me into his trailer and when I didn't oblige, he whacked me upside the head. He talked about putting me through a wood chipper. Needless to say, my husband wasn't pleased."

Myrtle's expression remained serious as she listened to Noles' story. During every conversation she had with Myrtle, it felt like Myrtle knew more than she was telling her. This waitress had known Barnes for years, and she had already shared some scary stories about the man. She looked serious and concerned, and she could have known that he would put Noles through a wood chipper if he had the chance. Maybe Myrtle knew of an instance where he had indeed put a woman through a wood chipper.

"I'm so sorry," she began, but caught herself. "I mean, I had no idea he would do this to you, but I knew he was a scary guy. I mean you aren't the first he's tried to kill."

"This isn't your fault," Noles said, reaching her hand out to Myrtle.

Myrtle clearly felt a sense of responsibility for what Noles had gone through. Maybe she felt she hadn't warned her, or told Noles enough stories to scare her straight. She took a deep breath, trying to clear her mind.

"So, what happens now?"

"Well, I've been in bed recovering at home. But it sounds like Detective Morgan is going to try and get Barnes for attempted murder based on this."

Noles pointed to her face before continuing.

"But based on his comments to me, it sounds like he could be a suspect in Anna's death."

Myrtle nodded slightly.

"DNA?"

"Well, we are waiting for it. That would close the case."

Myrtle sat for a while thinking and processing everything Noles was telling her. While Myrtle didn't have anything personally invested in the case, it was clear that she felt awful about Noles being beaten by Barnes. She had come to Myrtle for advice and information, and it was clear that she felt she hadn't warned her enough. Myrtle pointed to the plates with pancakes.

"Remember to eat now," she said, pushing the pancakes towards Noles.

Noles nodded and cut out small pieces of pancake. It hurt to chew so she would only take small bites. But her eating wasn't reflective of her appetite. She was starving and she wished she could chow down on the pancakes.

"When will you know more?"

"I'm not sure," Noles said. "The DNA results are currently holding everything up. And Barnes – we need to get him into custody."

"But not you," Myrtle said, showing her motherly side. "I'm guessing you are going home to bed."

Noles smiled at her, grateful that she was concerned for her. There was something comforting about the situation, especially since Myrtle knew Barnes.

"I should be in bed, yes. I only came out here to see you and to see if I could get some ideas on what to do next."

"What do you mean?"

"Maybe I could find something to help the case move forward, you know – while we wait for the DNA results."

She noticed Myrtle smile a bit.

"Well, while I can't help you with the case, I can tell you that the best thing to do when you don't know what to do is go back to the beginning."

Noles sat for a minute, processing what Myrtle was saying. In a puzzle, crossword, or any other brain puzzle, going back to the beginning was a great strategy, but for a crime or a murder? She already had the medical examiner working on Anna's body, and Anna was where it all started.

"I'm sure you will figure out," Myrtle said with a smile. "But I need to get back to work. Back to bed with you, young lady."

She winked as she walked away and Noles continued to eat the pancakes. It would take her almost half an hour to eat everything, but it was worth it. During that time, she could relax and think about the case. She couldn't shed Myrtle's comment about going back to the beginning. She could check in with the medical examiner, but then Morgan would know that she was working.

As she sipped the last bit of coffee, she contemplated just going back home. Her mind wasn't clear and she couldn't come up with any ideas. On the way out of the diner, she waved at Myrtle, who gladly waved back. Before leaving the diner's parking lot, Noles got out her phone and replied to Sam's text messages. He was checking in on her, asking her how she was doing.

She played around on her phone, opening several apps, including one of a map. The map around the diner revealed there were many smaller ponds in the area. She was intrigued and began exploring them on her phone. If she didn't have to work and had a few hours to burn, maybe she could explore the landscape around Beaverville.

As she browsed around the map, one wooded area stood out. As she zoomed in, her phone revealed the name - Lander's Lake. Immediately, she recognized the name from Anna's case file. This is where Anna was found. She put the address into her phone's GPS and started driving. She had never been out to Lander's Lake and she had no idea where, at Lander's Lake, Anna had been found. But her curiosity had gotten the best of her. She wanted to see this place for herself.

The drive out to Lander's Lake was beautiful, even though it was cloudy and a few raindrops had hit her windshield. As she drove through the country road, the trees began appearing taller. It was poetic out here and if Anna hadn't been found dead, she would think of this place as rather romantic. This was the kind of place where she and Sam would go hiking on the weekends.

The GPS informed her that she had reached her destination. She felt far away from civilization out here, especially since she hadn't seen a soul since leaving the diner's parking lot. As she turned into the wooded area, she felt slightly nervous. There had been a dead girl out here. That meant that a killer had been out here. She was in no way capable of defending herself should she run into some trouble.

She closed the car door and stood still. The sound of the trees and a few birds provided a great soundtrack for the landscape. It was peaceful and even though Anna had been found here, it wasn't a scary place. Perhaps her killer knew her and wanted to respect her by placing her here after killing her.

The crime scene tape was still up, from when Morgan had walked the perimeter. She didn't want to disrespect his investigation by entering the space. Plus, she knew that crime scene investigators had combed through the entire area and had found nothing.

Instead, she chose to take in the landscape. She began walking around the crime scene tape, taking in the air, the smells, and the scenery. After walking around the area for a few minutes, she spotted some tire tracks. They caught her by surprise, simply by the location. She looked around, and spotted a muddy area around her own car where investigators had parked. There was a clear parking space where she was parked, but these tracks didn't belong. They were untouched. No one had walked here. She took out her phone and took several photos of the tire tracks. Even though she wasn't supposed to work, she decided to call the crime scene investigators in the city to hear if they had gotten the tire tracks for their investigation.

"Hi, this is Detective Noles from Beaverville. I'm calling about the case of murdered Anna, little girl."

"Yes, how can I help you?"

Noles proceeded to explain her findings and the woman on the other end encouraged her to email the photos to the crime scene investigators so they could possibly find a match. It was a shot in the dark, but as far as she knew, the investigators had no idea about these tire tracks west of the crime scene.

After hanging up the phone, Noles stood still and listened to the sounds of Lander's Lake. She wondered whether these were the last sounds Anna heard before she died. She wondered who had placed her here. If she hadn't died here, where had she died? Noles had gone back to the beginning, and slowly, questions started to emerge.

- CHAPTER 27 -

He rolled over in the cot. It was a horrible bed to sleep in, but Morgan hadn't been home since he raped Jules on the floor of their shared home. He had told her to get out and leave, but he had been too ashamed to return to the home. He wasn't quite ready to face the consequences of his actions, just in case she hadn't left. Instead, he had stayed at the police station for about a week, sleeping on the cot when everyone else had gone home. No one knew about his new living arrangement, but he could hide it well as he had Anna's case to blame for the late nights of work.

It had been a week since Noles was attacked in the trailer park and he found himself in the office, working to find any clues as to where Barnes was the night Anna was killed. It was late afternoon on a Friday, which meant he had the entire station to himself. It had been quiet but he liked being away from everything. No one asked questions because he pretended to be very busy. But the nights were lonely. He found himself napping quite a bit, and this afternoon, he had primarily slept at the station.

Even though he was on his own, he had gone out to the trailer park to see if he could find Barnes. He wanted to confront him about what he had done to Noles, but he had disappeared. He hadn't been in or near his trailer, or he was hiding out somewhere in the park. But Morgan hadn't forgotten about his other suspects. Even though he wanted Maple to be the primary suspect, it was hard to deny that Donald Sukuti and Michael Barnes were higher on the list. Right now, his primary concern was getting Michael behind bars for aggravated assault, so he could have him in custody while he waited for the DNA results.

The DNA results could close this case. The medical examiner had revealed that DNA had been found under Anna's fingernails, possibly when she fought off her attacker. Right now, he was waiting for the results and he hoped he would get a letter saying that there had been a match.

It was hard to come up with something else, as Barnes was gone. Morgan felt he couldn't go see Sukuti because of the past. Sukuti would probably shut down and never utter another word. Noles had gotten him to talk slightly, so he would prefer that she be the point of contact once she returned.

Hopefully, Noles would come back to work soon. He had checked in with her a few times throughout the week, but she had been in bed recovering. They had discussed the case and she said she wanted to come back in a few days. He speculated that Sam was keeping her in bed, as she often texted him to check on with the case and offer up new ideas. She wanted to make a plan for when she returned, but both agreed that the DNA results would be great.

Noles had suggested that they try to find some of Barnes' family members or friends in the trailer park that could possibly provide details about his whereabouts when Anna went missing. It wasn't a bad idea and he contemplated whether to contact these individuals before Noles returned. He felt he was at a dead end so using Noles' ideas was something he contemplated.

His phone rang and the ringer was much louder than he anticipated. With the first ring, he jumped a bit out of his chair and he felt his heart racing. He had no idea who was calling him this late on a Friday. It couldn't be Jules as she would have reached out by now if she wanted to talk to him. It couldn't be Noles, as she'd never call him when Sam at home. And it couldn't be any of the investigators in the city working in the lab, unless it was of utmost importance.

He didn't recognize the number, but the area code was from the city nearby. He frowned a bit as he pondered who it could be before answering.

"Detective Morgan here."

"Ah yes, hello Detective Morgan. My name is Chris. I'm calling you in regards to some tire tracks results."

"For what?"

The gentleman on the other end sounded confused, as if he had been told that Morgan was expecting the call.

"Ah, let me see here…"

Morgan could hear him fumble with some papers, as he tried to find some answers.

"Ah, a Detective Watson sent in a photo of a set of tire tracks found near the crime scene at Lander's Lake. She was out there when she sent in the photos. I'm just calling you with the results."

Morgan didn't say anything, but felt slightly betrayed. Noles had called him several times about the case, but she hadn't mentioned going back out to the crime scene after she had been beaten up.

"From a thorough investigation and analysis, I can confidently say that the tracks are from tires, usually found on a BMW found in the X Series. It's an SUV. Now, keep in mind that the tires could also work on other SUVs and even other BMWs, but these tires are usually the ones on the car when it is sold brand new."

Morgan wrote down the information but felt a bit defeated. A BMW sounded like an expensive SUV. It didn't sound like something Sukuti or Barnes could afford to drive.

"Is this even something we can use?" Morgan asked.

"Uh, well, Detective Watson seemed to think it was important and worth exploring. I know nothing about the case, so I can't help. But should you need it, I can testify in court."

Morgan thanked Chris for working on a late Friday and risking his free time for a case he knew nothing about. These tire tracks could be completely pointless. Plenty of people went out to Lander's Lake to hike, so they could belong to yet a third person. He turned on his computer and went to the Internet. He typed in "BMW X Series" and got a set of pictures. He would never have been able to identify the car from the name alone.

The image of the vehicle confirmed his initial thoughts. Sukuti and Barnes could never afford to drive such a vehicle. While it could have been stolen, he didn't recall seeing such a vehicle in Beaverville. It would have stood out like a sore thumb. And if Barnes or Sukuti had stolen the car, where would they hide it? He hadn't seen such a car in the trailer park when he had been out there since Anna's disappearance.

And yet, there was something familiar about the car. He couldn't place it but he had seen it before. In frustration, he rubbed his eyes and turned off the computer again. It seemed like he was getting clues that didn't fit with anything he had worked on. The tire tracks seemed pointless.

He got up from his chair and went into the quiet lobby. It was lonely out here, as no one was working today. He put on some coffee and waited near the machine as the coffee was brewing. He still had a few hours before it got dark outside to work, and he contemplated what he could work on to move the case forward. As he waited for the coffee, he noticed a young man approaching the police station.

The young man looked at the exterior of the building, as if he wondered whether the station was open. He was wearing a backpack and seemed a bit confused. Morgan took a step forward, observing him from the dark police station. He didn't look familiar. Morgan was reminded of the pizza delivery guy from Moe's pizza – another young man in Beaverville he didn't recognize. Either more people were coming into the town without him noticing, or he wasn't paying attention to his town anymore.

He looked like a courier. He was wearing jeans, a sweater, a jacket on top of the sweater, and a baseball cap. There was a logo on the backpack and Morgan managed to get a glimpse of it as the man turned around to look at the parking lot. He was trying to figure out the street name. The young man couldn't see Morgan inside. He got out his phone and appeared to be verifying an address, as he looked at the building's street number.

While being distracted by his phone, Morgan walked up to the glass doors, knocking loudly, scaring the young man. He jumped back and put his hand on his chest to indicate that he had been terrified by the knock. Morgan unlocked the door and opened it slightly.

"Sheesh! You scared me!"

"Can I help you?" Morgan said, slightly sympathetic for the knock and scaring him.

"Yes, I'm here to deliver something for a … Detective Morgan."

He had to double-check the name on the envelope he was holding. Morgan reached out his hand for the envelope, but the young man held it back.

"Oh no, I'm going to need to see some ID."

Morgan looked at him, trying to stare him down. But it didn't work. The courier wasn't scared of him anymore and he wasn't going to simply hand over the document to him. Slowly, Morgan went back into his office and grabbed his identification. After a wordless confrontation with the courier, he got what he wanted. The courier had tried to be nice about interrupting Morgan's alone time, but he had merely closed and locked the door after receiving the envelope.

The envelope was from the laboratory and had the stamp "Confidential" on it. He took a deep breath before putting it down on the table. This was it. The name inside that envelope was the primary suspect in Anna's death. It would give them the biggest lead in the case thus far. It was someone who had fought with Anna before her death, as the DNA was under her fingernails. It was someone who hadn't come forward with an admission. If the name within was Maple, Sukuti or Barnes, an arrest would take place and the case could be closed. He could pass it on to someone else and retire.

The envelope was hard to open and he struggled to open it without ripping the paper within. When he finally got it out, he took a deep breath and closed his eyes before reading the letter with a soft mumble.

"Our laboratory sampled the skin cells under the victim's fingernails for DNA. All samples tested of the given variety were uniformly consistent and matched a person within our national CODIS system."

CODIS was the national Combined DNA Index System, where DNA samples were stored. The lab had already done the work for him. Morgan scanned the document for the name. There was a DNA match, but no name stood out.

"These results suggest the person identified was with the victim within hours of being found on location."

He continued to skim.

Details of the case were summarized on the second page. The person had written details about Anna and finally, he saw the line where it revealed what he wanted. A name finally stood out near the end of the second page, a name he hadn't expected. For the first time in this case, his mouth went dry and he felt his heart skip a beat. It wasn't a name that he had anticipated, but it was a name he recognized. And suddenly, he felt a sense of panic and urgency.

- CHAPTER 28 -

It had been a long few days for Noles, as she had been forced to stay in bed. Sam hadn't figured out that she had been out to Beaverville earlier in the week to see Myrtle and visited Lander's Lake, but it had been a close call. She had only just gotten home when Sam walked through the door. When he had touched her forehead, he had made the comment that she had been cold, so she had told him that she had spent some time on their balcony to cool down. There was no need for him to know that she drove all the way out to Beaverville.

It felt odd for her to keep this secret from Sam. She wanted to share everything with him, including how things were going in the case. She wished that she could legally discuss everything about Anna, about Maple, and her trips to the diner to see Myrtle. It would be nice to have someone to discuss things with, including a sparring partner. Morgan hadn't exactly been a great partner when exploring new theories or ideas, as he had been fairly narrow-minded so far. Sam had been her sparring partner in life, and they had often had deep conversations about everything from life to politics, food and work. But this was the first time where she couldn't include him. Like a psychologist, she was bound by confidentiality.

She turned on her side in their bed, looking out at the dark clouds. It had rained all day and the weather forecast did call for thunder. Nothing had happened yet and Noles had hoped it would soon happen, so she could enjoy the lightning from her bed. The clouds were moving fast and they looked like fluffy marshmallows. Some of them were dark grey, while others were light. Together, the sky looked like a beautiful oil painting.

She heard the key in the front door, as Sam unlocked their apartment door. As he opened the door, she turned around to lie back down on her back. She listened, as he walked into the apartment, put down some grocery bags, and removed his jacket. His breathing was heavy and she waited for him to either yell that he was home, or come into their bedroom.

His footsteps were loud as he walked towards the bedroom and he smiled when he saw her in bed. He had been somewhat quiet after coming home and he may have thought she was sleeping. But she hadn't slept all week because of the case. She had brainstormed, done research on her laptop and texted with Morgan to stay in touch. While she couldn't investigate Barnes' family members from her bed, she was planning on returning to work in a few days and hitting the ground running.

"Hey honey," Sam said as he sat down on the bed next to her.

"Hey you."

"How are you feeling?"

"Much better. All of this rest does the body and mind good," she lied. "I think I'm ready to go back to work on Monday."

His facial expression changed. Clearly, he wanted her to stay in bed for weeks. His medical background and his work as an emergency room doctor played a role in his behavior at home. He was treating her like a patient, not as his wife who had a need to get back to work.

"I went and got some groceries, so we can just hang out tonight. It's the weekend and we can just spend some time together the next few days."

"What's on the menu?" she asked in a flirtatious tone.

"Perhaps some fish tacos. The fish had just arrived at the store. I'll add some mango too. And maybe if you are lucky, some dessert."

"What a spoiled girl I am."

Sam looked over her shoulder to see the time on her bedside table. For years, she insisted on having a clock radio by her side. Even though the speakers didn't work anymore, she enjoyed being able to open one eye to see what time it was in the morning.

"I'm going to go start dinner," he said. "It will be a while. Why don't you go take a warm shower and just relax a bit? And then, when you are done, put on your sweatpants and come have some wine with me and find a movie for us."

She smiled and leaned in for a kiss. While she couldn't tell Sam about her work, she felt very lucky that he was so caring. He had turned down extra shifts this weekend to spend time with her, and he had made every effort to come home early. Now that it was Friday night, he was coming home prepared with groceries, so they could relax all weekend and rest up. He really wanted her to get better, so he was picking up the slack around the house.

He got up from the bed and walked towards the hallway, so he could start dinner. As he reached the door, he turned around and pointed to the bathroom. She nodded and started to crawl out of bed as Sam headed for the kitchen. As she walked away, she noticed her phone on her nightstand light up. She had turned the sound off, so the phone didn't say anything and it didn't vibrate either. As she stood in the door to the bathroom, she contemplated whether she should get it. The clock on her nightstand clearly indicated that it was after work hours and she didn't have the desire to speak to anyone right now. If urgent, the person would call back.

The shower tiles were cold and there was a draft from the bathroom window. She turned on the shower and let the water warm run before removing her clothes and stepping into the shower. The water was hot against her skin, but it relaxed her and she let her shoulders down. Since she hadn't worked all week, she felt restless. She was exhausted from being in bed all week. Other than her trip to Beaverville and Lander's Lake, she had stayed in bed and had made every effort to heal.

She shifted her body, so the warm water hit her face. Every day this week, the water had caused her wound to itch. But this time, it didn't hurt at all. The water could run down her face without hurting. The warm water was a soft massage on her face, and she closed her eyes and took a deep breath. After last week's assault, she was finally starting to feel normal again. No matter what Sam said about the situation, she wanted to get back to work.

As the water ran down her face and her body, she thought about the weekend. Sam wanted her to rest, she wanted to work, and Morgan was probably drinking the days away. Maybe this was the weekend to truly rest and then get back to work on Monday rather than spend the weekend researching. Given it was after hours now, Morgan wouldn't be working. She guessed he was at home drinking or somewhere at a bar. While she felt bad for Morgan as she had her suspicions that he was battling something much bigger than himself, she also reminded herself that they had a professional relationship.

Even though she wanted to ask him about his wife and his personal life, she often thought that she would open a can of worms that she didn't know if she could handle. Maybe once the case was over and he retired, they could have a different relationship with one another.

Through the door to the bedroom, she could see her phone light up. Someone was calling her again. The phone had been silent the whole day and now, after she had closed her laptop and Sam was home, someone was calling her constantly. If it had been during work hours, it could have been Morgan. Now that it was late, she had a hard time guessing who it was. Maybe Maple had a new tip she had to share.

She closed her eyes and directed her body and head under the water again. The warm water felt good. She could stand in the shower for hours if Sam allowed her to waste that much water. Any minute, he would come into the bathroom and tell her that dinner was ready. To avoid a lecture about saving the water, she turned it off and stepped out of the shower.

She reached out for a towel and dried herself quickly. It was cold in the bedroom as she pushed the door opened. From their closet, she grabbed a pair of navy sweatpants and a light grey t-shirt. She also put on a pair of socks and her slippers to avoid being cold. Finally, she dried her hair, and wrapped it up in a high bun so she didn't have to deal with it all night long.

Once dressed, she caught the distinct smell of Sam's famous fish tacos. She realized how hungry she was and she started skipping into the hallway before realizing she had forgotten her phone. Sam saw her skipping and her turning around, and he couldn't help but laugh at her. She laughed as well, realizing how ridiculous she must have looked. But she enjoyed how they could joke and laugh together. They had never really fought, possibly because they didn't take life too seriously. Their professions were serious enough, dealing with crime, health and trauma all day. It was relaxing and enjoyable to simply joke around and enjoy one another.

Her phone wasn't lit up as she walked into the bedroom. No one was calling her right now. As she reached her nightstand, she picked up her phone and pressed a button to activate the screen. She was surprised to see that she had 16 missed calls from Morgan and several text messages reading, "Urgent," and "911."

She smirked a bit in confusion. She hadn't expected to hear from Morgan, but based on his text messages and the number of calls, it appeared to be urgent. She tried to process everything that was happening, as she picked up the phone to call him back. As she heard the beeps waiting for Morgan to answer the phone, she contemplated what had happened. Did something happen to Maple? Did someone find another body? Did Barnes get arrested?

"Magnolia?" he answered.

"Hey! Yeah, it's me. I can see you called a few times. What's so urgent?"

"I've been trying to call you," he said, somewhat out of breath.

The whole situation seemed odd and his many phone calls had thrown her completely out of it. She had prepared for a nice night in with Sam, who was cooking dinner in their kitchen. Now, she was on the phone with Morgan, who sounded nervous and had texted her about an urgent situation.

"What's up? Did something happen?"

"I got the DNA results!"

Her eyes widened. Finally, there was some progress. It made sense that Morgan had called her 16 times if he had the DNA results. He carried the name that was linked to Anna. He possibly had the name of the killer.

"Okay, tell me."

"Watson," he began. "I don't know how to share this news. It's not what we had hoped."

Her facial expression changed, as she felt a sense of hope drain from her body. Immediately, she knew it wasn't Michael Barnes. After the assault, they had both hoped that he would be guilty, so they could get him off the streets. But Morgan's tone also indicated that it wasn't Donald Sukuti. Noles had guessed that Morgan would have enjoyed charging either of them with murder.

"Well, who? What's the name?"

"Watson…"

He kept the name from her. He struggled to tell her. She knew that he wanted her to know, but he couldn't get himself to tell her.

"What? Did Maple kill her own daughter?"

She struggled to make sense of the words she was saying. She couldn't imagine how Maple could hurt Anna, especially after seeing her break down as she learned about Anna being found near Lander's Lake. Noles couldn't get the pieces to fit. She couldn't figure out how Maple could get the body out to Lander's Lake. Nothing made sense.

"Noles, the name on the DNA results…"

He kept starting a sentence and cutting it off.

"Oh my god, Morgan. Just tell me."

His hesitation was scary. She felt unsure about her work, the case, Anna, and Morgan. She wasn't sure where she stood in the case. Her own partner couldn't share the DNA results.

"Noles, the name of the DNA results is Sam Watson."

She felt her breathing change. Her eyesight became blurry and she felt dizzy. Sam? Her Sam?

"Surely, there's another Sam Watson," she nervously chuckled, a bit unsure if she believed the results.

"Noles…"

She shook her head in denial.

"I don't understand this," she said, hoping Morgan could clarify the situation so she didn't jump to conclusions.

"Are you alone?"

"No, Sam is here. He's cooking."

"Noles, you need to get out."

She laughed a bit, shaking her head.

"It's not him. It's another Sam."

She could hear Morgan sigh on the other end. He was certain in his case. He knew it was her Sam that had killed Anna.

"How can you be so sure?"

She wanted to question his certainty. Surely, being from a small town, he was narrow-minded. He had been narrow-minded this entire case, focusing only on Maple and on criminals from his past he could get satisfaction from locking up. As soon as he saw a man named Sam Watson on the DNA results, he assumed it was her Sam.

"Noles. It's him. His DNA matched the skin cells we found under Anna's fingernails. I know it's him. He was already in the national DNA database and CODIS. His picture was there, Noles. He must have given up his DNA at some point because of his job."

Noles felt a tingle in her cheeks. Her mouth opened in shock as she tried to process everything he was telling her. Sam had been with Anna the night she disappeared. His DNA was under the fingernails. He broke her neck, killing her. He dumped her near Lander's Lake.

"Also, the tire tracks you sent in," Morgan continued. "The tracks match a BMW SUV, ideally from the X series. Does that ring a bell?"

Sam drove a BMW SUV. He had just purchased it last year because he was promoted and wanted to spoil himself. She had never noticed the tires' pattern. But she had been there with him, picking out the color and the features.

She felt her breathing slow down, as she tried to put the pieces together. The evidence all pointed to her husband being a killer. He was in the kitchen, preparing fish tacos and whipping up a dessert. Now, she had to go confront him. Did he really kill a little girl after they had talked so often about having a baby?

"What do I do?" Noles said, her voice shaky as she was on the verge of crying.

She felt herself slowly slip into a panicked state, not knowing what to do. The whole situation was overwhelming.

Everything she thought she knew about her husband was false. Her breathing got louder and she wanted to scream, but she didn't want Sam to come running. She had now become terrified of her own husband.

"Are you okay?" Morgan asked but continued to speak. "Noles, you need to get out of there."

She shook her head, trying to comprehend the situation.

"How? How can I get out of here?"

"I'm on my way! I've been driving for a good 45 minutes now. I found your address at the station. Just don't do anything stupid!"

Noles hung up the phone and looked at the door leading out of the bedroom. She could hear Sam whistling in the kitchen. Dinner was almost ready.

- CHAPTER 29 -

The fish had the perfect grilled look to them. Darkened grill marks were on both sides and the meat was tender. Without touching it, he knew it was near perfection. Sam Watson had always been proud of his work in the kitchen. During medical school, he would cook for the other students and he was often labeled as the live-in chef in his residential building. While it was a lot of work to cook for so many students, he had enjoyed it. Luckily for him, Noles wasn't a good cook so she allowed him to take over at home.

He had warmed the soft tortilla wraps for the tacos and had prepared a cabbage slaw as the filling. It was important for Sam that they ate healthy food, so he never fried the fish. Sam chopped up some cilantro as the final touch, adding chunks of mango to the slaw. He knew Noles would be impressed.

Magnolia had worked so hard on this case, but things had gone too far with Barnes. If she had just listened to him or Detective Morgan, this would never have happened. Sam was angry with Michael Barnes, who had beaten his wife to a pulp. For the past week, she had been in bed and had been uncomfortable as her body healed. Barnes hadn't thought about her loved ones, her husband, or her passion for life when he had beaten her with his gun, possibly trying to kill her. Now, Sam finally had some time off so they could enjoy the weekend together. This meal would only set the tone.

"Hey Noles, where are you?"

She had just been on her way into the kitchen when she forgot something in the bedroom, made a cute little skip jump and had gone back down the hall. It had been a few minutes now, and there had been nothing but silence. He opened up a bottle of red wine, pouring some into two wine glasses. He turned his attention to the fish fillets, removing them from the heat and placed them on a cutting board to rest.

"Hey you, the food is going to get cold!"

No answer. She had just been so happy and laughing, and now, she wasn't responding to his questions. His eyes were on the stove, and as soon as he had turned everything off, he removed the apron and turned around to go find her in the bedroom. However, as soon as he took one step, he saw her standing in the hallway. Her eyes were shiny as if she had been crying, and she had a terrified look on her face. Sam had never seen her that way before, and his heart dropped. She knew.

"What's wrong honey?" he asked while swallowing, clearly indicating that he was uncomfortable in the situation.

"You," she simply said. "You did this. You killed Anna."

Oh, she knew. She knew the one thing he had been trying to hide for weeks. Sam didn't think that she would be able to solve the case. She was a newbie and had never worked as a detective before. When he learned that she had been assigned to the case, he wasn't even worried. He had miscalculated her abilities.

"What are you talking about?" Sam asked, trying to laugh off her accusations.

"You killed a little girl. You dumped her in the woods. You broke her neck!"

Sam closed his eyes and clenched his teeth. His jaw got tight. She really did know. He was guilty of everything she was saying right now, but he had hoped that he could dump the girl in the woods and no one would have linked Anna to him.

"How?"

"DNA. Your DNA was under her fingernails."

He nodded. He was caught. It would be hard to talk his way out of this one. He thought for sure he had wiped everything down, but apparently not well enough.

"Look…" he said.

He wanted to say more to her as he took a step forward. But Noles pulled her gun out and held it up, pointing it right at his head. In a defensive gesture, he put his hands up to his chest as if he wanted to give up. The gun had surprised him. He had no idea she even had a gun as part of her new job.

"Wow, Noles!"

"Just stay right there," she said, keeping the gun steady.

"Honey, a gun? I'm not going to hurt you."

She didn't flinch. She really saw him as a threat, even though he would never hurt her. He could never hurt a hair on her head. And he didn't think he was capable of hurting anyone before Anna came into his life. It wasn't even supposed to happen.

"You killed a girl. I don't know who you are."

He sighed loudly, holding his hands up. He knew he had been caught, but he didn't want to lose Noles over this. She was his everything and he had no interest in ruining their marriage over this little girl.

"Can we talk about this?"

"Tell me what happened," she said.

Sam used his eyes to indicate that he wanted to sit down on the barstool next to the island. She allowed him to sit down, and he slowly walked over to the barstool. The juices from the fish fillets began running along the kitchen countertop and dripped down towards the floor, running down the cabinet door. He hadn't had the time to wrap them in foil before Noles confronted him. But she didn't seem to care about the mess. Noles looked at him, waiting for him to give his explanation of what had happened. Sam knew that she would eventually put the pieces together, so there was no reason to lie.

"Remember the accident, the major one on the highway a few weeks ago?" he asked her and she nodded.

"I had been working long hours and we had been doing CPR, smaller surgeries and stitches on the highway for hours. It was cold, and some people were dying. It was horrible."

He looked down at the floor, trying to remove his memories from his mind. That night, he had seen severe injuries and while he could have helped them in the emergency room, he didn't have all of the surgical tools on the road to save lives. People had died and he hadn't felt like a good doctor.

"When we had done everything we could, I drove home. It was through the countryside, close to Beaverville. I was tired."

Noles looked straight at him, tears slowly developing. He knew it was painful for her to listen to. If he had just told her what had happened, she wouldn't have gone through everything with Maple, Anna, and now this Barnes guy who had almost killed her. In addition to that, he had all of the answers to the questions she had been working to find since she started this new job.

"I hit her with my car. She ran right out on the road, chasing some white animal."

"A snow bunny…" Noles said while in a trance.

"I mean, it's possible," he replied. "I didn't see it."

Sam could tell she was putting the pieces together. The car had caused the blunt force trauma. Anna had been out there because of a snow bunny. A man or an angry ex-boyfriend hadn't kidnapped Anna. It had been Sam all along, and he had been hiding the truth right under her nose. He had known everything every night they had gone to bed, he had known the truth every time they had discussed the case, and he had known that he had killed Anna when she discussed possible suspects with him. Sam knew that his behavior was unforgivable.

"The neck…" she said suddenly, focusing her stare back at him.

Sam had hoped she would associate the neck with the car. He wasn't proud of his actions.

"She was still alive when I hit her with the car. She…"

He couldn't finish his sentence. He paused, look at Noles who had no sympathy in her eyes, and he realized that he needed to be honest for himself, for Anna, and for his possible future with Noles.

"She begged me to help her. But she was paralyzed. There was nothing I could have done."

"Nothing you could have done?" Noles cried, screaming at home. "What the fuck does that mean? She was alive!"

Noles clearly couldn't see it from his perspective. His medical career could have been over if people found out that he had hit a little girl in the middle of the road, paralyzing her, ruining her life. No one would ever trust him to care for a child or a patient, if he was labeled as someone who severely hurt a child with his car. It was irresponsible.

"I needed to remove the damage," he said suddenly in frustration, but immediately regretted his choice of words.

"The damage? She was a child! She was someone's daughter!"

Sam feared that Noles would lose control and shoot him by accident. He gestured for her to calm down and take it easy, but she didn't react like he had hoped. It was clear to him that she was trying to account for everything, as she would need to write a report about it later. She was crying now.

"I decided to break her neck to put her out of her misery," he explained, not looking at her. "She was in pain."
"You did it to save your career."

She was right. At that moment in time, Anna hadn't meant much to him. If she hadn't run out on the road in front of his car, he wouldn't have cared about her. But when she chose to follow that snow bunny across the road, she had become his liability. He couldn't let her poor decisions become his career's downfall. He chose to sit in silence, letting his lack of words confirm her theory. Yes, he had indeed killed her to save his own ass. A four-year-old girl running around on the country roads chasing a bunny wasn't going to ruin 20 years in the medical field.

"Your car," she said. "The damages."
"You were too busy to notice."

She looked straight at him, trying to make sense of it all. He felt bad, so he tried to give her a timeline of events.

"The night I hit her, the car was damaged but I could still drive home. I parked the car in my usual spot, but you could only see the backend of the car from your spot," he explained. "You were so busy with the case that you didn't notice the damages. I sent the car to the shop the day after the accident. That's why I got up early with you."

"Fixing the car takes days. You had the car back when you picked me up at the station after I was attacked," Noles began, but he interrupted her.

"I made sure to get a replacement car that matched in color and model."

Sam knew it was a sneaky move, but he felt he had to cover his tracks. He could tell she was stunned, probably wondering how her husband could have kept such a big secret from her. Or maybe she was blaming herself for not realizing what was going on, right under her nose.

"So, what now?" he asked her. "Can you please put the gun down so we can have some dinner?"

"Who are you?" she said, her voice shaking.

"I'm your husband, who just chose to sacrifice a lot for us and our lives together."

He got up from the chair, but his decision to stand up quickly scared her, and she repositioned the gun, pointing it at his head.

"Come on honey," he said, trying to undermine the situation. "Let's put the gun down and eat. I'm not going to hurt you."

"Were you ever going to tell me?" she asked.

"Yes, of course."

"When?"

She wasn't letting him off the hook that easily. Sam had never felt like he needed to prove himself to anyone and Noles wasn't giving him a break. He rolled his eyes before looking at her and smiling.

"Honey, look. Telling your wife that you killed the girl who is the focus of her first case isn't easy. I was trying to find a way, but I wanted you to get better first. I also wanted this conversation to go better than right now. I was hoping we could find some sort of resolution for this, for us, for the future.

"When?" she asked again.

He turned around and looked at the flowers in a vase he had put on their dining room table. They were new, as she hadn't seen them before. He must have picked them up at the market.

"Tonight," he said. "I was going to tell you tonight after dinner."

The flowers were her favorites and he had only bought them once before, the only other time he owed her an apology. Noles didn't get a chance to answer. The door buzzer rang and Sam jumped. He didn't anticipate company. He watched as Noles answered the door alarm, telling the person below to come up. She held the button to unlock the front door and shared their unit number.

"Noles, what are you doing?" Sam asked.

He was starting to panic. He was losing control of the situation. This wasn't how he wanted it to go. He wanted to discuss this with Noles after dinner, and see how they could possibly move on from this, never to speak about this again. Noles' expression changed from shock and anger to sadness and helplessness.

"I'm sorry, I can't help you."

Sam knew it was over. He was going away for murder.

- CHAPTER 30 -

Morgan felt his heart beating fast as he waited in the elevator of Watson's building. He had rushed to the city as fast as he could despite being tired. The DNA results had given him a rush of energy and adrenaline that was better than alcohol. He felt a sense of purpose, even though the answer to the crime had been close to home.

The elevator was moving rather slow, considering Noles had been in an apartment with her husband, who had become the prime suspect in a murder case. She had answered the doorbell, which meant she was alive and well. She sounded angry and terrified, and Morgan guessed that an altercation or confrontation had occurred. Noles was injured and after everything that happened with Barnes, she could be weak in comparison to her husband. He was antsy and felt more stressed the closer he got. The elevator would ding as another floor would pass, and each ding got him more agitated.

The elevator doors opened and Morgan ran as fast as he could down to the end of the hall where Noles' apartment was. He knocked on the door first, but chose to walk right in. He had his gun drawn, not realizing what he walked into. The apartment was modern, spacious and there was a delicious smell of fish tacos. He spotted the wine glasses on the counter. He then saw Sam with his hands up. Turning his head, he saw Noles with her gun drawn. She looked upset and sad, and Morgan suspected that she knew the whole story.

"Guilty?" Morgan asked and Noles nodded.

He turned his attention to Sam, who continued to stare at Noles in hopes of getting her attention. Grabbing his handcuffs, Morgan walked over to Sam and asked him to put his hands behind his back.

"You have the right to remain silent. Anything you say can and will be used against you in a court of law. You have the right to an attorney. If you cannot afford an attorney, one will be provided for you. Do you understand the rights I have just read to you? With these rights in mind, do you wish to speak to me?"

Sam ignored his Miranda Rights but nodded that he understood. Morgan didn't see the need to keep Sam in the apartment when he had a cruiser downstairs where he could place him. He wanted to talk to Noles privately, but Sam didn't have to listen.

"Let's go," he said, pushing Sam's foot, asking him to walk out of the apartment.

As he started walking, Sam forced Morgan to stop abruptly right by Noles, who had now put down her gun. Her eyes were filled with tears and Sam was choking up as well. Noles' hand covered her mouth, and it was clear she was trying to process everything that had just happened.

"Noles, I love you," Sam begged, hoping to hear those same words back.

But she didn't speak. She simply stood there in disbelief, refusing to give him her attention.

"Let's go," Morgan said again, pushing Sam out the front door of the apartment.

The elevator ride was silent, as Sam didn't say anything. He wasn't wearing shoes, but he didn't seem to care. Morgan realized that Noles' marriage was over, but his loyalty was with her. There was nothing he could say to Sam to fix his current situation. Plus, he had already read Sam his rights, so anything that was said between them could be used for his official record.

It was raining, as Sam walked over to the police cruiser parked right outside of their apartment building in socks. Sam cooperated and placed himself in the backseat of Morgan's cruiser. Before closing the door, Morgan leaned down.

"I'm going to go check on your wife to make sure she's alright after tonight."

Sam nodded, and replied, "Please do."

At least both men were in agreement that Noles was a top priority right now. While Sam was worried about their relationship, Morgan didn't know if she was going to go off the rails like he had done in his own life.

The apartment hallway was silent, as Morgan surfaced again. This time, he wasn't in a rush to get to Noles' apartment, but didn't walk slowly either. He was nervous as to what he would find inside.

Noles had placed herself on a chair, her face buried in her hands. She was crying when Morgan surfaced again. He had never been good at handling emotional situations, but Noles could be injured.

"What happened? Are you okay?" Morgan asked her, trying to remove her hands from her face to see if Sam had physically injured her.

"He didn't hurt me," Noles said, telling Morgan everything that Sam had told her about hitting Anna in the early morning hours, and how he had snapped her neck to discard of her to avoid ruining his career.

Morgan pulled up a chair and sat down next to her. He didn't know what to say to make her feel any better. It had been a rough time for both of them over the past couple of weeks. When they met, they had both been happily married. But both marriages had been based on lies, and plagued by children being killed.

"He didn't mean to do it," Noles said. "But he didn't tell me. He killed her when he could have saved her life. Him, out of all people, should have tried to save her life"

"Do you want me to try and get bail for him?" Morgan asked. "It's a shot in the dark, but it's possible."

Noles shook her head.

"I don't even know the man. I didn't marry a killer. I don't feel safe in my own home with him."

Morgan nodded, not quite sure if he should give her a hug. He felt odd about the whole thing. At the beginning of the case, he had warned Noles not to get too close to the victims, but this was as close as one could get. This was personal.

"If you want, I can tell Maple everything," he offered.

"No, I want to talk to her. My husband is the reason why her daughter is gone," Noles said firmly. "I owe her that much. If you talked to her, I'd be a coward."

Morgan didn't quite see the connection.

"And I want to hold a funeral for Anna," Noles continued, to which Morgan's facial expression showed concern.

She was getting too close to the victims again.

"You can't do that," Morgan said, but he was quickly interrupted.

"It's not up for discussion."

Morgan looked around the apartment, noticing the tacos on the kitchen counter. She was clearly devastated by everything she had gone through and there was nothing more she could do. The case would be handed over to someone else, and she could focus on herself.

"Look, eat some tacos. Clean up here. Enjoy the flowers," Morgan said, pointing to the beautiful bouquet that Sam had gotten her earlier.

Noles let out a small chuckle through the tears.

"You know, he told me he was going to tell me everything tonight. I think he's lying, but I want to believe him."

Morgan smiled a bit at her.

"Life is crap sometimes. It's how we deal with the cards we are given that defines us. You did nothing wrong here, but don't end up like me, drinking your sorrows away. You are stronger than that."

Noles looked at him through her tears, and he felt emotional about the whole thing. The case had come to a dramatic end, an end that neither one of them had expected or guessed. He had lost his wife, and he was now consoling his partner, who was going through that same loss. Neither of them would be the same after this case, but he hoped Noles would find a better way to grieve.

"I'll see you on Monday if you are ready," Morgan said, standing up to leave the apartment.

"I'm not so sure," Noles began.

Morgan could tell she was questioning her career as a detective. How could she label herself a detective when she couldn't see the answer that was right under her nose? Morgan didn't blame her, but wanted her to know that it wasn't her fault.

"It's not your fault," he began. "It can happen to the best of us. Take your time and let me know."

"And Sam?" she asked.

"He's no longer our problem. I have to hand him over to the authorities here in the city."

She nodded, realizing that there was nothing she could do about the situation.

Morgan didn't say anything as he got up to leave, and he closed the front door behind him as he walked out of her home. As Noles tried to make sense of everything that had just happened, she got up and went over to examine the flowers her husband had bought for her. Maybe he was going to apologize for his behavior, his lies, and him killing an innocent little girl. As she looked at the bouquet, she spotted a small card inside. She opened the envelope.

"To my beautiful detective wife, who is going to get that scumbag off the streets, and behind bars for a senseless murder. Here's to a glorious career, our bright future together, and our everlasting love."